THE ADVENTURES OF MAD GAD THE BARD

JAMES COYLE

The Adventures of Mad Gad the Bard

ISBN: 979-8-35094-286-6

TABLE OF CONTENTS

The Adventures of Mad Gad the Bard

A chair flew overhead, crashing into a wall with a small explosion of splinters and noise. Our not-quite-hero and his faithful friend huddled together—perhaps cowering—but bravely behind an overturned table on the edge of the room. The first floor of the tavern was in chaos; the drunk and the angry, small slights and old grudges, far too many emotions were being expressed with hearty violence across a crowded room.

Gadriel, or Mad Gad as he had come to be known within the circles he often found himself, thought of himself a free spirit that just wanted to enjoy life. Gadriel liked playing for a crowd, and his idea of a nice evening was a cozy inn, a roaring fire, a small stage, and a lot of tips. Or getting rich the cheapest way possible. Gadriel wasn't the tallest man, nor the shortest. Chestnut hair was free to fall to his mostly square jaw that was crooked into a grin most of the time. His dark brown eyes were always searching and his voice was smooth, and it stuck with those who heard it like a dark, wildflower honey.

Laughing, Gadriel said, not for the first time and likely not the last, "Shanks, this one is not my fault." Shanks, Gadriel's best friend and most (only) trusted ally, just shook his head, cowering beside Gadriel, trying to make themselves as small of a target as possible. As they did, they heard a mostly wet thud overhead on the wall behind them; Shanks looked down to see most of a fish had fallen there amongst the remnants of a broken plate.

Shanks proceeded with the best course of action, casually picking up the fish and slapping Gadriel right in the face with it, to which Gadriel responded, "Hey, okay; this one might be my fault," then stuck his tongue out to lick the side of his mouth and face, not unlike a child.

"Aw, Shanks, you should've had the fish—it's a mint sauce; I have just had the pleasure."

Gadriel didn't know Shanks's real name, and as far as Gadriel was concerned, he didn't need it. Shanks was Shanks: small, spunky, dependable, always looked far too young for his age, and, well, Shanks never left.

"You want to turtle over to the door like that one time?" Gadriel tried to say as quietly as was possible over the din of the crowd. Shanks stared at Gadriel blankly, then began clearly looking for another fish.

"I think we should carry the table like a turtle over to the door like that one time."

Shanks attempted to peek over the table but was immediately forced back down behind cover by thrown debris. "Okay, we're going to turtle." Shanks simply sighed, blowing black strands of hair from his face in exasperation.

As if without needing to communicate with each other, Gadriel and Shanks switched places behind the table so Gadriel, being the taller of the two, could lift the front leg of the table just enough for "team turtle" to scoot over to an exit without getting stabbed, at least this was their plan.

"On three? One, two . . . wait, wait, wait. I'm forgetting something . . ."

Gadriel looked down frantically at broken dishes and upturned furniture while patting himself down. Shanks widened his eyes with both shock and incredulity. Gadriel simply held up a finger in an assuring way. Dropping back down on his hands and knees, Gadriel began quickly moving debris in search of . . . right there, a small fabric pouch between two large feet. Gadriel looked up and up and up until he saw the grinning face of Turf looking down at him.

"Oy pretty man, looks like not everything be going yer way tonight, ey?"

As Turf picked up his blocky foot to simply stomp on his target, a chair from one direction high and a rageful Shanks from another low slammed into an unsuspecting Turf, and the small giant crumpled. Turf's merry band of awful criminals saw this, however, and our non-heroes were quickly running out of time to escape this situation unscathed. Shanks, not one to lose knives he doesn't have to, joined the crowd and began throwing what was convenient at the two men; this only slowed them, however. Gadriel quickly snatched the pouch and placed it inside his jacket, joyfully springing up to his full height, only to be knocked back down by an errant plate of food.

"Another FISH!?" Gadriel complained to no one in particular.

Gadriel said loudly, abandoning all attempts at stealth, "Shanks! My good man! We have overstayed our welcome!"

Making eye contact with each other, Shanks didn't hesitate to evade, as was their way, and dove out a near first-floor window.

"So I guess we don't get to turtle like that one time," Gadriel muttered to himself as he crawled on his belly toward his overturned table for cover; he did not want to make the mistake of standing up again and being assaulted by another finned supper.

Again, Gadriel began making his way toward the exit, but so did Turf's agents. About halfway toward freedom, Gadriel covered in ale, spirits, and Mother knows what, the three met, and none were happy to see one another. Gadriel was afforded the opportunity to stand up to his full height, and the three were able to chat:

Gadriel: "Good evening, gents, what assistance may I provide? Might I say, you both smell nice."

Thug 1: "Give it ere' then, Mad Lad."

Thug 2: "Naw, Munty, it's Mad Gad."

Munty: "Mad Gad? What are you on about?"

Thug 2: "It's not Lad; it's Gad—we're professionals now."

Munty: "Oh, oh, thanks, Dint. All right, give it 'ere, Gad."

Gadriel: "Give what?"

Dint: "You know what we want, now hand it over."

Gadriel: ". . . hand what over?"

While Gadriel was attempting to use this opportunity to stall and walk backwards towards his goal of escape, this fact was not lost on thugs Dint and Munty. Dint demonstrated this understanding by slamming a chair leg into Gadriel's thigh, hard enough to hobble the man.

"Oh you know, that helped me remember—you mean this pouch?" which he produced from his jacket.

"Yes, that's the exact one right there, then," Munty said, moving forward without hesitation.

Gadriel threw the pouch over their heads toward the back of the room. "Ah ya knob," said Dint, who began moving in the direction of the pouch.

Gadriel's second attempt at taking the thugs for fools was foiled by the barest of intelligence again. Munty said, "Go find it, Dint. I'll stay here with the knob; boss will want to talk to him."

"So have you ever thought about changing careers? I hear executioning is nice this time of year," asked Gadriel pleasantly.

"Shut your mouth, pricklick. I've got a knot on my head because of you," demanded Munty.

"I've got the bag!" shouted Dint, and in a deeper, louder baritone, rejoining the evening and plucking the bag from Dint's hand, Turf shouted, "No, I'VE the bag, you idiots! And it's not all 'ere."

"But boss, it's full of coin," pleaded Dint.

"I said, it's not all 'ere," Turf repeated, but slower. Both men then began making their way to Munty, who had ahold of Gadriel's arm.

"We'll search him and help him tell us where the rest of it is," said Turf with the smile of a man who was about to enjoy his life's purpose.

"FIRE!! FIRE!!!" shouted men and women from the back of the great room as smoke began to pour in from the back of the building. Turf shouted "GRAB HIM!" over the panic of the crowd, but Munty's grip loosened, allowing Gadriel to break free.

Turf's hand reached for him as smoke began to envelop the group, but he howled in pain as his hand suddenly became bent in an interestingly wrong way. Gadriel, as shocked as Turf, looked over to find a cloaked woman with wavy auburn hair recovering from her swing.

"Let's go, pisser!" and Gadriel grinned.

1

The Port Town of Lulin

Three days earlier, Gadriel and Shanks arrived at the small merchant town of Lulin with little more than the clothes on their backs and small coin in their pockets. Lulin specialized in exports of goods and the saltwater fishing of their own. Villages and smaller townships transported goods to Lulin up their canals, and being a port town, would facilitate shipping them out to sea on larger ships. If Gadriel and Shanks had liked to be still, Lulin would be a lovely place at first glance. Not too filthy and rundown, which meant not too corrupt in their book—usually a good thing for their purposes. A quaint, small clocktower in the center of town with what Gadriel thought were beautiful chimes could be seen from canals. Gadriel decided that Lulin tried very hard to be grown up, something he knew plenty about, so he decided he liked it. Gadriel had his favorite flute, Shanks his favorite knives. As he mentioned many times on the roads and canals alike, Gadriel was determined to have a good time. And it started at a bakery.

"Shanks, do you smell that?" If someone could nod hungrily, it is what Shanks managed to do. Gadriel quickly straightened himself up using his reflection in shop windows, then followed his nose (and his stomach) to the door of a small shop where he found fresh breads and sausage rolls cooling from being removed from their oven.

"Sweet, glorious Mother, have I died? Shanks, am I dead?"

"What's that, sir?" said a young man, standing up from behind the counter. He was young, likely twenty years old to Gadriel's twenty-eight, with shortly cropped blond hair and green eyes that were self-serving when they weren't kind.

"Oh, hello, my companion and I were brought in by your heavenly aroma . . . of your bakery, I mean," said Gadriel.

The man smiled and looked at Gadriel inquisitively. "Well, we're glad you've come in today. I'm Julien. My family and I are proud of our craft and its . . . aroma," he said.

Julien had a beautiful face and an upper body one receives when moving sacks of flour for the family bakery and kneading dough by hand every day. Gadriel grinned.

A belly full of sausage rolls later and incredibly pleased with himself, Gadriel let out a contented sigh while he swaggered down Lulin's high street. Shanks, walking along beside Gadriel and never one for many words, made a statement with half a shrug and a shake of their head.

Gadriel smirked and responded, "Why, yes? dear Shanks?"

As was his way, Shanks shook his head some more in response. Gadriel and Shanks were headed toward the Wooden Leg, Lulin's largest tavern of illest repute. Gadriel and Shanks's idea of a good time also involved work, because Gadriel and Shanks liked coin.

Gadriel was a talented musician and singer; Shanks was a loyal friend talented in other ways who did not mind hours of pub chatter. Establishments such as these were a place where Gadriel could perform leisurely, allowing for him and Shanks to observe groups coming and going; more importantly, they could listen to them talking, as everyone seems to ignore the help (or in this case, the bard).

Gadriel played his favorite flute and sang his favorite tunes on and off for two chimes before calling it an evening the first night. Our heroes didn't make it too late of an evening, having been travelers a few short chimes before. One wouldn't normally stay in an inn like this one if he had anything of value, but seeing as he and Shanks did not, it seemed like a great place to lay their heads.

"Innkeep, my good man, my companion and I would like a room if one within this fine establishment would be available please, sir."

The man looked nearly confused at Gadriel, a look of which he was used to receiving.

"Two of your finest beds please, good sir."

The man stared at him a little longer, then looked around. Gadriel knew it was late, but it wasn't that late; he was worried for the man.

After a few short moments of additional silence, Gadriel said, not slowly or loudly, just clearly, "Two beds. One room?" to which the innkeeper sprung into motion in response.

"Right this way. Right-o!"

Gadriel slept fitfully most nights, and that night was no exception. Shanks slept lightly but easily and was straight to sleep. Gadriel knew he wasn't alone in the room, but this didn't keep shadows or nightmares at bay for him. Some nights he couldn't escape the fire; others he was never afforded the opportunity to try. Waking up sweaty shortly after daybreak, Shanks was already sitting up watching the sunrise.

"Did I talk again?" Shanks nodded. "Was it embarrassing?" Shanks nodded again, then both smiled.

In addition to an exhausting vocabulary, a mouth that often got him into trouble, and light madness, some might say our not-quite-hero was somewhat of a vain man, and Gadriel could not do without a proper bath. Shanks? Not so much. Shanks preferred to bathe when it was warranted or about once a week, as was normal. Though both would often argue concerning the expense, Shanks often relented as Gadriel seemed to use his exceptional cleanliness to their advantage often, much like the day before.

After Gadriel finished primping and preening, he and Shanks hit the town in search of jobs or other happenings of interest. Their first stop was a town bulletin board. Shanks quickly leaned in to tap a notice of a public bath, using the tip of his finger to tap the much cheaper cost.

"You think I'm going to subject myself to a . . . a . . . a public bath?! A people soup!? Heavens Below. Keep reading, you mountain person."

Advertisements for more well-to-do trading posts and specialized merchants, help wanted ads for dock labor (the hardest job of which Gadriel could imagine, so it certainly wasn't for him) . . . after a few moments of perusing, both of their attentions seemed to be caught at the same time by an interesting notice:

Reward!

for the return of

Lost green jewel!

try not to touch it

It'll know it when you see it!

seriously, don't touch it

By decree of the Governor!

"This may need our attention and expertise," said Gadriel.

Shanks nodded after he finished rubbing his chin in thought. "I wonder if any of *those* are errors?" Gadriel said while waggling his finger across the notice.

Shanks slowly shook his head, tapped the drawing of the stone, then tapped *"don't touch it"* three times.

Gadriel said, "ooh fiiine, it's like I'm getting in trouble for something I haven't even done yet."

After a few additional moments of awkward silence and cut eye from Shanks, Gadriel ripped down the notice with a flick of his wrist and two fingers.

As the two began to walk away, a voice from behind them shouted, "Oy, sir!"

Gadriel said over his shoulder, "No, it's okay, son, I've got it."

This evidently confused the man sheerly from not expecting it. "No, sir, you can't just be walkin' about taking whatever ya want."

Gadriel quickly turned around, still holding the notice by two fingers but away from his body, saying far too loudly, "It is COVERED in urine! You take it, here you go, have it."

The man quickly relented, "Aw, no sir, sorry sir, thanks for the help," to which Gadriel indignantly folded up the notice and placed it inside his jacket, sniffed the air, turned on a heel, and continued his walk with Shanks.

"So, it'll know it when you see it and we shouldn't touch it . . ." Gadriel said and they both paused. "Yeah yeah, I shouldn't touch it. We should try learning more about this."

Shanks nodded, spread his arms in a searching gesture and turned in one circle, then looked at Gadriel, to which Gadriel replied, "Yeah, I've never been here before; I don't know where to start either. Or maybe we do—are you hungry?"

Around twenty minutes later, Gadriel and Shanks were standing in front of the Lulin Bake Shop, Lulin's Oldest Bakery. Shanks gave Gadriel a side eye'd glance with an eyebrow to match.

"We're just here for information about the Governor and this gem, and perhaps some sausage rolls; simmer down, sir."

As Gadriel entered he was again hit with the heavenly aroma of this shop and the fine skills of Julien and his family. Gadriel was looking forward to seeing Julien, not for special personal purposes, but simply because he was pretty to look at.

Gadriel was surprised to find not Julien, but a young woman of similar age and features entering the shop from the back.

"Good day, what can I get you?" she said to Gadriel, to which he responded, "Good morrow, my lady. If my growling stomach were to be trusted, I would take one of everything, but that's a terrible idea—tried it once . . ."

Gadriel paused in thought, staring off into nowhere in particular; the young lady grew concerned by the second until Shanks kicked his leg under the counter.

"YES, yes . . . anyway. I was wondering if Julien were about? We met yesterday."

The young woman appeared disappointed, but in a flash it was gone. "Aye, Julien is my brother, twin actually, but I'm prettier, you see. My name is Rose, after my mother."

Gadriel offered his hand in a noble way, which Rose quickly gripped tightly in a working way. "Nice to meet'cha," she said with a smile.

Rose stood up a little straighter and said, "I regret to inform you, sir, that Julien and his blond locks are not around at present. May there be something with which I may assist?"

It wasn't lost on Gadriel that Rose chose to speak this way, thereby displaying she had at least some of an education. And an opportunity to speak and be understood by someone other than Shanks? That was too good for Gadriel to pass up. Shanks simply sighed . . . loudly.

"Pity that, my lady. For I hoped to speak with the young lad concerning mysterious goings-on about the town?" said Gadriel.

"Aye, my lord," Rose responded. "What sort of mysterious happenings dost thou wish to discuss?"

Gadriel produced the folded notice from his jacket, handing it to Rose. Rose studied the note long enough for her to recognize she was already familiar with town gossip and handed it back to Gadriel, completely ignoring Shanks.

Giving Gadriel a warm smile, she said, "Sorry, handsome. I'm a baker; well, a baker's daughter. All I know is that our Governor has a lot of shiny stuff for a man who doesn't work. And I know about as much about this as you do."

Right then, a man ran up to the door of the shop speaking hurriedly. "Rose! Rose! Some sissy priss just pissed all over the town board! Watch out for the fancy pisser! We're warning everybody! Gotta go!" And then he ran off.

Rose looked slowly in Gadriel and Shanks's direction and asked, "You wouldn't happen to know anything about that?" to which Gadriel responded, "My good lady, do I look like the kind of man that would relieve oneself on a town bulletin board?"

"Not in the daytime," Rose quipped.

Before Gadriel could retort, Rose asked, "Will there be anything else, sir? I should really go talk some sense into this group searching for a 'fancy pisser.'"

"Just when might Julien be back, ma'am?" Gadriel asked politely.

"I told you, handsome. I'm the pretty one," said Rose. "How about I ask around about your mystery and meet you at the Wooden Leg this midday?"

"Now how would you know we were staying there?" asked Gadriel.

With a wink, Rose said, "Clearly word travels fast in Lulin, fancy pisser."

With that, Rose shooed Gadriel and Shanks out of the shop, for which Gadriel received a sharp backhand to the chest from Shanks for forgetting sausage rolls. This only caused Gadriel to slap himself on the forehead in shame.

"I must make this up to you. Tavern chatter?"

Shanks appeared to quickly forgive and with excitement he mimed "no, Tavern food," rubbing his hands together.

Determined to learn more about the town, our duo did not return to the Wooden Leg and decided instead to visit a tavern by the name of The Thirsty Goat, known for its fish and chips when the sun was up and fistfights when the sun was down—a perfect place for both of our not-so-much-heroes.

As they walked, they often talked to work a problem, to replay a conversation, or to form plans. On this afternoon, they did all three, attempting to casually discuss the gem near townsfolk hoping to spark interest, attempting to then eavesdrop. Gadriel even wagered Shanks that Rose would not show at The Wooden Leg that evening.

On their way into The Thirsty Goat, however, an angry goat, who may or may not have been thirsty, stomped its hooves in frustration as it stood there tied up to a pole while local drunkards poured ale near its face as if offering it a drink.

"You know, I think that goat wants to drink," observed Gadriel.

"Oy, what's that then?" said a shining member of the community standing just out of reach of the goat and its rope.

"I was talking to the goat, sir."

Confused, the men took a break from taunting the goat and continued to stare at Gadriel, who continued to walk toward the entrance to the tavern. A few moments later, the inquisitor bellowed in pain as the goat rammed him where no man would want to be rammed, rope broken cleanly enough as to have been cut.

Shanks was suddenly to Gadriel's left with a contented smile on his face. As they walked through the door, Gadriel said in a murmur, "Was that you? because I loved that for them," to which Shanks responded with only snicker.

Taking a table not too close to the bar and not too far from the back of the room, Gadriel ordered two helpings of fish and chips from a lady barkeep of middling years who wouldn't have minded speaking with Gadriel for longer.

"I hope you're hungry sir. This be the best chippy you'll find in three ports."

The somewhat matronly and kind barkeep was growing gray through her black hair like tinsel but wore it with pride. Her apron was seasoned by years of hard work; her hands and arms were built with wired muscle by those same years. Her olive skin was beginning to wrinkle, but her light brown eyes showed no signs of slowing down anytime soon. This woman knew who she was and quickly gained a good idea of who others were. Running this tavern appeared to Gadriel exactly where she needed to be, and it was exactly appropriate.

"May I have your name, ma'am?" asked Gadriel.

"Louanne, sir, but please call me Lou. What might I be calling you?"

"Of course, Lou, my name is Gadriel, and this is Shanks."

"Shanks?" Lou asked.

"Yes, family name, you see," Gadriel added quickly. "Might we ask what you may know about this missing stone that seems to have Lulin aflutter?"

Lou smiled and said, "Ah, you wouldn't be the sign pisser would ya? You do be lookin' fancy."

Gadriel nearly blushed, but of course he did not. Gadriel said, "I do hope dearly that they catch this scoundrel, whoever they may be." After a pause, he continued, "Is there love lost for the Governor?"

Lou responded, "Well, it be lookin like the Governor's been losin' a lot of tings lately; but no, sir, I don't be knowin' special about it."

"I thank you so much for your time, Lou."

Gadriel ate his helping and discussed the day with Shanks. "So from what we've heard on the street, from Rose, from Lou, not much is known about this stone, gem, whatever. And it also sounds like the Governor isn't anyone's favorite person."

Shanks nodded.

"Whether he is malevolent or his cronies are, it doesn't appear as though anyone will answer direct questions to outsiders like us."

Shanks agreed.

"What do you say we head to The Wooden Leg and start an honest evening's work? Perhaps Rose does stop by and surprises us both," asked Gadriel.

In response, Shanks simply stood up. Gadriel settled the tab with Lou and thanked her again, leaving a generous overpayment for her, not only to be thoughtful, but to purchase information in the future. A woman like Lou knew a lot and heard a lot; Gadriel could appreciate this.

Chimes later, Gadriel and Shanks found themselves practicing familiar routines at The Wooden Leg—Gadriel singing and playing off and on, telling the occasional bawdy joke, Shanks taking a seat at a rear wall not too far from the stage.

There was a man ere' who was messy
There was no hope for his wife, so named Bessy
For he would not take a bath
And he could not make her laugh
And that's how I know Bessy's cranny!

With chuckles all around, even from Shanks, Gadriel noticed auburn hair struck red by last of the day's sunlight coming into the Wooden Leg. Across the smoky tavern floor, Gadriel spotted Rose standing at the bar near the entrance to the great room, looking intently at Gadriel, and Gadriel realized he was smiling. Quickly he waved and motioned for her to join them at his table. Rose made her way carefully across the room with a grace most often seen in cats, not often in people; she took a seat as if taking a throne, saying hello as if finishing a lesson.

Rose had wavy auburn hair just past her shoulders that she often put up for work, with green mischievous eyes not unlike her brother. If her handshake earlier that afternoon were any indication, she had the upper-body strength of her brother too. Rose was not exaggerating, however, when she insisted that she was the prettier sibling. Rose, not unlike her namesake, seemed to have adorably dimpled and often-flushed cheeks under a collection of freckles about a buttoned nose. She wore a merchant's dress of dark green, changing out of her working clothes and apron she wore earlier. And when Gadriel noticed, it was apparent she had been sizing him up just as much as he'd been evaluating her appearance.

"Any luck catching the pisser, then?" Rose asked with a smirk.

Gadriel responded, "No, my lady. Unfortunately we have not been able to nail down this disgusting scoundrel. We will remain ever vigilant, of course."

Rose barked a quick laugh, then said, "I'm sure you will, sir."

After a moment's awkward pause, Gadriel, exasperated, said, "You know I told that man I was taking something covered in piss? Not that I pissed on anything? Yokels."

Gadriel turned slightly red at the thought of his perfect deflection backfiring on him in a potentially disastrous way should this grow out of hand. The table could not help but laugh at Gadriel's embarrassment.

Shanks tapped a comforting hand on Gadriel's shoulder. "Aw, thanks."

Rose offered the table information they had not had this afternoon. "I did some asking and learned a little about your mysterious mystery."

Gadriel and Shanks perked up into rapt attention, which gave Rose no small amount of pleasure. She continued, "Apparently this jewel did indeed belong to the Governor, and he kept it on display in his office for business. It is gone now, but it was very important to him; this is all I know, unfortunately."

Gadriel's eyes brightened. "Unfortunately? My dear lady, this is more than we knew; this is great information. Do you know if he kept it on display or secured in his office?"

Rose responded, "That I do not know, I'm afraid."

Gadriel shrugged. "Well, tomorrow is another day. May we buy you a drink?"

Rose said, "Of course sir, what kind of lady would I be to refuse?"

Rose and Gadriel continued to talk for several hours, without saying too much about themselves, which wasn't lost on either of them; Shanks seemed to melt away like he usually did, which was fine for him. Rose and Julien were indeed twins who had claimed the life of their mother during their birth. They both helped run the bakery with their father, but it was no life Rose wanted.

"There's far too much of the world for me to stare at the same balls of dough all day." Gadriel nodded both knowingly and just as longingly.

Gadriel's childhood was far from normal, but whose ever is? An orphan at a house of iniquity. His mother also passed during his birth; he never knew his father. Gadriel wasn't quick to leave his childhood home; he loved and felt protective over his little family. The world called to him, however.

"And Shanks has been with me longer than I can remember!" Gadriel said over his third drink in as many hours.

"Shanks, huh?" Rose said over her first and unfinished ale. "Sometime you'll have to tell me about . . . them?" Rose suggested.

"Yes! Yes, someday. But we're not in the mood for sad stories; let's talk about daring and impressive things!"

And they did. And for once, Gadriel made a friend. He thought.

2

Turf, Munty, and Dint

The next day started the same, just slightly more hung over than the last. Shanks hadn't gone to bed any earlier than Gadriel, but he certainly appeared more rested. The two got ready to attack the day and hit the streets of Lulin with purpose. The purpose of the day was to gather more information on this stone or, if that failed, to find other ventures.

Much like how he preferred to work, Gadriel wanted to be where the people were. He liked hearing their stories, their plans, about their days. Walking down high street, Gadriel and Shanks came to a rather busy establishment named The Kitchen.

Gadriel leaned over to Shanks and murmured, "An eating establishment called 'The Kitchen.' Must be pretty good; look at all the people."

As they sat, a young lady by the name of Anne greeted them with, "What'll it be, what can I get'cha?"

Gadriel responded, "We've been told the . . . coff . . . ffee is something to have here."

"Aye, we think you'll like it; we just started getting it from a place across the sea. Are you expecting someone else?" Anne asked.

Gadriel said, "No ma'am, we'll take two 'coff-ffee's, please."

Anne simply nodded and entered The Kitchen.

Anne looked to be a lovely young woman who appeared to be born into a merchant life and was not quite considered the "help." Though she was of a merchant class she still worked for a living, and this showed on her clothes and by how she deftly assisted customers. Anne's thick black hair was pulled tightly back into a bun, and her dark skin only became more beautiful as the sun climbed higher in the sky. Violet was clearly Anne's favorite color judging by the ribbons and her apron, but her blue eyes contradicted this.

Before Gadriel was lost in thought, Anne delivered two hot cups of a dark black liquid that smelled delicious. Anne smiled and said, "Start with a sip I think, sir."

And so he did. Gadriel sipped the bitter liquid and it burned his tongue and throat all the way down to his belly; he liked the little shiver it gave him. The Kitchen was a delightful little establishment. Sitting on a terrace surrounded by wrought iron, the cafe overlooked most of the town square. The sun came up slowly to light up the outside of the shop and all the guests enjoying their food and drink; the gray cold stone became a warm orange as the clock chimed its seventh chime of the morning. He could steal peeks of the inside, which was filled with dark hardwood, but Gadriel wanted to be where the people were, and the people liked the terrace.

"And then she said—" . . . "God rest him, he had taken all the—" . . . "Mother that's funny, just like my dog Br—"

Conversations flowed around him, and Gadriel began to close his eyes. Shanks did nothing in particular, just sat back and relaxed in the cool morning air, enjoying the surroundings.

"I didn't take it—I thought you were going to?" . . . "I was but I didn't!! A lot of people were going to but it weren't me!" . . . "Oh, Lara!"

Gadriel's eyes sprung open at the sounds of this hushed, almost frenetic conversation. Two women, who appeared to be maids or servants of a sort, were at a side entrance to The Kitchen, likely for workers of this station. It was clear that Shanks heard this conversation as well, as he stood up slowly but with purpose with Gadriel, leaving coin on the table for Anne.

Gadriel and Shanks calmly waited for whomever Lara and the other women might have been to begin leaving the area to follow them, a difficult task this early in the morning. However, the two decided that when the ladies began moving in a direction, because Lulin was laid out in a sun pattern from the town square, they would simply walk faster and ahead of the women, then wait at some point for the ladies to pass them, doubling the tail time moving half the distance to avoid suspicion.

In a way, this gambit worked, as they were not discovered and they identified where the women were going. Shanks pointed out that it was nothing they did in particular that allowed for this, however, as the women stated, "See you later at the Governor's mansion, Anne!" while carrying a basket from The Kitchen when leaving. Gadriel was never one to throw away victories, however small. Gadriel and Shanks knew that service staff of a house typically knew almost everything happening in such a house, and if Lara and her cohort didn't know who took the stone, they felt it was likely service staff did not take it, even if they might have wanted to.

There was a sudden tap on Gadriel's shoulder, which caused him to yelp in the most rugged and manly way possible. He turned around to find none other than Rose standing there with a great big grin.

"Following the Governor's servants, ey?" she asked.

"No, madam, I were simply listening to something interesting," Gadriel said.

"Oh, so you think it was an inside job?" Rose smiled conspiratorially.

"How may we help you, madam?" asked Gadriel.

"We?" Rose asked.

"Yes, yes, Shanks is my most trusted ally and helps me do jobs even for sneaky beautiful women."

"Huh," she said curiously, but as a statement, not so much a question. She then continued, "Well, I'll be meeting new importers at the docks this afternoon and was wondering if you'd like to come with me? It isn't always a safe proposition, so I will pay you in sausage rolls."

Before Gadriel had a chance to respond, his ear was suddenly flicked, hard, by someone next to him that wasn't Rose.

"Ye-YES. I was going to say yes! Anyway!"

"Excellent!" Rose said with a genuine smile.

Several hours later, the trio found themselves walking along one of Lulin's canals, past its locks, and toward its docks. The Lulin docks and harbor were a marvel for a town its size. Being a seaport, Lulin made good use of its canals to transport imported goods to the rest of its duchy; it also made excellent use of tariffs to maintain its substantial docks, which included two dry docks, canal locks, cargo lifts, and several large berths for high traffic. The warm hardwood of the Lulin docks had withstood the test of time and no longer creaked as much as balked at the weight of man and his devices. Walking past the Dockmaster's Office, they descended the seawall on stairs with a railing worn smooth from a lifetime of use. The steps had been replaced as needed, but this railing, a helpful boundary, had outlived generations.

A young porter ran by as the three made their way toward the end of the dock, as was arranged by the flour importer. There was one small ship and two empty berths at the end of the docks. Shanks took special notice of the boy then special notice of the lack of other porters, longshoreman, and sailors in the area at midday. Shanks then tapped Gadriel and made an abortive gesture. Rose continued her confident pace toward the end of the docks, which caused Gadriel to shrug and silently motion toward Rose, eventually giving up trying to silently communicate and saying in a defeated tone, "Oh it's not like we haven't done this before; of course we're being ambushed."

Alarmed, Rose asked, "What's that?"

From overhead on top of the seawall, several men quickly climbed and jumped down behind them, cutting off a quick getaway, surprised to see multiple adversaries instead of one lady merchant, but enjoying the element of surprise all the same. From the gangplank of the ship swaggered a middle-aged woman with a dagger on each of her hips. Dark brown, braided hair was knotted back into something not easily grabbed. Her billowing black blouse looked like something to confuse her opponent in a fight as much as it did appear fashionable. She wore her men's trousers and boots in a way that suggested men were doing it wrong, and there was no mistaking that this was her ship.

Following just behind her must have been many of her crew; Gadriel and Shanks stopped counting after six, and they were all pleased with themselves.

"Well, well, well. Look here, boyos, it's Lulin's thorny Rose, and she's duped some help?"

Gadriel, as much as he wanted to stay quiet and find out why Rose was thorny, could not help himself. "Hey, we weren't duped, we volunteered."

Rose said, "Hello, Tamara," followed by a very dry, "oh no, what an unexpected surprise."

"Told you," a slight man behind Tamara said too loudly.

"Shut it, Think," the captain said.

"If it pleases the captain—" cut in Gadriel; "It does *not*," cut off Rose.

"I'm here to speak with Thorny, not her *help*," said Captain Tamara.

"What'll it be, Thorny?" asked Captain Tamara.

"Well, seeing as how you just got into town, I thought maybe you might be interested in some information," Rose said, dripping with intrigue.

Gadriel and Shanks stood there like lost children.

"And what information might that be? I've been disappointed before, Thorny," the captain asked skeptically.

"Oh, about the Governor's little treasure," said Rose.

From behind Tamara, Think hissed, "Cap't, the Whisper Stone."

"And I said *shut it*, Thinker. What about his lump of green glass, Thorny?"

"Only that it's gone missing," said Rose, sweetly.

Gadriel raised his hand as politely as possible, clearing his throat. "Ladies, may we be excused?"

Both Rose and Tamara loudly said, "No!"

Tamara then asked, "Who is the pretty one anyway?"

Rose said, "Just a friend with which to take pleasant afternoon walks on the dock."

"Tool, got it," Tamara responded, then continued, "Well, why don't you join me on my ship where it's 'safer' [making air quotes]; we'll discuss business, then one or both of us can be on our merry ways?" she said cheerily. And before anyone could respond, Tamara then calmly said, "Now."

The men behind Gadriel began moving forward. Captain Tamara was clearly not accustomed to being disobeyed, whether or not she was standing on the deck of her ship.

As Gadriel, Shanks, and Rose walked toward the gangplank, up which Captain Tamara had already traversed, Gadriel admired the dark wood and sleek lines of this ship, which appeared to be very fast. Across the prow read the word "Midnight." The top halves of its sails were storm-cloud gray; the bottoms were inky black. As Gadriel walked alongside the ship, he realized the hull, where he could not see dark wood, was patterned with dark blue and dark gray paint over tarred sealant, and it occurred to him the ship would be near impossible to see at night—an excellent advantage for a smuggler or a pirate, of which he believed the good captain to be both. Even the crew of the Midnight wore dark clothing, and something told Gadriel that the man called Thinker was likely responsible.

The deck of the Midnight was dark hardwood, and as much as Shanks loved ships and wanted to explore, he loved getting left behind less. So as curious as Shanks usually was, he kept a close pace with Rose and Captain Tamara. At the door of what Gadriel presumed was the captain's quarters, Tamara welcomed in Rose as promised. However, Gadriel and Shanks were not afforded this hospitality and were told to wait on the deck.

As the door began to close, Captain Tamara gave Gadriel a wry wink and a smile, then shut the door harshly. Gadriel and Shanks found themselves surrounded by six men; the one called Thinker appeared to be First Mate Thinker, considering the deference afforded him by his fellow crew.

Several moments passed by in silence. The crew stared in silence, blinking on occasion. Gadriel's mouth was in dangerous territory, the kind that got him into worse trouble than he already was. But, as he always thought, life was boring.

"So boys—MEN! . . . Thinkerrr."

He paused. No one responded or moved. "Okay, all right," said Gadriel, who was kicked by Shanks with zero nonchalance. "Okay so this woodpecker walks into a bar. The bartender says, 'what'll it be?' The woodpecker says, 'something stiff,' and the bartender says, 'so like a drink or like a wooden lady?'. . . ehh? eh? Wow, tough crowd, a pecker joke and everything."

Gadriel lit up for a moment and exclaimed, "OH! I know what this needs, may I?" and slowly moved his hand to his flute that he kept with him for just such an occasion.

Shanks just put his face in his hands.

After blowing a merry upbeat tune, Gadriel opined:

There was an old crone
Who sat on an old throne
Who much preferred the light of the night
The old matron was royalty
But paid for her loyalty
For the sight of her was quite the fright
She had strange wants all told hear
Something to do with her rear
And one lad she thought was a delight
This poor lad didn't know
That's not where it goes
And his wit forever smelled of shite!

Though a few members of the crew tried to stifle laughter, which pleased Gadriel, Thinker officially broke the crew's silence, if only to stop another song. "How do you know Rose . . . Gadriel, correct?"

"Yes, sir," Gadriel responded, "we actually met a day or so ago; my companion and I just arrived in Lulin not two days ago."

"Companion?" inquired Thinker.

"Yes, Shanks is my man—basically an assassin, everything I'm not, you see, a man of few words."

"Ah, yes, of course. Some of our crew have heard of you, so is it true that you're mad? I mean no offense" asked Thinker.

"How do we know it isn't everyone else who is mad, I say," retorted Gadriel, crossing his arms not unlike a child.

"You really don't know Rose, do you?" said Thinker with a smile.

Before Gadriel could ask Thinker to elaborate, the captain's quarters opened and Tamara and Rose exited. In a commanding voice, Tamara announced, "All right, boyos! These civilians are free to leave! *Today*! Now, if you would be so kind as to get off my ship; she doesn't like visitors, at least ones that aren't paying rent."

Our non-heroes did not need to be told twice and carefully made their way down the gangplank, not nearly as gracefully as any of the crew. Rose, however, moved down the gangplank more gracefully than she moved through a crowded, smoky tavern.

The three made their way down the dock toward the stairs of the sea wall. Once they were out of what Gadriel felt was earshot of the crew, both Gadriel and Shanks stared daggers at Rose.

"What in the Heavens Below was that about, Rose?" asked Gadriel.

"They weren't flour importers, I suppose?" responded Rose unconvincingly.

Gadriel said slowly and clearly, but without quite losing his temper, "Tell us the truth or we're no longer friends or acquaintances."

"Fine, fine," said Rose, making a calming gesture. "I knew that Tamara and her ship would be at the docks today; they arrived late yesterday and I wanted to speak with the captain."

"Okay, what did you need us for, then?" asked Gadriel.

"Well, to be honest, it's a lot harder to make two people disappear than it is one person. Also, just because I thought she'd be willing to have a conversation doesn't mean my walk through the dock district would've been any safer. I'm sorry for not being truthful; I just needed your help."

Gadriel and Shanks looked at one another while continuing to walk beside Rose, as if having a conversation with each other in silence.

"Well? Do you forgive me?" asked Rose.

"Will you wait just a minute? We're discussing it," said Gadriel, turning back to Shanks. Rose forced patience but only in strict definition.

"Okay fine. We've decided that it is okay ONLY because we would've done the same thing to someone else in similar circumstances and hypocrites are just the worst."

"Thank you," said Rose. A much more business-like Gadriel then asked, "Now, what is going on?"

Several chimes later, Gadriel and Shanks found themselves back at The Wooden Leg for the evening. Rose had gone home to help Julien and her father with the following day's prep for the shop. By now, one in three conversations they overheard mentioned the missing stone. Shanks gleefully pointed out to Gadriel that about one in five conversations mentioned the "fancy" or "sign pisser," which Gadriel could only roll his eyes at in annoyance.

Occasionally taking requests from the crowd and telling the occasional joke, tips were good that evening. When tips were good and business appeared normal, it made eavesdropping much easier for the duo. However, sometimes they don't need that level of subterfuge. Around the twelfth chime, a small giant and a small man entered The Wooden Leg and took a conspicuous table near the hearth, near the stairs, and away from the main bar. The two were either dock workers or from a merchant boat that ran canals, judging by their appearance and attitude. Both Gadriel and Shanks thought the pair's attempts to be clandestine were laughable. The two appeared to be waiting for one or more people to join them, and the man in charge, named Turf, kept demanding his partner remain quiet, while he himself did nothing of the sort.

Shortly before the first chime, a man entered wearing a cloak, and he did not remove his hood. Turf and Munty, whom Gadriel had identified through inane discussion, had been drinking plenty; this was bad form for good crime. But thus far, Gadriel and Shanks had gathered over the last chime that the two men were waiting for a third, then were leaving for what was likely a burglary; why this needed three men and not one our not-quite-heroes couldn't wait to discover.

"Ah, this must be our thug," Gadriel said quietly while cleaning his flute at a table far enough away so as to barely hear the conspirators. To alleviate suspicion, Gadriel had already left the stage for the evening.

Upon sitting down, Turf roughly pulled down the cloak off the man and said, "Way to get attention to yerself, Dint, ya litt'l shite."

Dint quickly said, "Sorry Turf, just tryna be careful."

"Whatever, you need a drink before we get to it, then?" asked Turf.

"How thoughtful," murmured Gadriel.

"Nah, I had one before I came—just left the docks, looks clear," said Dint.

"Good, let's get on, then," said Turf as the three stood up and walked toward the front doors together.

Gadriel and Shanks patiently stayed in their seats and then patiently arose, collecting their things as if going up to their room. Instead of taking the stairs, however, they continued past the stairs and out a back exit of The Wooden Leg, quickly circling around the side of the building to observe Turf and company—and there they were, trudging with purpose along the canal and back toward the docks. Gadriel and Shanks followed at a safe distance, crossing the canal to use the moving water to help conceal the sounds of their feet as they caught up.

At the sea wall and main stairs to the docks where Gadriel and Shanks were earlier that day sat the Dockmaster's Office, which appeared to be the building of interest for Turf's caper.

Gadriel mouthed "Tariffs?" to Shanks to which Shanks nodded.

Munty acted as a lookout while Turf and Dint, who couldn't have been more than eighteen years old, broke into the small standalone office by way of what appeared to be simply prying the locks. Before the door was opened, Gadriel and Shanks noticed two town guards on patrol moving toward the Dockmaster's Office from the direction of the canal, where Munty was not looking.

Completely disappointed in their ability to achieve even simple crime, Gadriel couldn't help himself. He picked up a small stone and lobbed it overhand across the canal to direct Munty's attention in the correct direction. As it did so, Munty's eyes widened, and he made a clicking noise with his mouth, dropped down on all fours, and covered himself with a cloak in shadow. Turf and Dint, having heard this signal, stopped, ducked, and moved behind the Dockmaster's Office, listening for the steps of the guards, slowly moving around the building using it as cover while Munty laid still and silent. Gadriel looked at Shanks and silently clapped in mock admiration.

Back to work, Turf finished prying the locks of the office, then the two quickly entered. Inside, they did not use any lights, using only moonlight through windows to guide them, which is also how Gadriel and Shanks observed them; there was nothing mock about their appreciation for this decision. A short minute later the three men were walking away from the Dockmaster's Office and back towards Lulin's center districts, not along the same canal route, but not along the seawall bound to have dock guards, either.

The three men never had the chance to finish their plans due to several black-and-gray–clad men armed with clubs, among other weapons, who intercepted and rushed Turf and his gang in an immediate clash of violence in the middle of a side street. Munty was clubbed and folded in on himself instantly, Turf turned to Dint and said, "GO!" and Dint didn't hesitate; the young man with his small frame was fast, and he fled in the opposite direction of this trouble. Turf was hit in the back with a club, which cracked the weapon, but not Turf. In response, Turf grabbed the man and used him as a weapon, swinging the screaming man wildly.

One of the men dressed in black wearing a black mask was patting down the incapacitated Munty. In the middle of his search, Munty began to fight back, and in response, the searching man stabbed Munty in the side with a small, flat knife, just for this purpose.

The man leaned down amongst the chaos of the fight and said calmly, "I'll use small words to be clear. Fight me again and I'll twist this and you'll die. Reach for my face again and I'll pull the blade out, you'll bleed out, and you'll die. Lay still, and you'll live."

Munty was pale with fear but understood the man clearly. The man finished his search, disappointed to not find what he was looking for, and turned his attention to Turf, holding his own against four aggressors.

The man in the black mask approached Turf with purpose, who was still using a grown man as a ram, sweeping him back and forth and screaming with rage. Giving Turf a wide berth, the man dressed in all black positioned himself quietly behind Turf, then calmly walked up behind him and stabbed him in his giant hamstrings, dead center—not to permanently maim, but to incapacitate for now. Turf dropped to his knees and dropped the poor man, who looked like he would sick up at any moment.

Breathing heavily, Turf knew if he could not stand up he could not fight them all, and now that he was losing his rage, he realized they weren't killing him deliberately. They attacked him with clubs, not blades.

The man who hobbled him spoke clearly and directly. "Where is it?"

"Where's what, then," said Turf, more of a statement than a question. In response, Turf didn't hear a voice, but a long, slow, metallic scrape of a short sword being drawn from a belt harness. Nothing else was said. Turf was simply clubbed in the back of the head with the butt of the heavy sword.

Dint was long gone while the fight raged on, and he did not stop until he was several districts away and sure he wasn't being followed. Except he had been followed, of course, by Shanks and Gadriel. The boy took up a position to rest in the shadow of the corner of a textile building, figuring buildings with lots of people sleeping inside would somehow be safer. Our maybe-heroes decided that this boy was so far out of his depth and so inept at crime, that he likely still had the purse containing tariffs on him instead of ditching it in a prearranged location and they could probably relieve him of his burdens the old-fashioned way.

After catching his breath, Dint began moving more calmly, with the pace and movements of a normal, non-terrified human being toward the town center. Gadriel and Shanks began moving across the street to intercept overtly, pretending to have enjoyed a night on the town.

Gadriel said, half shouting, "Hey! Heyyy! It's that guyyyy! Hey guy, give us a hug and a kiss!" While passersby laughed, Dint did not and only became more nervous. This did not matter, however, as Gadriel simply bumped into the boy then apologized, "*hick* I'm sorry lad, I better call it a night, You're not my type now that we're up close."

Of course Gadriel wanted neither hugs, nor kisses from an awful little criminal. He wanted to pickpocket the boy, and that he did. What Gadriel now had in his possession was a purse full of the previous day's Dockmaster's tariffs. Or so he thought.

3

The Return of Lara

GADRIEL and Shanks played it as cool as they always did, calmly making their way back to The Wooden Leg. Waiting until it was clear, they used the rear entrance for quick access to the stairs, and in turn their room, and they called it a night with little additional witnesses. Their favorite part of any job was the pay, and this was one of the times they got to dump it all out to take a look. Only this time when they turned over the purse onto Shanks's bed, it was not only coin they found. They also found a small, green stone, about the size of an egg, that glowed faintly. Both men stared at it intently, as if briefly lost in its light, and Gadriel was sure he heard something that made him want to reach for—

Pain, sharp pain lanced up Gadriel's hand where Shanks slapped, what Gadriel figured was as hard as he could.

"Right. You're right, we shouldn't touch it. Not even me," Gadriel agreed.

"Thanks," he said in a rare moment of sincerity.

Both men somehow knew it would be a bad idea to touch the glowing stone, regardless of the warnings on some bulletin posting. Some of the coin they added to their own pockets, but most went back into the purse; the two men then carefully placed the stone back into the purse without touching it with their hands—which became much easier when they realized they could cover their hands with fabric to move it.

It was time to start the day, and their task of the day was figuring out what to do with this stone. Would they turn it in for the reward? Would they tell Rose about it? Captain Tamara? Would they fence it themselves? Blackmail the Dockmaster? Why did he have it? So many questions. What they did know is they didn't want to carry it on them, and there wasn't anyone in Lulin they could trust, not really.

Fortunately, Gadriel and Shanks made a habit of meticulously hollowing out furniture legs, particularly beds, with a block blade when staying in new places for just such occasions. Shanks had it down to such a practiced art that if the wood were soft, he could make this hiding spot on the first night and still get a good night's sleep, so inside the furniture the purse was hidden. And down the stairs our kind-of-heroes went.

Gadriel decided to appreciate another sunrise at The Kitchen and enjoy Anne's coff-ffee, and they did. Gadriel again appreciated the hot, steaming, bitter liquid as it warmed up his insides on a chilly seaport morning. He liked how the wrought iron glowed when the sun rose just for him. How from where he was sitting he could see the breaths of other patrons and how they would float out differently when someone was laughing or breathing out their nose. He also enjoyed watching Anne help people and how she seemed to enjoy her work. She liked it when she could get something complicated delivered correctly—she beamed, which brought Gadriel a rare sorrowful smile, with the memory of someone or perhaps time, lost long ago.

After finishing their coff-ffee, Shanks and Gadriel excused themselves after paying Anne and began walking toward the Bake Shop to speak with

Rose. When they were about to enter the neighboring district and away from crowds, they were both caught completely off guard—hooded, gagged, and restrained. Knowing someone got the better of them and that kicking and screaming would likely result in beatings, Gadriel and Shanks tried to be good prisoners for the time being.

After traveling what seemed like not too long of a distance, perhaps only one and a half districts away, it felt as though they entered a building, hearing people, but none seemed alarmed at the presence of hooded restrained men. Walking down a hallway or corridor of sorts, Gadriel was being guided by the elbow by a very large man, as well as by the back by what was likely also a very large man. Eventually Gadriel and Shanks were placed in chairs with hoods and gags removed, but not restraints.

Getting a look at their surroundings, Gadriel sat in an ornate office of rich woods, green velvets, and lush rugs atop beautiful, polished wood floors. The back wall of the room was bookcase after bookcase filled with priceless knowledge, and directly in front of him was a large desk with a large chair, behind which was a large hearth and fireplace. To his right was a great window that covered most of the wall, well over half. And to his left were the double-doored entrance and more bookcases with more knowledge. Gadriel noticed at the front of the desk sat a small case with an empty stand, and he presumed this must be the Governor's office and that was where the green stone was usually displayed.

In the chair sat a tall, large man with steepled fingers, few of which contained rings of gold. The man was not inherently ugly, but his demeanor, the way he looked at others, and Gadriel guessed the way he treated others made him a very ugly man indeed. Hair of solid white was styled fashionably, and his buttoned squared chin often took your attention away from too-small brown eyes.

I bet this man is a prick, Gadriel thought to himself and smiled slightly.

"Hello, bard," said the large man in the large chair at the large desk.

Yeah, prick, thought Gadriel, again to himself.

"Hello, sir?" said Gadriel.

"Yes, I am Governor Matteson. And to confirm, you are?" said the Governor.

"Good morrow, sir, I am Gadriel and yes I do bard from time to time. This is my companion, Shanks," Gadriel said, nodding over to his best man.

"Ah, yes, Mad Gad, as they say," quipped the Governor. "Do you know why you're here, Gadriel?"

"Well, no, sir," said Gadriel. Although he knew very well why he might be there, he absolutely wasn't going to admit it.

"You really can't think of any reason why you would be here, in front of me, right now?" asked the Governor again.

"No-nnnnope. Not all my songs are great, but I hardly think that's a reason to bag us off the street," said Gadriel.

"I've received a great many reports that a newcomer in town approximately two to three days ago relieved himself on our town notice board; do you know anything about it?" asked the Governor, without a hint of amusement on his face.

Internally relieved, then annoyed, Gadriel piped up too quickly, "Yes, I've heard of the sign pisser."

"I believe he has been referred to as a 'fancy pisser' due to his attire and demeanor," said the Governor.

"Yes I've also heard that reference as well," said Gadriel, exhaustively.

"Mr. Gadriel, you look plenty fancy to me—you arrived in my town three days ago, did you not?" asked Governor Matteson.

"Sir, I did not relieve myself on your notice board. The only honest-to-goodness involvement I have had involving your notice board was that I removed an item that appeared to already be covered in urine. Who may have supplied that urine is lost on me—"

Before Gadriel could finish, the Governor shouted, "ENOUGH," then continued, "We're a port town, Mad Gad. We have new people in, new people out. My father helped build Lulin into what it is today; that was his job. What my job is now, is to not let new people come in with the intent to harm what my father built. Do you understand?" said Governor Matteson.

"Yes sir, but I—"

The Governor again interrupted. "No I do not think you do. You have a reputation; you're a vagrant that smells better. I don't give a shit about your charming songs or rank jokes. I don't want you here—in fact, I want you gone today. You may leave on your own, or my men will help you at the sixth chime; is that understood?"

"Absolutely, sir," stated Gadriel clearly.

Shanks nodded. "Good. You're dismissed," decreed Governor Matteson.

Gadriel and Shanks were walked out the back of the Governor's mansion much more roughly than they were walked in, but they were not hooded and gagged. On their way past the kitchen, Gadriel caught the view of the kitchen staff and decided to say "Hi Lara" in a cheerful tone while being marched right past a corridor toward a rear exit. He laughed as he could hear other staff asking Lara, "*Lara! You know the pisser!?*"

Gadriel was pushed out a back door into a small semi-open courtyard still in his restraints. As he fell onto his front, the heavy door was slammed shut and locked with two loud, dull clicks. He quickly rolled over to welcome Shanks, who was sure to follow.

"Shanks my boy, I'll catch you!" he said, spreading his legs in an oddly welcoming gesture. Shanks opted for the ground and landed on his front in much of the same fashion; his belt knives clinked on the ground shortly after. After good teamwork, both were on their feet in a short minute. After bribing a few street kids with a promise of fresh bread, they were free from their restraints, then on their way to the Bake Shop. Though both were searched before entry to the Governor's mansion, their own money purse was checked then roughly stuffed back into Gadriel's jacket pocket; the Governor's men were professional, Gadriel would give them that. And though Gadriel could pay the children outright, he could not shake the feeling that all of their predicaments lately were directly related to Rose, so she could pay these hungry children.

When Gadriel, Shanks, and three hungry little mouths arrived at the Bake Shop, both Julien and Rose were working the counter. Gadriel and his little band waited patiently in line like other patrons, but when they arrived at the front counter, Gadriel announced in a saintly voice, "Children, this is Mother Rose, the absolute angel in human form we discussed. Choose any breads your bellies need—she won't charge you, probably ever."

He quickly stood up, giving her more eyebrow than lip.

Rose was off-balance for only a moment before stating, "Yes children, please fill yourselves, *today*, not probably ever. Julien could you help these boys while I speak with our customers."

"Sure thing, everything okay?" asked Julien, looking at Gadriel and smiling genuinely. When Gadriel made eye contact with Julien, his face softened into a genuine smile of his own.

Rose responded, "Yes, brother, all is fine, we'll just have a quick discussion outside."

On their way out the door, Shanks looked longingly at the sausage rolls, sniffing the air without shame as the three casually walked around the corner of the Bake Shop to discuss recent events. Gadriel did not want to reveal they had the Governor's stone, but he needed to know how Rose knew Turf would be breaking into the Dockmaster's Office. Rose didn't reveal it to Gadriel and Shanks, but it was clear that Captain Tamara's men intercepted Turf and his men in search of their prize shortly after. It was easy for Gadriel and Shanks to make the short logical leap when discussing their day falling asleep, one of Gadriel's favorite nightly rituals and something they had done since their recovery from the Sapphire incident.

Gadriel decided to go directly, but also vague: "So what the Heavens happened last night?"

"I should ask you the same question," stated Rose. She continued, "I wasn't a guest of honor with the Governor this morning; what was that about?"

The coolness between the two continued. Gadriel responded "Oh yes, he needed to discuss with me rumors of a sign pisser, something I'm sure others did a great job of quelling in these money districts."

Gadriel conveniently left out the Governor's threats if he did not leave by the end of day.

"And?" Rose asked, with a "continue" hand motion.

"And WHAT, Rose, I didn't piss on a sign, no one did!"

"And we all know that, Gadriel, but does the Governor know that? He can be an obsessive man," asked Rose.

"He may, or he may have a kitchen servant by the name of Lara who gets fired today, but she's a thief, so, oh well."

To which Rose was very confused and said, "Wh-what?"

Gadriel cut back in. "Not important; what happened last night?"

"Not here," said Rose.

Half a chime later, Gadriel and Shanks found themselves in the sitting room of a small but high-end home in an upscale district of Lulin, likely filled with successful merchants and old money, but not quite nobles who had their own and different class of district altogether. Upon entering the home, they met an incredibly polite older man with dusty lightly colored hair, pale eyes, and a hunched, bad back. The man appeared to be almost too old to be Rose and Julien's father, who had put in a lifetime of work at the bakery. Gadriel could tell this man did not like to stay still, losing his hearing and sight, and perhaps other faculties be damned, and was surely excited to have guests. Rose introduced him as Jerald, her father. Jerald was glad to grasp Gadriel's hand tightly, then gave a slight bow to Shanks, for which Shanks beamed, gently grabbing the man's hands and bowing lower.

"Hello to you, sir!" said Jerald. Shanked bowed again in happy appreciation.

"Father that's . . . he's so glad you're here . . . that's enough. How about some tea for all of us, hmm?" said Rose, a little uneasily.

"Ah! Ah. yes. Tea. Tea is good. Right-o." And Jerald excused himself from the room, retreating to the back of the home.

"Sweet man," said Gadriel, and Shanks nodded quickly. The three took seats, and a moment of silence passed. Clinking and clanking could be heard from the back of the home—hopefully just tea was being made, but it sounded like more.

"So," Rose started. "Last night I heard there was a disturbance by the docks."

"You may have heard of a disturbance, Rose, but you already knew it would happen," suggested Gadriel.

"I had a good idea," said Rose, continuing. "The shop is used as the bakery and supplier for a great many houses throughout the town, at times for the Governor. I had learned tariffs were late, and this had attracted the wrong kind of attention. If it wasn't Turf, it would have soon been someone else at the Dockmaster's Office."

Gadriel nodded, then asked, "Why didn't you just break into office yourself?" to which Rose replied, "For the same reason I talk my brother into carrying the flour," which Gadriel was quick to understand.

"So you involved Captain Tamara to, what?" asked Gadriel.

"Carry more flour," Rose stated simply. "I owed captain Tamara coin from a failed business venture the last time I tried to get out of Lulin. This deal I hoped to work out to clean my slate with her, and in hopes to work with her again in the future."

"I see," said Gadriel.

Just then, a shaky tray of tea cups entered the room followed by a sweet, hunched Jerald, and the smell of fresh, baking bread followed him that nearly made Shanks float out of his chair.

Jerald sat down long enough to pour the tea and smile. Rose, Gadriel, and Shanks, especially Shanks, smiled with deep appreciation for Jerald's efforts.

"Father, you're baking bread?"

"Ah! Yes! Bread!" exclaimed the old man, who sprung up with the energy of a man half his age and shuffled back into the rear of the home.

Gadriel wasn't sure how much of Rose's story to believe, being a generally suspicious man, but it appeared logical without knowing how deep Rose may have been in with Captain Tamara, as there was a small fortune in tariffs, not including the green stone. He was confident, however, that she knew much of what occurred the night before.

"We better be going; we don't want to put your father out, who has been a wonderful host."

Rose arose and said, "I'll pass along your appreciation for him; he does love company. I should also get back to the shop; it should be our midday rush."

Gadriel nodded and said, "It might do you well to steer clear of Turf and his men in the immediate future, for safety," to which Rose said, "Oh, I intend to."

Rose walked our anti-hero-duo out the front door then softly closed it behind them. Shanks appeared disappointed both in leaving the old man and with passing up another meal. As they walked toward the town center, they discussed what was learned.

"She knows everything," Shanks said by tapping his hand to his head, fingers swirling in the air.

Gadriel nodded confidently. "Even knew the names of the thugs," to which Shanks nodded.

"Do you think she knows about the stone?" asked Gadriel, speaking low as to not be overheard. Shanks rubbed his chin in thought, then nodded, then looked up at Gadriel as though asking what he thought.

Gadriel said, "I think it's likely—too much of this is a coincidence, and I think Rose has learned that it's easier to survive keeping valuable information to yourself; she's done it to us twice." Shanks nodded.

Gadriel and Shanks continued down a side alley until reaching Lulin's high street, turning toward The Wooden Leg. Much more aware of what was behind them, it did not appear they would be bagged again this day, at least for now.

"Shanks, question," Gadriel said, to which Shanks again looked up. "The stone, last night, did you . . . hear it say anything?"

Shanks paused in thought, then shook his head. Gadriel reiterated, "You didn't hear any voices or whispers; did you notice it glow?" Shanks leaned back away from Gadriel dramatically as to suggest he was madder than usual.

Gadriel then explained, "The stone once in sight began to glow a deep green; but as though to show me just how deep the stone really was. Almost as if one could fall into it. The longer I stared, the more I felt like the floor shifted. The longer I stared, the more I could hear . . . something. I thought I heard voices; I thought I heard the stone call to me. What started as a whisper that knew me grew louder and more distinct the closer I reached for it. Thankfully your slap snapped me out of it! Goodness, who knows what would happen if you touched that thing. It does not strike me as benevolent."

While Gadriel explained this, with a vacant distant expression, Shanks felt the need to snap their friend out of this too, and he did so by tapping his chest with the back of his hand. When Gadriel looked down at his friend, Shanks tapped his own chest, signaling that maybe he should carry the stone.

"No, no, dear Shanks. No need to risk us both. I simply won't touch it, and that is that." Shanks rolled his eyes and snorted, which caused Gadriel to laugh, which caused passersby to cross the street away from the pair.

Our mostly-heroes decided it would be a good idea to remain mobile most of the day and then leave town closer to their deadline. This way they could catch the canal boats heading away from the direction they came, and they wouldn't be found where they were known, like The Wooden Leg, The Thirsty Goat, or the Bake Shop, and should they be caught unawares, they would not have the stone in their possession at that time. As the sun settled into the horizon, however, it was time to gather their things and find a canal boat out of town. During their day on foot, they decided they would learn more about the stone and likely fence it in another city where it would be more difficult to trace back to themselves. With any luck, perhaps they would never work again. Of course the pair would always want to work, but this could afford them the luxury to take only jobs they really wanted—what a life that could be.

Approaching The Wooden Leg with caution as dusk claimed Lulin, they noticed little Dint standing on the opposite corner of the Wooden Leg acting as a lookout. Being able to maneuver around him without engaging him was easy enough, but more importantly, this told them that it was not perfectly safe inside The Wooden Leg. They needed to access their room, however. The first floor of the tavern was raised, so it was more like a first-and-a-half floor, meaning the second floor, where their room was, was a second-and-a-half floor, a riskier exit if it came to that, and also a riskier climb. Shanks and Gadriel decided to cautiously enter the back of the tavern and hopefully climb the stairs without notice.

Shanks entered first being smaller, noticing Turf sitting very near the rear entrance, near the hearth, so he could observe the entire great room, but his back was to them and he could not observe the stairs at the same time. Gadriel and Shanks slowly made their way behind Turf, who was drinking ale and leaning back in his chair, steaming, waiting for his targets. How he knew to look for them, Gadriel didn't know, likely because of their afternoon's interrogation by the Governor, but he was sure he'd end up finding out. The duo made their way up the stairs, not needing to be as quiet as possible with the noise of a crowded tavern, but they were as quiet as could be all the same.

After slowly ascending the stairs, Gadriel and Shanks found Munty waiting outside their room. This wasn't surprising; The Wooden Leg wasn't the most reputable establishment, and they had met the inn-keep. Munty was overlooking the great room floor, occasionally laughing at drunkard antics below. Like a true professional, he had his back to the staircase. Munty was too close to the door to their room but he was not too close to the door of the neighboring room, which, lucky for Gadriel and Shanks, was unlocked. They carefully let themselves inside, which was thankfully empty. They then carefully climbed out the window, then back into the window of their room, with Munty none the wiser.

What they found was what they expected. Their room and few belongings were completely tossed and trashed. Mattresses cut open, each of their single bags overturned. Pillows in shreds and an overturned simple writers' desk. But what were not overturned were the bed frames and one hollowed leg containing one purse and one green stone (and a substantial amount of coin). Gadriel and Shanks quietly collected their items, Gadriel placed the purse with the stone inside his jacket, and back out the window they went.

Peeking out the door of the neighboring room, they found Munty's back was still to the stairs. And rather than taking their chances going out the window, Gadriel and Shanks figured why not leave the way they came in, which they proceeded to do. Slowly but surely down the stairs, they rounded the bottom of the landing and made their way behind Turf, near the hearth and nearly to the rear entrance, when a screech pierced the crowded tavern. "SIGN PISSER, YOU OWE ME A JOB, YOU SON OF A WHORE!"

Gadriel, Shanks, and much of everyone froze for a moment and looked around to identify the source of the accusation, only to find a distraught Lara, one of the Governor's now former kitchen servants. Turf was quickly to his feet and turned around with a grin on his face.

Gadriel addressed Lara first. "Lara, we should talk, but let's not bring her into this." Then "Turf, sir, nice to meet you."

Turf responded by saying, "'Ello pisser!" then immediately grabbing Gadriel by the front of his jacket. Gadriel then let out a rugged and manly squeal. Turf threw Gadriel toward the middle of the room, knocking over several tables. Knocking food and drink and drunk men and women into more drunk men and women started a chain reaction that was easy to foresee, at least easy for Gadriel and Shanks to foresee.

Shanks ran toward Gadriel, stomping on Turf's foot along the way. "OUCH, WHAT!?" he shouted.

Shanks maneuvered between the alarmed patrons and overturned furniture alike. Shouts and screams begged Munty's attention from upstairs, and he began running down steps two at a time, as fast as his wrapped side would allow to join the fray Turf had just created. Turf was marching toward Gadriel with violent purpose. As Turf reached Gadriel, Munty reached Turf, and both were hit with a bench seat thrown by someone (or someones), and the two fell to the ground. Dint entered the tavern in time to observe his partners hit the ground; part of him wanted to turn around and run, but the larger part of him did not want to face Turf after having done so, so in Dint went.

Gadriel, pleased with this stroke of luck, stood up and moved to leave the tavern, only to have little Dint jump on his back and begin poorly trying to strike him about the head. At about this time Turf began to stand back up.

Gadriel screamed in his rugged and manly way, "HERE, YOU TAKE HIM!" and he jumped toward Turf back first, smashing Dint between the two of them. The impact knocked the wind out of poor awful criminal Dint, letting go of Gadriel, who was quick to his feet, but not before throwing as many elbows behind him, striking wherever they may have landed, preferably below some belts. Shanks kept Munty busy by tripping him several times as he fell over several times in the chaos. Shanks did not want to draw his knives and escalate the entire room to a level of violence no one wanted.

Turf, sick of what he felt was taking far too long to accomplish a simple goal against a coward, wanted an advantage of numbers and picked up Dint and tossed him in Munty's direction, saying, "Get. Him. Then. Get. Him," motioning toward Gadriel.

Gadriel, for his credit, attempted to take this chance to evade, which was foiled by a flying end table thrown by the large Turf, which forced Gadriel to take cover behind a large table, where he was soon followed by Shanks. Just then, a chair flew overhead, crashing into a wall with a small explosion of splinters and noise. Huddled together, cowering bravely, Gadriel couldn't help but laugh as he said, "Shanks, this one is not my fault."

4

The Sapphire

Five years before the fire at The Wooden Leg allowed Shanks and Gadriel to be bravely rescued by a girl, they experienced a much different fire, one that would bond them forever. Before Gadriel was ever Mad Gad, before he preferred to travel by canal and wagon, Gadriel preferred to sail. He loved the open water, despite his inability to fastidiously clean himself and served on the crew of what he thought was the most glorious ship he'd ever seen, the merchant ship Sapphire. The Sapphire won awards for her speed and specialized in moving precious cargo fast, far too fast to be run down by pirates or opportunist naval vessels.

Gadriel would play his flute on the deck for his crewmates and sing out rowing songs to keep the crew's rowing pace when the occasion called for all the speed they could muster from their narrow jewel of the sea. Gadriel's good nature and filthy sense of humor made him a favorite among the crew and its officers. He had been serving on the Sapphire for close to a year when he and

Shanks met. Shanks was nineteen if he was twenty years old at the time and mostly skin and bones. Six months of three squares, even if half the time it was salt pork, biscuits, and limes, filled out young Shanks quickly.

One night shortly before sundown and after supper, the Sapphire had been underway for two weeks, due to arrive at the port of Pope within days. Gadriel was playing his flute for the interested on the deck and as usual, Shanks could be found not far away. Before Gadriel called it an evening, he took time for one of his favorite activities, which was watching moonlight bounce on the water while the Sapphire's exposed keel cut it with her speed. Relaxing near the prow, Shanks approached Gadriel and asked if he could sit.

"Of course, dear Shanks, this is your ship as well as mine."

Shanks smiled then asked, "Why did you decide to join the Sapphire? You've been here for two years, right?"

Gadriel smiled. This was an ages-old question sailors asked one another, either an incredibly intimate one as to be an insult for asking, or an incredibly dull question as to not be worth asking. Gadriel's answer was somewhere in the middle.

"Well, my boy, I never knew my father, and to be honest, I was born in a whorehouse; my mother passed during my birth."

"Heavens Below, I'm sorry, sir," apologized Shanks.

"Oh, please don't," assured Gadriel. He continued, "There are plenty of hungry children with worse childhoods than my own. I was raised by wonderful people who educated me, took care of me, and for whom I cared deeply. But I eventually reached an age where the ladies didn't really need me at the brothel anymore, and it was just time for me to cut out on my own, you know?" Shanks nodded.

"So, being in a small port town, we were mostly a trading hub with little wares of our own, hence the whorehouse. I fell in love with ships. As a younger lad I laid eyes on the Sapphire just once and resolved to crew a ship like it someday. Well, the Sapphire happened to dock around the time I was leaving and I met her first mate at the brothel and begged him for a job."

"That's all it took?" Shanks said curiously.

"No, I honestly don't believe I would've got the job if it weren't for the ladies taking special care of him. They knew I loved the ship."

"Oh wow . . . That was . . . nice of them," Shanks said sheepishly.

Gadriel just laughed. "Oh it's just sex, dear Shanks. You're a sailor, after all. If you laugh at half of my jokes then that part of the story shouldn't blush you." Shanks nodded.

"What about you?" asked Gadriel.

"Nothing so interesting," said Shanks.

"Oh come off it—everyone is interesting in their own way," responded Gadriel.

Shank's smile widened. "Well, honestly I'd been serving as a porter when I joined the Sapphire, but it wasn't really enough to make ends meet when a larger man insists you owe him money when you don't."

Gadriel nodded. "Familiar with that trick."

Shanks continued, "I am rather talented with my knives, really much about them. And I hustle throwing them for small wagers around the docks so I could eat. As you can imagine, this is why I 'owed' someone money." Gadriel nodded again.

"One of the Sapphire's officers was impressed with my handiwork and asked if I could climb, and I said sure thing. So I guess I'm here because I'm small, can climb our masts, and have a talent for knives?" finished Shanks.

"See! That's incredibly interesting," smiled Gadriel. "Which port did you leave when you joined? It'll be fun to go back with your new family when that man tries to collect his false debt," added Gadriel with a wink.

"Oh Heavens Below, I hadn't thought of that, yes! I was born and joined from the town of Woodport."

"Excellent, I'll make a mental note of that one," said Gadriel, then added, "well, you better hit the bunk, young sir. If the winds are favorable there's a chance we reach Pope a day early tomorrow, and I know the cap't will row it the last leg if that means arriving early. Reputations are valuable."

"Oh thanks sir, but I have crow duty tonight, but no one will be sneaking up on us tonight—how could they anyway, but I've got a job to do all the same," said Shanks with a smile.

"That you do. Good night, young sir," said Gadriel.

The next morning, true to Gadriel's assumption, the salty first mate stood next to the Sapphire's captain from the quarter deck. The first mate struck the Sapphire's bell sharply four times, signaling for row crews to ready themselves.

"OY! YOU SALTY SONS A SOW! YOU SEE THAT LAND!? THE CAP'T WANTS IT!" the crew screamed. "BY MOTHER WE'LL TAKE IT!" then howled at the top of their lungs, even Gadriel himself.

The first mate and helmsman could not help themselves but crack predatory grins from the quarterdeck; the stoic captain cracked a small but noticeable smile, cap tight and low to keep sea and spray out of his eyes.

Before heading below decks, Gadriel noticed Shanks still in his crow's nest, at least eight hours after he started his watch, bellowing his support with the crew, apparently volunteering to continue his watch. Gadriel placed his feet on the sides of the railing and slid downstairs quickly, running around a short corridor, past the gundeck, and down another set of railings to the row deck. Gadriel quickly took a seat with his crewmates, and at the sound of four more sharp bells, presented oars and began to row, hard.

After fifteen minutes of hard rowing by most of the Sapphire's crew, Shanks still sat on his knees atop the crow's nest. It was not typically a station when underway like this, but visibility was low—not so low as to not see the port of Pope, but a light fog at sea cut visibility for much of their surroundings, so Shanks volunteered for the dangerous duty. With the excitement of a race against only themselves, Shanks was no longer tired. Abuzz with adrenaline, he remained ever-vigilant at his post, holding his spyglass, carefully scanning 360 degrees around the ship as far as the visibility would allow about once every tock. Around his sixteenth pass, Shanks thought he saw something behind them. Worried at first that he was seeing things due to fatigue, he used the back of his hands and rubbed firmly at his eyes; he then raised the spyglass back to his face. And there it was, a dark ship piercing the fog, and incredibly, somehow, gaining on them.

Shanks nearly panicked, frantically searching his belt for his crows' horn. Gadriel and the rest heard three high-pitched horn blasts from the crow's nest; young Shanks had observed a ship in pursuit of them.

How was this possible? thought Gadriel. Not only were they one of the fastest ships in the great open sea, they were also adding manpower to their speed. Another four sharp strikes of the ship's bell indicated to the crew that they should continue rowing. This made the most sense to Gadriel—a ship like the Sapphire didn't need to fight when they could easily outrun its enemies. The crew was picking up the pace, just not fast enough. Gadriel tried to help in a way he knew how:

Oh it's been several months since I've seen or heard from home
And I might as well be lost since my lady's all alone
My wife and kids are fed which is what a man desires
It's why I toil away on the crew of the Sapphire

The first mate, helmsman, and captain felt an energy, a rumble from the men returning Gadriel's song as they suddenly picked up enough speed that the first mate moved his right foot backward an inch. Another three high-pitched horn blasts, Shanks indicated to the crew that their pursuer was still picking up speed. Gadriel roared his Sapphire song again, and the crew bellowed back. Gadriel knew they could not keep up this pace, and they were likely about out of it as it were. Just then, eight rapid sharp strikes of the bell sounded, followed by eight more rapid sharp strikes. Gadriel almost didn't recognize it because of how rare it was for the crew to need to take up arms in general quarters and prepare for a fight.

The crew in practiced and efficient fashion pulled in their oars and closed ports, then followed one another in an orderly march up either set of stairs leading out of the row deck. The Master at Arms led the way to the armory while the gun crews made their way to the gun deck. Gadriel was never much for fighting but would for his family, and he was issued a belt containing a short sword and a dagger; not knowing what else to do with it, he shoved his flute into his boot and strapped on the belt.

The Sapphire had only nine gun ports, with six cannon total, and they were not of a particularly large size. Its gundeck contained two chase gun ports on its stern, as it was always most likely to need to shoot behind it at pursuers, one chase gun port on its bow, should it need to chase down a smaller, lighter ship, and three port and starboard broadside gunports, paltry in comparison to most ships. However, this is because the Sapphire wasn't a fighting ship, it was a racing ship that ran away from fighting ships—which continued to beg the question, what ship could be catching up to them so quickly.

As Gadriel arrived on deck, a long horn from the crow's nest sounded to be one long blast with all the air young Shanks could muster, and Gadriel could now see why. A terrifyingly large black ship, easily twice the size of the Sapphire, was nearly on top of them. At a shout and motion of the Captain's arm, followed by signals from flaggers, both stern guns fired the heaviest rounds the Sapphire carried; this did not deter their pursuer. In response, the black ship expertly fired a single chase gun from their bow, striking the Sapphire's stern squarely, smashing through and into its gundeck. Gadriel's nightmares usually begin with the screams of the Sapphire's gun crews.

Not wanting to lose any more men and now having no hope of outrunning nor winning a fight against this enemy ship, the Sapphire's Captain struck down the Sapphire's flag and raised a white flag in surrender, retracting her guns with the remaining gun crew alive enough to do so. Hoping all they had to do now was wait, Gadriel for a moment wanted to run away, until he laughed at himself realizing that was not an option. He and many other crewmates were confused, however. This black ship did not slow down and appeared to be steering closer to the Sapphire, almost as if to ram her with its larger size. Eight sharp rapid strikes on the ship's bell, the crew looked over to see the captain holding its rope in one hand and his rapier in another. He shouted with the utmost authority, "GENERAL QUARTERS, LADS! PREPARE TO BE BOARDED! TAKE NO SHITE, MY BOYS! THINK OF HOME!"

Shanks's blood ran cold at hearing the pronouncement. He didn't believe he could be seen from where he was and was sure he wouldn't be expected to be in the nest. He didn't want to be a coward, but he was terrified. He didn't think Mr. Gadriel would act this way, and he decided that Mr. Gadriel wouldn't. So he got back up on his knees and continued his duty, shouting updates from the attacking ship. "TWENTY MEN READY BOARDING PORTSIDE PLANKS AND ROPES! AXES AND CLUBS!" The first mate shouted "AYE, CROW!" and repeated the observation to the crew.

Gadriel's blood was just as cold, likely as cold as everyone else's. But when he thought of home, when he thought of his family, his crew, that blood boiled. His spine was no longer rigid, his wrist no longer shaking. He drew his sword in one hand, which did not leave its holster with a rattle, but with a slick, confident metal on metal slice. A wall of black wood ominously blocked everyone's view of the Sapphire's portside as the black ship positioned itself to board the Sapphire with force. "REPEL BOARDERS, GENTS!" Gadriel screamed, not knowing what else to do with himself; this set off a chain reaction of roars from the Sapphire's much smaller crew.

All of them knew what they were in for, what was about to happen. There was a strength to be had in numbers, and this ship dwarfed the Sapphire; it was easy to assume its crew did as well. That did not mean they would not fight as ferociously as possible. The first of the grappled ropes broke the gray sky between the ships; all the men froze momentarily. Then three ran toward where the grapple was about to hook the side of their ship and frantically cut at the rope. All knew this was futile, however, as ten more grappled ropes flew through the sky, few missing purchase on the rails of the Sapphire. Though it felt impossible, quickly the larger ship was even closer and more on top of the Sapphire. One, two, four, six planks fell between the ships, although with the height of the larger ships, the planks weren't very necessary. The invaders were able to use ropes, or simply jump from their deck to the other, to board the Sapphire just as easily.

Gadriel's shock was fleeting—he did not have a choice. Gadriel and his crew were suddenly engaged in fighting for their lives. They did not know why they were being run down and boarded, only that they were going to die if they did not fight. A young man to Gadriel's left was brutally clubbed in the face, caving in what looked like the boy's eye socket. Gadriel knew little about sword play but stabbed at the club-wielding boarder, running him through his belly, to the shock of both men. Gadriel didn't know what to do next and began apologizing to the man who wailed in pain, dropping his club. Gadriel tried pulling his blade out frantically and apologizing the same way, eventually scream-crying in the confusion.

Gadriel eventually couldn't take it anymore, letting go of his sword, letting the man fall over and die, a slick of red and stench spreading out from underneath his body. Gadriel grabbed the man's club from the ground and looked for his crew, noticing that fires had broken out on the deck, along with smoke coming up from below deck. Looking to his right following the sound of cracks and squeaks, he observed a boarder using an axe to chop through a locked door, assuming his crew were behind it. Gadriel ran toward the man, rearing back and swinging the club as hard as he could, connecting with the man's hip, resulting in a sickening crunch.

The man dropped the axe and screamed in pain; Gadriel screamed in fear, striking the man over and over again with the club while he was on the ground until he was unrecognizable, tears streaming down his face.

His hoarse throat croaked at the door, "Boys, it's Gad, the ship is on fire, we have to abandon."

A small young voice from the inside said, "I can't."

Gadriel tried to look through cracks made by the breaching axe and realized the young man behind the door had barricaded himself in. Gadriel shook his head, backing away knowing the young man wouldn't leave the room and he had no hope of getting him out, at least not timely.

Gadriel began moving backwards, away from the barricaded boy and another dead body, turning in search of more crew, to find a flash of bright white pain blind his vision for a moment, his blood-covered club dropping and rolling away from him, arm now broken by an invader. When his vision cleared, he saw a man standing near a center mast holding a club, clearly pleased with the damage he inflicted upon Gadriel. With his uninjured arm, Gadriel drew his dagger issued to him by the Master at Arms before the fight began, holding it out in front of him; he knew this was of no use against this more experienced man and such a weapon.

Even if it were of use, Gadriel didn't want to kill anymore. He wasn't sure he wanted to live with himself over what he had done these last ten minutes. He found resolve and solace, however, when he reminded himself he did not do those things for himself, but for his crew, for his ship, and for his home. The boarder began marching toward Gadriel with a smile, until a blur of a figure landed on him from above and began rapidly stabbing him in the neck with a small dagger. The figure rode the boarder to the ground and wiped his blade off on his clothes before adding it to his belt.

"Mr. Gadriel! You're okay!" said a relieved Shanks.

"Shanks! My boy!" breathed Gadriel.

Both men ducked behind barrels of salt pork, too heavy and too worthless to raid from a moving and burning ship. Gadriel observed a man exit the captain's quarters, holding a bag, followed by the captain in restraints.

"Mr. Gadriel, your arm!" a concerned Shanks pointed out.

"Let's not worry about that now," winced Gadriel, as he cradled his right arm.

One long horn blared from the black ship. In practiced form, the boarders retreated to their ship, many hauling treasures and trophies pillaged from the Sapphire; most had none at all, seemingly content with enjoying the event itself.

As the last of the invaders made their way up their boarding planks, they smoothly retracted the planks and cut their ropes free, smoothly steering away from the destroyed Sapphire.

"What do we do?" A worried Shanks asked.

"Well, ship's on fire," which caused Gadriel to laugh. "It's funny, get it, because we're surrounded by water?"

"Uh, yes, sir, funny," Shanks said nervously.

Gadriel coughed and apologized, "Sorry, it's probably just shock. We've got to get to one of the tenders, the one on the starboard side as our port was likely smashed."

"On it sir, let me check."

The sails were catching fire, along with two of the masts now, making breathing difficult. The smoke coming from below decks was also thick and billowing; Gadriel hoped this wasn't from the powder magazine below.

A few moments later, Shanks returned excited and saying, "Gadriel, it looks like the tender is still there!"

"Excellent, Shanks. Let us make our way there but keep a look out for any of our crew."

Gadriel heard young screams coming from his left that drew his attention while he walked along with Shanks's help; it was the boy in the cabin, which was now ablaze. Gadriel felt something sour creep into his mouth, not realizing he felt both sick and a lump in his throat at the same time.

On their way to the tender, which was a small ship attached to the Sapphire that could more quickly "tend" to its smaller needs, they came across one of their crew alive, the Master at Arms, suffering from what appeared to be a vicious axe wound to his leg.

"Gadriel, we take him with us?"

"Absolutely, young sir."

And with three good arms, the men lifted the Master at Arms and continued on their way to the tender. Along the way, they found one more crew member alive and with a fourth man were able to move faster.

"C'mon gents, we don't have much time." And as Gadriel uttered this jinx, their time ran out.

The thick smoke was from cannon fuse storage on the gun deck, which was kept in crates outside the powder magazine, the secure dry storage of their black powder. Likely a fire that was started on purpose for this reason. The explosion sent the men soaring off the deck, and they were the lucky ones (depending on how one looked at the situation). Anyone below deck was, mostly, instantly obliterated. The Sapphire's captain was made to watch his ship burn and die from the deck of his captors', and what he saw were the final seconds of his home disintegrate into flame and a shockwave that rocked the deck on which he stood.

Gadriel hit the freezing cold water, which shocked him so badly he forgot about his broken arm and, for a moment, was in blinding pain for having tried to swim with such a damaged arm. Looking around himself, he could not tell which way was up until he noticed the direction bubbles were moving and could orient himself. From there he looked up and saw what looked like sunlight pleasantly warming the surface of the water; but it wasn't sunlight, it was fire. Gadriel kicked and kicked, holding his broken arm to his chest, using his good arm to move sinking debris. He broke the surface of the water and began gulping air only to be forced back underwater by the flames. Swimming down several feet, he found an open area to surface, and he did so.

Gadriel was treading water, frantically looking around, calling out for Shanks but could hear no one. Using one good arm, he swam toward the larger pieces of wreckage of the ship in hopes to find crew clinging to it or somehow having survived the explosion on it; he did not know what else to do. To his complete shock, as he swam closer and, after moving some unfortunate souls, he found Shanks exhausted and nearly unconscious on a large piece of hull, about the size of a small skiff. Concerned for shock, Gadriel cried with relief trying to keep the boy awake.

"Shanks! Shanks, young sir! Stay with me now. We've made it! Look, we can see the shore with our naked eye!"

Shanks smiled and then appeared to pass out. Gadriel said to himself that it was going to be all right.

Climbing onto the large piece of hull, which contained a concave in the middle, not unlike a small boat, just with not much of a stern and only half a bow, Gadriel pulled up Shanks with him and positioned him as best and as comfortably as he could considering the circumstances. Grabbing an errant piece of wood in the water to use as an oar of sorts, Gadriel began paddling toward Pope. Gadriel didn't lie; he could see the shore from the site of the wreckage, but they were still at least a league away and both terribly injured.

Gadriel dutifully paddled as long as he could with one arm. At a point past exhaustion, he checked on Shanks, whose lips had turned purple. Worried for shock or worse, he hugged the boy to share as much of his body heat as he could, which was not much, considering they were both thigh deep in sea water. Gadriel eventually passed out cradling the boy who saved his life, adrift, he hoped, toward land.

5

The Whisper Stone Caper

Rose, Gadriel, and Shanks made their way out the front doors of The Wooden Leg through a crowd that was already forming and did not stop moving until they were safely behind the locked doors of the Bake Shop two districts away.

"When you boys sneak into a place you surely make an entrance, don't you," Rose said with a smirk.

"Actually, it was a grand attempt at an exit foiled by a kitchen servant," Gadriel indignantly responded.

"Ah, yes, Lara, I heard."

"She didn't hear; she sent her."

"Shanks?"

Shanks tilted his head in response, letting Gadriel know they had not said anything. Gadriel then ignored himself and redirected his attention to Rose.

"Rose, I'm never one to criticize a rescue, but setting the tavern ablaze, was that perhaps a little extreme?" asked Gadriel.

"Oh, no, I wouldn't set fire to a building full of people like that. I just climbed up on the roof and placed a pot over the flue of the chimney; in chaos like that it's easy to think it would be a fire."

"You started a fake fire, with a kitchen pot?" asked Gadriel, incredulous.

"Yep," Rose said simply. All three began to laugh at such an absurd, effective, and simple plan.

"How long have you known how to use a staff, Shanks and I both wonder?" asked Gadriel.

"When I was younger my father said I needed to take a form of dance; something about fitting in with the other girls in our district. Well the bow staff is like a form of dance, and I found it much more preferable."

"I see," said Gadriel.

"Ask her why she broke her own man's hand."

"What??" Gadriel said to Shanks. To which Shanks stuck their hands out in an exhausted gesture, which caused Gadriel to stick his hands out in an exhaustive gesture, as neither knew what to make of what was happening.

Rose stood there watching Gadriel, wheels evidently turning in her head. "You have the stone!" she exclaimed. "You have the stone and you touched it!!"

Shanks began looking around at the ground, likely for another fish. Gadriel's eyes widened just enough to tell Rose she was correct. Finding no fish and no sausage rolls to calm his nerves, Shanks settled for a classic back-hand to the chest of their best friend.

"I told you she knows everything"

"Oh, what do you mean, you told me she knows everything? Shanks told me that," Gadriel tried to say privately between himself and Shanks. This was fruitless, however, as Rose clearly heard him.

"So it talks to you?" she asked, excitedly.

Gadriel, not enjoying a single moment of this exchange and becoming increasingly upset with a supposed friend, Rose, turned to her with a look not so much in anger, but it certainly wasn't happy.

"If you're so excited about this stone, it wants me to ask you why you broke your own man's hand tonight—you want to answer that question?"

It was now Rose's turn for her eyes to widen.

"It wasn't hard to guess, madam, but this is also not funny."

After a moment's pause, Rose said in what appeared to be an earnest way, "Do you have the stone on you now, or is it still at The Wooden Leg?"

Gadriel only looked at her with incredulity. "No, all joking aside. I'll be completely honest with you moving forward. I now have no desires on the stone—no, no, I did, but now I don't."

Rose assured him, "I want to help. You've bonded with it. It should be of no use to anyone else now."

Gadriel thought about it, and it was clear to him Rose knew plenty more about this stone than he did. He decided to take a risk and produce the stone from his jacket; without its protective purse, it sat in his ungloved hand, producing a distinctly different and brighter light at every point it touched Gadriel's unprotected skin. You could see where the glow of the stone reflected beautifully in Rose's green eyes to produce a nearly golden glow. It even changed the color of Shanks's eyes, who found it difficult to look away. Noticing this, Gadriel put the stone away back into his jacket. The trance seemed to diminish from his cohorts.

"There, now you know I have it, now you've seen it, you've no doubt been trying to get your hands on it for days—why?" asked Gadriel.

"Well, for days I've wanted the stone for selling; I haven't lied to you often, Gadriel. I do wish to leave this place and seek adventure of my own. I love my family but no longer wish to be a baker's daughter; it is Julien's calling, not mine."

Gadriel understood and strangely believed her. "For a number of reasons I don't like this object so close to me, and since it is also a prized possession of such an understanding Governor, I don't casually want it on my person. Do you have anywhere I could keep it safe?" asked Gadriel.

"Of course!" Rose said excitedly.

Rose motioned for the two to follow her further into the bakery. In the dry storage room were sacks of flour among many other baker's supplies to run a successful busy bakery.

"May I have it for a moment? So I may hide it."

She stuck out her open hand with a handkerchief in her palm, which Gadriel placed the stone in the middle. Rose carefully wrapped the stone in the cloth and placed it deep inside a bag of flour in the back of the stack, then shook the bag so the flour would settle on top, hiding the trace of her hiding spot.

"If someone is thorough enough to open sacks of flour, they better be ready to open many of them and then sift through the lot."

Gadriel grinned again at the simplicity of Rose's approach to a problem. There was no extravagance to her solution, but if it wasn't effective.

"I think we should leave here so that your family isn't drawn into this mess," said Gadriel.

"That's sweet of you. But I think we should leave here because Captain Tamara's men from the Midnight are looking for you and will likely look here after they see what has happened to the Wooden Leg."

Gadriel scowled. "And here I was going to suggest we get out of here because it's past sixth chime and I've been threatened by the Governor that I better be out of town by now."

Rose chuckled and said, "You've been in town for what, three days? You're a busy man."

"If we could get to an inn and tavern called The Thirsty Goat, we may be all right for the night," Gadriel thought out loud.

"You know Lou?" asked Rose.

"Not really, we've never been here before. But we met the other day, and she seemed like a sort whose honesty could be purchased."

"That it can," agreed Rose.

In the same tone, just more quiet, if not muffled, Gadriel heard: *"Ask her about what happened the last time she worked with Captain Tamara."*

Gadriel attempted to ignore it, but what unsettled him more is that he knew exactly where the stone was among at least fourteen sacks of flour, inside a storage room, in the back of the bakery as they were leaving the front, and this awareness persisted as they moved about Lulin.

At present the group was one district away from the town center with merchant shops and eateries. In Lulin, the further you traveled away from the town center, the more industrious, dangerous, and/or rundown the districts became; the Governor and nobles lived in the city center, as an example. In Lulin there were a total of six districts not including the docks, which were nearly their own economy. As Gadriel and Shanks learned the first day, Lulin was laid out in a mostly sunburst pattern with the center or noble district in the middle, meaning subsequent districts were more or less crescent shapes. All this to say, The Thirsty Goat was at the edge of the city closest to the docks, a dangerous area at night, but just as dangerous was the distance they must travel with so many parties actively searching for Gadriel and company.

They made it three districts over, passing behind The Wooden Leg and its crowd of drunken brawlers tending to their wounds while the town fire brigade fought the "fire" Rose started. They saw no one familiar but were sure Captain Tamara and the Governor had agents in the crowd. Two more districts and they found themselves near canals and mercantile or other workhouses. *Nearly there,* Gadriel thought.

"What an incredibly lucky evening we've had," Gadriel said aloud, cheerfully, to which Shanks slapped himself in the face and Rose slowly turned around to give him a look of disbelief.

"What, it's true," Gadriel said defensively.

Just then, around the corner of a workhouse in full swing despite the hour, the three heard heavy footfalls from a group of what were likely men. The three froze, then turned to hurriedly move to the other edge of the building, where they heard more people. The three were now trapped between a building, two groups of unknown people large enough to be considered groups, and a canal with one pole barge, likely belonging to the workhouse.

The louder group moving with no stealth rounded the corner first and turned out to be a group of guards on patrol. Whether they were looking for Gadriel or simply walking a beat, they couldn't know. But the other group that appeared to be traveling/following in the same direction as Gadriel, Rose, and Shanks appeared to be Captain Tamara's men led by the man in the black mask. Who were not in the middle were Gadriel, Rose, and Shanks, who opted to quietly enter the canal, not known for its cleanliness, to hide behind the pole barge and listen.

"Who that's be there out and about this late, is that a mask, what the bloody Mother do you think you're carrying?" exclaimed a member of the guard.

It seemed the longer the man looked at the crew, the more he found suspicious and undesirable things about them. The crew of the Midnight, or whom they presumed to be the crew of the Midnight, carried clubs and dressed in their dark clothing, the same Gadriel observed them in the night before, and the day before on the deck of their ship.

Several of the crewmates did not round the corner, making their party look smaller as the man in the mask, who appeared to be unarmed, calmly approached the speaking guard who was likely the patrol captain. Gadriel began to hear rapidly clicking behind him, which turned out to be poor Rose's teeth chattering. They had not gotten their heads wet, and Shanks motioned for Rose to put a braid of her hair in her mouth, which simply confused everyone.

"Hello, sirs, may we help you this evening? It is why we're here, as you ask," said the man in the black mask.

"What's that?" asked the guard captain.

"We are simply concerned citizens fed up with the rampant crime in our district sirs, and we know how overworked you are. We only want to help so we formed our . . . citizens patrol."

"Citizen's patrol, eh?" asked the guard captain.

"Yes, sir. We thought it best to patrol our homes and the workhouses to keep the orphans safer, you see. We know you do a good job, but there's only so many of you," said the man in the black mask smoothly, and earnestly.

Gadriel thought he was doing a wonderful job, even though he was likely searching for him and it would be helpful if the man were stopped.

"Aw, well, you boys ought not be doin' that, best leave patrolling to the guard. Clubs and drink never mix well," said the guard captain much more softly.

"We completely understand, sir; let us assure you we are as sober as a sister in cold pants, but we will heed your excellent point and call it an evening if it is best for the guard," placating the man in the mask.

"There's good boys, then. Head straight home; it's already first chime then. And as much as we appreciate you, please leave the patrollin' to us, eh?" said the guard captain.

"Absolutely sir, we appreciate *you*," said the man as he turned and motioned for his crew to begin back the way they came.

"Damn, that was really good," whispered Gadriel.

Rose whispered back, through chattering teeth "Y-y-yeah, that was Th-th-thhinker, he's d-d-done well to earn his n-name."

"Let's get out of this water and get to The Thirsty Goat where there's warmth and hopefully baths," said Gadriel, to which Rose nodded emphatically.

The three climbed out of the canal on the opposite side, saving their time walking to the nearest bridge crossing. The trio then made it to The Thirsty Goat without further incident and the coast appeared clear; no one would necessarily know to look for them here, as Gadriel and Shanks visited The Thirsty Goat for food while exploring the town before ever getting involved with anyone.

Finding a rear entrance all the same, Rose entered the building half wet and came back out with Lou. Lou, surprised and happy to see Gadriel, brightened at his wet and uncomfortable face.

"Oh it's you! The pretty crazy boy with all the money," she said with a beaming smile on her face. Rose looked back and forth with a wry smile.

"I am pretty and crazy most days, ma'am," said Gadriel, then continued, "Might you have a room for us, we hope with a fireplace and a bath basin?"

Lou chuckled, "We can't do you much about a bath basin 'round 'ere, but I can give ya a room with a hearth, yes. I suspect ya not wanted to be disturbed considerin' where we be standin'?"

to which Gadriel replied, "Yes, please my lady."

"Hah! D'ya 'ere that? 'My lady.' I might as well be the fancy pisser. C'mon then, I can take you upstairs through the kitchen."

Gadriel, Shanks, and Rose followed Lou through the back entrance, up the stairs, and to a surprisingly large room with two beds, several chairs, a table, and a large fireplace, likely the largest room the establishment had to offer. As the four entered the room, Lou set to lighting lamps and getting a fire started in the hearth. Gadriel prepared Lou's payment with his back to the room—old habits.

"You be smellin' something awful, you knowin' that?" Lou asked.

Rose said, "Oh, uh, yeah, we had to go for a swim where ya ought not."

"Aye," said Lou, then she added, "If you give me your clothes, I can have them clean for ya by mornin.'"

The three were first very excited then very bashful.

"Uhm, madam, do you happen to have gowns or, something?" asked Gadriel.

"Do I be lookin' like your mother? No, fancy man. We have plenty of blankets. I'm sure you can figure it out."

After a few awkward minutes, and a few extra coin, Lou was gone with their wet, filthy clothing, and the three sat around a roaring fire, each wrapped in a blanket for both warmth and modesty. Shanks tapped his belly longingly.

Gadriel said, "I hope she brings us food too; we should have asked."

Rose smiled, "I bet she will; she's sweet on you."

"Doubtful," said Gadriel. "She is certainly sweet on money, though, and that I understand clearly." Gadriel continued, in a nearly accusatory fashion, "Rose, you said you'd be honest, and I think it's time for that."

Rose nodded slowly, looking down, and said, "Right . . . As you know, our shop supplies many of the houses in central Lulin, including the Governor's mansion from time to time. The Governor doesn't exclusively work with anyone; I believe him to be paranoid, but father has said it's to be fair to his 'subjects'; I don't believe the man has ever cared for fairness. But whether infrequent or every day, you come to know workers, and you get to learn things from people.

The green gem, or the 'Whisper Stone,' as it is known to people familiar with the gem, has sat on the Governor's desk for years after he came by it from a ship's captain passing through Lulin. No one knows how he obtained it, but one day it was displayed on his desk. And one thing was clear: some people were 'affected' by it more than others. Some people hear things from it, some people see lights within it; the Governor appeared none too affected by it, but enjoyed the discomforting effect it would have on visitors to his office, so he enjoyed keeping it on display; I'm not even sure he was familiar with the legends of stones like it.

"Because most people who visited the Governor's office were visiting dignitaries, ship captains, and higher-ranking members of the town staff, there weren't a great many people who knew of the stone, let alone many who wanted to talk about something that made them so uneasy and could not explain why. Well, one of the acquaintances I made over the years was Lara, who had routinely delivered the Governor's morning coffee and bread and was routinely near the stone every time she delivered his breakfast to his office.

"I learned about the stone roughly eight months ago. And while I spent several of those months learning everything I could about the stone, I only tried convincing Lara to steal it very recently; this time was spent at the docks hoping to learn more about its mysteries, and more importantly for my purposes, its value."

"So you figured out it was valuable and tried to get your friend to steal it for you?" asked Gadriel.

"I never said she was a friend," countered Rose. "Lara was an acquaintance of mine and not the greatest of people. But she had information I wanted, and I was able to get it for the price of bread and the occasional evening, a trade in my favor, in my opinion," she said.

"Sorry, go on."

"I learned a great many things about the Whisper Stone, such as that it is not the only one of its kind. These stones were made long ago, not found this way. And these stones are, in a way, alive. Not like you or I, but, a sort of spirit to them. When I asked if it bonded with you, I assumed it was talking with you, attempting to carry conversations?"

"Well, yes, but I attempted to ignore it," said Gadriel.

"So it HAS bonded with you!" said Rose excitedly.

"Excuse me, this is not fun for me, what does this mean?" chastised Gadriel.

"Sorry," she apologized. "I'm sorry, I've just spent a long time learning about this stone, and now I'm finally seeing things about it confirmed, is all . . . The stone apparently only bonds with one person at a time and chooses the person with which it bonds. But most of what I've learned indicates that most who ever can bond with one are quick to go mad. It did not bond with the Governor, and I would assume he tried, likely many times—"

Gadriel cut in, "Okay, well how do I *unbond* with it?!" He began to raise his voice.

Just then a knock at the door silenced the group, and Lou entered with a tray.

"Sorry to interrupt, kids" said Lou cheerfully. "Handsome, you be lookin' fancy even without clothes," she said with a wink, to which Gadriel unconsciously drew in his blanket slightly closer and turned slightly more red.

What Lou uncovered on her tray was a sight for hungry eyes and rumbling stomachs. On the table sat a tray filled with The Thirsty Goat's specialty—fresh, hot, salty fish and chips, likely enough for six people. Everyone's mouth began immediately watering, and Gadriel suddenly could not recall the last time he ate something.

"I figured it be best to bring extra to avoid suspicion on the number of people in this room, and I be doubtin' it go to waste." They all nodded.

"Oh, handsome? I brought a special for ya.'"

Lou left the room and returned from the hallway shortly after with a steaming pot of water and a cloth hanging from its side.

"It don't be a bath, but it be the closest thing I could muster for you."

Gadriel couldn't help but grin. "Oh dear woman, I could kiss you!"

Lou spread he arms slightly and said, "Well, I be standin' right 'ere, handsome," for which Gadriel rose from his chair and planted a big kiss on her cheek; it was now Lou's turn to blush.

Lou left the group be, and after hanging the pot over the fire to keep the water nice and hot, Gadriel and Rose opted to wash themselves first before feasting; Shanks did no such thing and began gorging himself immediately. Everyone had an agreement to keep their backs to the hearth while others cleaned themselves, which no one broke, not even Gadriel. While washing and eating, Rose continued her honesty.

"Where was I . . . Yes! So knowing you have bonded with it, we know the Governor did not bond with it, and at least I assume it was not for lack of trying."

"Where does Captain Tamara fit into all this?" asked Gadriel, to which Rose responded, "Do you want to hear about the stone and learn about the last three days, or do you want to hear about the past and how it doesn't matter right now?"

"Okay, well, I'll want to know about that eventually; they are a pretty violent sort," he said.

"Lara was preparing to take the stone, which the Governor was arrogant enough to leave unsecured, in an unlocked case on display in his office. A member of his staff did attempt to steal it once—what the Governor did to him, well, I can see why he would believe no one would attempt to take it again. Lara was unable to take the stone, however, because someone else did."

"The dockmaster?" guessed Gadriel.

"Correct," said Rose.

"How di—"

"Uh mbu-bu-bu I'm getting there," interrupted Rose.

"Before Lara had a chance to take the stone, someone else did—the day you arrived in fact, but it occurred before canal boats arrived that day, which is one of the only reasons I can imagine you haven't been tortured as a new face in town after the questioning of the Governor's staff."

Shanks, who was sitting on the floor in front of the fire, belly absolutely full of fish and chips, nodded appreciatively at the prospect of torturing someone in their position should they had arrived in town earlier.

Rose continued, "There are few people allowed in the Governor's office without the Governor present; not even most of his staff are allowed to be inside it without him present, including Lara. For the most part, trusted city officials who deliver taxes and tariffs and have access to the Governor's safe can access the office when he isn't there, and this is only to expedite the flow of coin into the Governor's coffers.

"Though I had not known who had taken the stone, I had known the stone was on the move. I had also known Tamara was in port who captained the kind of ship who would smuggle cargo or a passenger like that out of Lulin, so I thought it important to pay her a visit. This is when I learned that the dockmaster had already arranged for passage on the Midnight when they left, and two plus two equals four.

"I had not revealed to Tamara that I didn't know where the stone was, but upon divulging the dockmaster's plans to run, I began to think of places it might be. At that point I told Tamara that I would arrange for some idiots to have the stone that night and that I would send word on where her men could intercept them, asking we split profits from its sale. Tamara asked me why she should work with me at all now that she knows the dockmaster will have the stone and be on her ship? I said it was because someone would probably mention to the dockmaster that her ship was no longer safe, taking me now would certainly advertise her ship was no longer safe, and attacking the dockmaster within Lulin wasn't a good idea as he was still a high-ranking town official."

Gadriel and Shanks nodded with smirks, "Well played."

"Yes, Tamara thought so too!" said Rose, proud of herself. She then continued, nearing the end of her story.

"So being fairly familiar with the docks and most of its porters, I was familiar with little Dint and knew he had been following around Turf and Munty. Dint, being young and likely not corrupted, was a runner responsible for the dockmaster's errands. I decided to pay Dint coin to pay attention to the dockmaster's purse, telling him it would be our little secret, and Turf and Munty didn't need to know about it.

Dint informed me the purse looked to have not been emptied in days, and he thought the dockmaster's office was haunted by a ghost. And that told me everything I needed to know about the dockmaster's plans. He was keeping the stone in his office along with plans to steal withheld tariffs, and he would pick it up on his way out of port onto the Midnight, never having his goods on himself until the last possible moment.

So I met with Turf with a proposition to steal the purse, explaining to him he could keep the coin, but the deal was there was going to be a stone, he could not touch it, and that's what I wanted. Turf appeared effective for his role in this, because what I did next was send word to Tamara that Turf and his crew would be stealing the stone, where to find them, and about when, so her men could ambush Turf."

"Why didn't you just steal the stone with Turf?" asked Gadriel, now also full and relaxing by the fire, but in a chair.

"Because I needed to settle a debt with Captain Tamara. And if it wasn't this stone, I likely wouldn't repay the debt," answered Rose.

Gadriel nodded. "I think that brings us up to speed, my dear. The Governor wants his stone back but does not know where it is. Tamara believes we have the stone after having followed Turf and likely that you have double-crossed her, since you so easily double-crossed Turf. And Shanks and I are stuck in the middle because . . . what? No one in this town can do crime honestly?"

Rose gawked for a moment "Honestly?? Who was the one who followed Turf? You did the same thing—I just planned better. At least you were just my backup patsies. I liked you best." Rose ended her statement sweetly.

"*COME ON OUT, THORNY!*"

6

Captain Tamara

"I KNOW YOU'RE UP THERE, YA DOUBLE CROSSIN' SOW!" Gadriel, Rose, and Shanks froze at the sound of Captain Tamara's voice from the main floor. Gadriel felt the sensation that someone else was speaking to him but could not hear it.

Rose's eyes grew larger and said in a hushed tone, "We could run."

"We're naked and have very little, ma'am," pointed out Gadriel. Shanks made two swift striking motions with a knife in each hand, because only Shanks would think knife fighting naked were appropriate, Gadriel thought.

"I don't believe Lou would betray us. If we leave, she'll be harmed, and I'm not sure I want to live with that, as much as I'd like to live" said Gadriel.

"You're serious?" said Rose, as a statement in as much of a question.

"I am," Gadriel responded, devoid of his usual sarcasm and charm. Gadriel stood up, business-like, as did Shanks. Gadriel took his blanket from his shoulders and wrapped it tightly around his waist. Rose took a cue from this and wrapped her blanket tightly around her torso, folding it as best she could under her arms.

Gadriel exited their room first with as much dignity as a naked man could muster, followed by Rose and then Shanks. True to his assumption, Lou was being held by Thinker and it would appear she did not tell them where they were or if they were there.

Gadriel broke the immediate silence. "Here we are, please let Lou go?"

The good captain said, "Aw, Lou, is that yer name, deary? Get down here, now!"

Gadriel held his blanket with one hand and raised the other in a surrendering gesture.

The three made their way downstairs and joined Captain Tamara, Thinker, and five more armed members of her crew on the main floor of The Thirsty Goat. This group wasn't armed with clubs to fool guard captains. This group was armed to destroy guard captains and much of anyone else between them and their objective, which Gadriel suddenly realized was himself and the stone.

Upon reaching the captain, Gadriel also realized the main floor was devoid of other patrons. They likely cleared out at the sight of Tamara and her men, wanting no part of whatever was about to happen. Captain Tamara signaled for the release of Lou, which Thinker did immediately. The captain then commanded all of them to sit; she remained standing, as did her men.

"Before we get started, may I have my clothes? This doesn't feel like a fair negotiation," said Gadriel.

"Shut your fancy mouth, you blighter," clipped the captain, and Gadriel did indeed.

"How did you find us?" asked Rose, genuinely curious.

"How did I?" Captain Tamara began to respond, then adopted an over-the-top mocking tone, "Ohh, how did I find you . . . where would the man who willingly stayed at a place like The Wooden Leg go, if not for a worse tavern even closer to the docks with a similar reputation?" She finished with a disgusted "Ugh" then a very quiet "Good job, Think," to which Think gave the barest of nods.

"Thorny, I'm disappointed, really I am," stated Tamara.

"Why? I haven't done anything to disappoint you," said Rose.

"Oh, we're going to do it that way? Fine," said Tamara. "Where is the stone?" she demanded, removing a blade from her belt.

"Why don't you ask Turf—we certainly don't have it; we're naked, for Mothers' sake!" Rose countered.

"Don't you play about with me, girly. Two of my men are injured. My crew has been possibly identified twice tonight by town guards. You almost burned down a tavern, and with this Governor, who likes to blame everything on the newest visitor, might want to start looking at my ship, and Lulin is an important port for us. It's late, I'm angry, I will break things, and I don't mean exclusively you."

"The stone is worthless now," Gadriel interrupted.

Rose just hung her head. Shanks stewed stoically.

"What's that, boyo?" asked the captain.

"The stone—I have a limited understanding, but it shouldn't be worth anything now." Rose started to shake her head.

"What makes you say that?" Captain Tamara said with a smile.

"It's been bonded," Gadriel answered.

"Oh it's been bonded you say? With whom?" asked the captain.

Gadriel realized the conversation was not going at all how he'd hoped and wanted badly to change the subject. Rose attempted to do just that by adding, "He doesn't know what he's talking about; I fed him a bunch of horse shit about the stone and—"

"Shut ya mouth, Thorny," cut off the captain.

"With whom has the stone bonded, sir?" asked Captain Tamara slowly, putting her hands on Gadriel's knees, leaning in close to his face. At this distance he could see flecks of gold in her deep, dark, hazel eyes. This close he could see crow's feet from her laughter, deep smile lines, and also frown lines upon her face, weathered by the sun and time she spent on the deck of her ship.

Captain Tamara was a complicated woman. In addition to her black jacket, which contained her captain's stripes in midnight blue on either arm, she wore her captain's cap, adorned with four midnight-blue stripes on its left brim. A woman like Tamara did not need her cap to command the respect from her crew; she had earned that long ago as evidenced by such hard men standing behind her now. But a captain's cap did command some respect from civilians, guardsman, and soldiers alike, which Gadriel assumed is why she wore this now.

"I wouldn't know with whom the stone has been bound," said Gadriel.

"Aw, oh no deary, oh you poor thing. It's *you*," accused Captain Tamara in a sad way.

Gadriel attempted to protest but the good captain ignored this, addressing Rose. "Thorny, please tell the nice boy why it's such a shame, would you?"

Rose, keeping her head rather low, and in a defeated tone stated, "Because, should the stone become bound to a living person, then that person becomes just as valuable if not more so than the stone by itself. Additionally, it is just as easy to kill the person to unbind their connection with the stone to maintain its former value."

Captain Tamara began clapping slowly for Rose. Thinker allowed for a rare smile to grace his face. "Well, that interrogation went well. Thank you Mr. Tool; true to your name, aren't we. Now, that went so *swimmingly* well, get it? Because we're . . . ? Aw you're all boring. Anyway that went so well, why don't we just tell us where you've hidden the stone just as easily and no one gets hurt and maybe some of you get to leave peacefully," Tamara offered.

"Really, you'll let us go?" asked Gadriel. "Oh not you, boyo, you're not going anywhere but right back to my ship, with me and my men."

"What'll it be, anyone? Anyone?" asked Captain Tamara. "Lovely. As suspected. Get 'em up" she commanded. Her men sprang into action, two of them flanking the captain, two of them picking up Gadriel and restraining his hands in front of him, securing a rope around his waist to keep his blanket in place, and a fifth standing with Thinker. Rose tried to quickly rise to protest, but quicker than her eyes could adjust to her new height, Captain Tamara had drawn her cutlass and placed it on the tip of Rose's nose.

"You had your chance, deary, now let me be clear: You're alive because you have something I want. And I like your moxie. And you've got nice legs, if we're all being honest. You failed to work with me straight, again. It is second chime now. You have until daybreak, about four chimes, to bring me that stone, on my ship, with an apology, or I'll come find it, and I'll burn down the places I look. I'll start with your home . . ."

After a moment's silence, she commanded "Nod" while pressing the very tip of her blade down enough to draw a small amount of blood. And Rose did nod that she understood, pulling away from the captain's sword.

"We're gone boyos. Egress quietly, but we stop for no one, got it?" A resounding "Yes Cap't" was the response.

As the Midnight's crew moved out of The Thirsty Goat, Shanks simply moved to follow them and no one stopped him, leaving Rose alone in the middle of the tavern's main floor. She sat there taking these moments for herself, looking into the main hearth.

"I've seen that look before, I think," said Lou, a little knowingly from behind Rose.

Rose jumped slightly, if only because she was alone and she suddenly was not.

"We be thinking about leaving everything, including your man, and runnin', don'tcha?"

And right then, Lou's use of 'we' connected something for Rose. She thought to herself, *if there was one man who could . . .*

"Lou, I'm so sorry this has happened, and I'm sorry to ask for anything right now, but may I have our clothes please?" Lou smiled and said, "Aw, if you be askin' for both yer clothes then it's no bother atall dear. None atall."

A short time later, Rose was in wet dress, running through districts barefoot as quickly and as silently as she could. She had with her Gadriel's bag, his too-damp clothes shoved into the top of it. While Rose dressed at The Thirsty Goat, Lou retrieved their belongings from their room, and despite being a place like The Thirsty Goat, she somehow knew Lou wouldn't rob them. Gadriel had purchased Lou's honesty fair and square; Rose gathered he paid handsomely for it. Lou did insist Rose take a small sharp object she called a Hideaway Knife, which Lou tucked away in Rose's beltline.

According to Lou, "Ohh, on you? Men might even miss it during a search. You use it when there be no other options, you put this in your hand and don't stop swingin' till yer free, y'hear?"

Rose more than ran, she darted from cover to cover through the districts. When she moved side to side, she pranced like a dancer, never slowing—past The Wooden Leg, which was back in operation, just much more quiet now closer to the third chime of the night. Rose floated past the outskirts of the town center, being sure to not connect with guard patrols and run-of-the-mill ruffians on the streets at such a chime. Gasping for air, she arrived at the Bake Shop and let herself inside.

Closing and locking the door behind herself to catch her breath for a moment, she was startled by the voice of her brother Julien.

"Rosey, what's going on??" a very concerned Julien asked her.

"HEAVENS Below!" Rose began to shout with a fright. "Julien!? What are you doing here?" she demanded.

"It's the third chime, and I work here, remember?" he said, confused. "Sister, there was a woman at the house last night looking for you; she might have been a guard captain? Or member of the guard? I couldn't see who was with her but it looked like a whole guard patrol. I got to the door before father did, but what is happening?" Julien pleaded.

Rose said, "I know, brother, this is over soon—"

"WHAT is over soon?" Julien surprised Rose with anger, clearly from a place of fear. "You've been out all night for days; you haven't been in the shop. We both know father doesn't know you're gone, but that doesn't mean he doesn't worry when you're not around. If you need help I'll handle the shop and I can help you, but what is happening?" he pleaded, again.

"Brother, I cannot tell you what's happening; you wouldn't be safe. What I need now is a change of clothes, a drink of water, and a moment alone in the dry storage room," said Rose.

"A moment alon— you know, fine." Julien threw up his hands and stepped aside from the edge of the counter.

As Rose passed she said, "I promise, this is over tonight if I can help it."

In a few short minutes Rose returned with her work clothes on, a simple white blouse and trousers; she tucked the Hideaway Knife in her belt how Lou showed her, but she took an additional knife from the bakery—one of their sharper ones, so not great for fighting, but not knowing what else to do, she slid this into her belt as well.

Julien had not moved much while his sister prepared. When she came out from the back of the shop in her work clothes and boots, Julien wasn't confused by why she had a knife in her belt—he was confused by why one of her arms was covered in flour up to the elbow.

Before Rose ran out the door, she wrapped her arms around her brother and hugged him tightly, trying to tell him a lot without saying much. She had imagined this hug many times before, but it was the night she was "escaping" this place, as if her life were some sort of prison. No, now it was with the hopes of getting back to him and helping him bake bread, at least for a little while longer. And it wasn't too long before Julien was returning her hug just as tightly.

Just before the sun broke the horizon, Rose stood outside the Midnight at the end of the dock in Lulin's seventh, unofficial district. Under one arm was Gadriel's bag, clothes dryer now, and in her right pocket sat a green faintly glowing stone. She could hear men on the deck, and knew she was seen by several as she approached the ship. But she stood there patiently. And she waited. And half a chime later as the sun broke the horizon, Rose was still waiting. However, when the first rays of light struck the harbor, you could hear the Midnight spring to life. In what sounded more like ritual than warning, she heard a "Gaaang way!" before she heard a wooden, sliding *thump, thump, thump* of a gang plank being quickly extended from the deck of the Midnight down to the dock. The first to exit the ship was Captain Tamara in her traditional swagger, without a care in the world. The captain was followed by Thinker, of course, and they were then followed by a handful of crew members, likely the men that were with them at The Thirsty Goat a few chimes ago.

"Thorny! It's nice to see you, deary, how have you been?"

"Is Gadriel okay?" asked Rose, ignoring the captain's faux pleasantries.

"Oh that old sap? He hasn't been saying much, 'cept to himself. At first it was, 'leave Thorny alone, blah blah blah,' then the sod just kinda stopped talking. He is mad, right? If he ain't you found yourself a good actor."

"I want to see him," said Rose.

"And I want to retire on a tropical island filled with beautiful boys and girls that take care of my every need. But I work for a living with these smelly bastards, don't I?" One of her men shifted on his feet. "OH Calm Dowwwn, Clancy, xo xo and all that. Besides, I already won the smelliest competition did'n'i? Ya' moody brutes."

"I'll get on your ship. I just want to see him," offered Rose.

"You'll get on my ship exactly when I want you there," said Captain Tamara, losing some of her jovial demeanor, adding, "Show me the stone or I'll throw your ungrateful ass into the harbor, right Mother damn now."

"I want to see Gadriel!" Rose argued defiantly, showing her inexperience holding little leverage considering her priorities. Tamara's eyes filled with something like rage and she began marching toward Rose, whose eyes widened in fear, not expecting Tamara to make good on such a threat so immediately.

Captain Tamara's curses matched in time with stomps of her boots. "Bloody. Mother. Damn. Piece'A. Shit. Amateur. Trash."

When the captain was getting close to Rose, she didn't know what to do and began backing up and promptly tripped on her own feet. With one hand, Captain Tamara reached out and grabbed a handful of Rose's shirt, stopping her from falling. With the other, she deftly removed the kitchen knife from her belt, smoothly throwing it into the harbor. Just as smoothly, Tamara then turned ninety degrees on a heel to her right and began dragging Rose toward the edge of the dock, making good on her threat, still muttering the language of her people.

"Don't know why in the Heavens Below I gotta work with lame idiots, repeating myself all the bloody time—like I've never thrown anyone in a Mother damn harbor before."

"Okay! OKAY!" squeaked Rose. "AND I'M SORRY! YOU WANTED AN APOLOGY—I'm sorry! I truly am sorryyyy!" Rose rapidly pleaded, stopping Captain Tamara a mere four steps away from the edge of the dock.

She slowly looked down at the young Rose and grinned, saying, "That's a very good start. All someone needs to do is to pay attention and to listen. Now!"

Letting go of Rose, she fell a step and a half to the wood of the dock; not expecting the height of the fall it made it difficult to breathe for a moment.

"May I presume you have the stone, seeing as how you've begun your apology." said Captain Tamara.

Rose climbed to her feet and caught her breath with her hands on her knees. She produced the Whisper Stone from her right pocket and showed it to the captain, Thinker nearly moved forward to take it. When the morning light struck the stone, it appeared to both amplify it and consume it, depending on the angle in which one viewed the stone. Rose and the crew of the Midnight could see a bright flood of light alongside the hull of the ship, but she could also look down and see the light of the sun simply disappear into the stone.

"Excellent!" said Captain Tamara. "We'll be takin' that from ya' but first, your proper apology, please," added the captain.

"I thought I did apologize," asked a confused Rose.

"No, Thorny, I want a proper apology, where you tell me why you're sorry, and you ask for forgiveness and tell me how you'll repent for your behavior, you see. That's what my dear mum taught me, MOTHER REST HER—"

"MOTHER REST HER," was echoed by her crew.

"Okay, well," started Rose, "Tamara—"

Just then one of her crew immediately and violently cleared his throat, which frightened Rose.

"Captain! Tamara . . . I very much apologize for failing to inform you of who I believed to have the stone when I believed for them to have it. As partners I should have come to you with information. I don't feel great, but to be honest I also don't feel that bad about having double-crossed so many parties in such a short amount of time. I will try not to do it to you again, at least, and I am truly sorry," she finished, and not knowing what else to do, which was becoming a usual for Rose, she added a small bow.

"That . . . deary . . . was one of the best, most proper and honest apologies this captain has ever heard. I will not hug you, but if you hadn't double-crossed me not five chimes ago, I might," Captain Tamara said beaming. "Alright everyone, all aboard, we set sail in a quarter chime." Looking over, the captain added, "C'mon deary," patting her legs like one would after a dog.

"What do you mean, set sail?" a frightened Rose asked.

"Well, the Governor is likely to suspect the Midnight will be responsible for too many of his woes after last night; I don't want to be here for that. Thinker needs time to study the stone, and your boyfriend, unless you'd like for us to kill 'em. And I'm certainly not leaving you here to send Mother-knows-who after us. So you, the stone, and your mad attractive friend come with us."

"May I send a runner with word to my brother? He will worry, and that may attract attention you don't want. You're welcome to read the note; this is not a trick."

Captain Tamara responded only by loudly snapping her fingers together four times. Rose turned and whistled loudly, and shortly after a boy ran up to her.

"What'll it be ma'am," he stated more than asked.

"I need a message delivered to Julien at Lulin's Oldest Bake Shop in the merchant district.

"Yes, ma'am, you be needin' paper?" asked the boy.

"Yes, please," said Rose.

"That be extra," he said, looking up, trying to be much older than his likely age of eight. Captain Tamara thumbed the boy a silver. "OH, ma'am, Captain, ma'am. I don't have enough to—"

"It's yours, boyo," said the captain. "You and the boys enjoy a tug and full bellies tonight."

"Thanks, ma'am, Captain ma'am!" the boy said, nearly running away with his good fortune. Rose showed Tamara the note:

Julien,

I had hoped to finish this adventure last night once and for all, but it will be a little while longer. I must leave but please don't worry, I'll be home soon.

With love,

Rose

Captain Tamara nodded her approval. Rose folded the note and handed it to the boy, reiterating its destination. "Julien, The Oldest Bake Shop in Lulin, Merchant District."

"Yes ma'am!" said the boy, turning to run as hard as his little legs would allow.

"Let's go, deary, time to leave before trouble comes," said Captain Tamara. Now that they were out of earshot of the crew, she was a little different, not by much, but slightly softer.

"I'm sorry about your knife; I hope it wasn't important."

"Oh, no, it was just something I grabbed on my way out the door not knowing what else to take with me," said Rose.

"Excellent," the captain said cheerily, removing something from behind her back evidently from her belt line. "You should have one of these anyhow, much better than a kitchen knife," added the captain, producing what appeared to Rose a fine dagger much larger than her kitchen knife. How the captain had it so hidden behind her she couldn't know.

"We're about to spend the better part of three weeks on my ship traveling to the Port of Saints Rock. If you can't use that dagger by the time we arrive, I will take it back and throw you in that harbor." Rose laughed; the captain did not.

True to the captain's timeline, fourteen tocks later, the Midnight was underway. Her large, magnificent sails were unfurled catching fine favorable wind, harbor speed courtesy be damned. Rose looked up, mystified by how the sails were dyed, and in awe at the speed and efficiency with which the crew of the Midnight worked. Thinker barked orders from the quarterdeck, using the ship's bell to communicate orders as well as shout them. As the Midnight navigated its way out of the harbor, much faster than other ships, both in lack of courtesy and superior ability, Thinker shouted orders to the helmsman, which were repeated back with the same effort.

Contrary to captains Rose read about in stories and in books while with her tutors, Captain Tamara was not on her quarterdeck with her first mate, nor was she in her quarters recuperating from what was likely over thirty chimes without rest. No, Captain Tamara stood at the front of her ship, one boot leaning on her bowsprit while the Midnight's keel cut through waves and lifted from the water as she picked up speed. Tamara doffed her hat for a moment to untie her hair that had been tightly wound into braids and bun. Once loosened, she affixed her cap back on tightly and low to protect her eyes, in a captain's way, but what trailed her now was a sight: beautiful, dark, wavy in places, bent in others, streaming like a kite's tail, glowing in the morning sun while the Midnight cut faster and faster through the water.

As they broke the edge of the harbor, the waves increased in size and number considerably. Rose had never been on a large ship, let alone out past the harbor, and this terrified her to no end. The Midnight was a large and narrow ship, a smugglers' ship, and a fast one, known for passing inspections and never losing cargo. Some waves it cut through, which was jarring for someone like Rose who did not have her sea legs, as they had come to be known to her. Reaching the open ocean is where Rose's anxieties really took hold. The Midnight did not cut through all waves; it couldn't for it wasn't that type of ship nor heavy enough.

The Midnight took a wave, and Rose would've sworn they flew from the water. Captain Tamara did not move from her chosen post, hands behind her back, and for a moment all Rose could see in front of Tamara was sky above the horizon, then the sea below the horizon. She was sure they had not flown, but the impact drove Rose to her knees—not the crew of the Midnight, however, who continued their work. Not the captain. Who remained at her post and simply straightened her left arm in a signal across the deck to her first mate and driver.

"HELMSMAN! FORTY-FIVE DEGREES TO PORT!" shouted Thinker.

"AYE! FORTY-FIVE DEGREES TO PORT, AYE!" returned Helmsman.

Before long, further out into the open ocean, with Lulin's harbor growing smaller and smaller off the Midnight's stern, the ride became much smoother for Rose—either that or she was becoming much more accustomed to being on a ship. Before long, Captain Tamara turned on her heel and marched down the deck and toward her quarters.

Before entering she addressed her first mate: "Mr. Thinker, I'll be entering my quarters for a time. The ship is yours till I return."

"Aye," said Thinker.

Before reaching for the door, captain Tamara turned to Rose and said, "Just a moment," whistling sharply one time. A short time later a young woman climbed onto the deck from one of the stairwells below.

"Rose, this is Violet; she is my valet. Yes, yes, you're both named for flowers, Violet the Valet rhymes, I want to never hear bad humor again." Rose simply nodded.

"Violet will sort you out for now. You'll be sharing guest quarters with your boyfriend until such time as it becomes more appropriate for you to have separate quarters; we run a tight ship."

Rose nodded again, and the captain continued, "I've received reports that he was sleeping before you arrived on the dock, but has been acting very peculiar since you arrived; Thinker assumes it is closer proximity to the stone. Speaking of which—" The captain held out her hand.

"OH!" exclaimed Rose and handed the captain the stone, which she briefly held up to the dull light of the overcast day. "Interesting," she muttered to herself.

"That'll be all for now; we have a galley if you're hungry, and luckily you bathed before we left! I'd catch some sleep now if you can; who knows what the sea will bring later." And with that statement, the captain doffed her cap once more, entered her quarters, and closed the door behind her.

7

VIOLET AND THINKER

VIOLET signaled for Rose to follow her. As they descended the stairs below deck, Rose politely began introducing herself. "Hello, I'm Ros—"

Violet interrupted her. "I feel we must level-set expectations. I will be as polite to you as my lady instructs. Right now that is as polite as a merchant woman from a city with moderate traffic would be accustomed."

"Okay," Rose responded, her feelings slightly hurt, and she wasn't sure why as she didn't know this woman, and, well, she technically did betray the crew of the Midnight.

"Please see me should you find yourself in need of anything on this ship. That is also an order for my lady. Do not wander, do not solve your own problems. See me, if you would . . . please."

"Yes, ma'am," Rose responded.

"I'm not a ma'am; I'm a valet,'" said Violet.

"Mr. Gadriel is already in your quarters, which contains two bunks of two beds each as one of our larger guest quarters. You'll have privacy but not from each other unless you arrange for it amongst yourselves. Stay away from the crew quarters. Stay away from decks below this one. The galley is just beyond this corridor. My quarters are the first door we passed, the door that says 'Violet' on it. Do not touch the door that says 'Think' on it, understood?"

"Yes, Violet," said Rose, not knowing what else to say.

Before leaving Rose, Violet added, "I suggest you heed the captain's advice and attempt to get rest. When we have an opportunity for it, it is good to take it. Just because you are guests here does not mean you won't work. Unless, you've paid for your passage?"

Rose could only mutter, "Uhh, we were ab . . . duc . . . ted," to which Violet said, "I didn't think so. Rest. Cook will prepare midday meals in about three chimes; you'll hear it with two quick bells; they'll do it twice in case you miss it the first time."

"Thank you," said Rose.

"Don't than . . . You're welcome, ma'am," Violet said, with a slight bow, taking a step backwards, then walking away.

Rose lightly knocked on the door to her cabin. She heard "Y-yes" in a distracted voice. Upon entering she found Gadriel sitting up on a bed. Shanks was laying on the top bunk above him with his arms behind his head. Gadriel looked up and said, "Oh good, Rose, you're okay."

"Are you okay??" Rose asked, concerned.

"Ye . . . I think so. I take it you've brought the stone aboard?"

"Yes, it is with Captain Tamara, and probably Thinker now," Rose said, then asked, "Can you feel it? Or what is happening?"

"Yes I can feel it, I can hear it, that's the problem—it won't stop talking," Gadriel said, resting his head in his hands.

"It calms down a bit and becomes more conversational when I talk to it, but how am I to know if that is wise? When I try to ignore it, all it does is whisper things it shouldn't know about the people around it or, something. Sometimes it's secrets, sometimes it's embarrassing facts. Sometimes it feels like I've upset it when I go too long ignoring it. I haven't been able to sleep since you arrived . . . uh.. No offense," said Gadriel.

"None . . . taken," said Rose slowly, then asked, "What if we placed it in another cargo container to quiet it?"

"It was pretty angry from the bag of flour; I'd rather not piss it off again," responded Gadriel.

"Well. Have you tried asking it if it would let you sleep?" asked Rose, innocently and out of genuine curiosity.

"What?" asked Gadriel.

"It seems to be of an intelligence. You're not even the one that placed it in the flour sack. What if you introduced yourself and asked it if you could sleep?" shrugged Rose.

An exhausted Gadriel blinked at Rose, as did Shanks who had rolled over to stare at her. "Go on, try, I believe the stone is right above us with the captain. So, ask . . . gentlemanly," Rose said.

Gadriel: "Hello, uhm, Whisper Stone."

"Well, hello. Look who finally decided to accept their new partnership."

Gadriel: "My name is Gadriel, what is yours?"

"I know what your name is; I'm inside your head, you dolt. Look who's all polite all the sudden."

Gadriel: "I apologize. What is your name?"

"My name's Roderick, but don't call me Roderick, call me Rod."

Gadriel: "I see. Rod. I've had a day. I've been slapped with fishes, plural. I've been abducted. I've been thrown. I've been jumped upon and choked. I've been kicked, and kneed. I've been soaked and run ragged. And biggest of all, I have become your new best friend."

"Uh-huh," Rod said, somehow conveying a pleasant smile to Gadriel.

Gadriel: "If it wouldn't be too much to ask, would it be okay if I rested for a bit? I have no intention of ignoring you again."

Rod: *"Are you sure about that?"*

Gadriel: "Very sure, yes. I didn't know what to do before and I was rude. I apologize."

Rod: *"Okay, it'll be hard, I've been in this stone a llllong time, Gadriel. But go ahead, sleep."*

Gadriel: "Thank you, sir."

Rod: *"It isn't 'sir,' just Rod."*

Gadriel: "Yes— Rod. Thank you."

Rose, having only heard Gadriel's half of the conversation, sat on the edge of the bed across from Gadriel with her mouth agape. Gadriel, for his part, simply fell backward onto his bed, head hitting the pillow, and fell straight to sleep. Shanks was able to do the same. Rose, not wanting to disturb him, quietly laid down and tried to take the captain and Violet's advice and rest.

Some three chimes later, two sharp rings of the ship's bell sounded. This roused Rose awake to find Gadriel's bunk empty. Feeling much better than earlier, she stretched and collected her knives she placed under her pillow, both the dagger given to her by Captain Tamara and the hideaway knife from Lou, tucking them into her belt. She exited her cabin and, following Violet's instructions, followed the corridor toward what she hoped was the galley.

It wasn't long until she was sure she was going in the right direction as she smelled what she thought was a beef stew and heard laughter from a number of crew.

There was a one-legged pirate named John
With a one-legged story and song
John once misbehaved by his captain he was saved
And now he's a one-legged pirate named John
John used to have two legs you see
Cap'ts orders he didn't always heed

One day he thought better
And he fell from his tether
And now he's also the pirate with no pecker named John

Rose entered the galley to raucous laughter and applause. Still somewhat bewildered from having woken up, the wall of noise hit her abruptly. As she walked in, she saw Gadriel sitting atop one of the tables surrounded by several men while he told jokes and sang songs with his flute. Occasionally he would look down and mutter, but others he would speak freely to his right.

Scanning the room, Rose noticed Thinker standing in the corner nearest Cook, arms crossed, observing the room quietly. Rose did not see the captain in attendance, but from what she read, captains didn't usually eat in galleys; they ate in their quarters, sometimes with their officers. Rose slowly made her way to Thinker, trying to make herself as small and unnoticed as possible. As though she made a noise she knew she did not make, Gadriel looked over directly at her and smiled; she waved.

Upon reaching Thinker, she asked him, "Have you spoken with him yet?" to which Thinker responded, "No, once I heard he had left your cabin, I've been observing in here, only for a quarter chime or so."

Rose knew Thinker had a significant academic interest in the stone and Gadriel now that he knew they were bonded. Thinker had an engineer's mind. He'd been intrigued by the stone for as long as Rose had known him, not for its value, but for its mystery and practical applications and what it might be able to do. And everything he knew about it just changed, with Gadriel at the center.

Thinker said to Rose, "You should eat something before Cook allows second helpings. I'll be in my cabin. If you would, please ask Gadriel to meet me there when he is finished here. It is apparent he is talking to it; I have the stone with me." Softly patting his jacket pocket, he added, "I'd like to perform a number of tests."

Rose nodded. With that Thinker quietly left the galley and back up the corridor from where she came. Rose winced at another round of laughter and approached Cook.

"Hello, may I ha—" Rose was cut off by two reasonably loud thuds: one of a wooden bowl hitting Cook's counter, the second of a large spoon slapping stew into the same bowl. It was then scooted over to her in a motion just as delicate as it was served. Cook said nothing, only maintained a furrowed brow before and after the interaction and nodded. Rose simply said, "Thank you."

Rose, out of her element and uncomfortable as ever, stood at the edge of the room slowly scooping spoonfuls of stew into her mouth and chewing in a daze. The food was actually quite good, much better than she would have imagined on a ship. Startled, again, by someone clearing their throat, Rose looked over to find Violet standing next to her and laughing along with the crew. Her dark-purple noble servant's dress appeared very out of place in such an environment, but it fit her well. Violet's dress did not billow or flow luxuriously, despite being constructed of a luxurious material Rose could not identify. Violet's white-gold hair was kept in a single thick braid behind her head, which did not contrast much with her pale skin. Her violet eyes, likely her namesake, were piercing, as were her sharp facial features.

Rose had met people, and not always women, like Violet before. Not at the Governor's mansion or within his staff; the Governor wasn't important enough of a man for a servant of Violet's caliber. Violet and those like her were highly trained, highly sought-after servants from a culture far away from Rose's own. This culture placed respect and service to others in their highest regards and echelons of their society, and many who wished to leave were trained to serve others this way. For Captain Tamara to have Violet in service to her, let alone in such a dangerous and as harsh of an environment as a ship like the Midnight, was one of the most impressive things Rose had ever heard or seen.

"You should try to enjoy it now," said Violet to Rose, but not looking over at her; it was the crew's turn to tell jokes.

"Enjoy what?" asked Rose.

"The food," responded Violet. She continued, "The food will always be more fresh the sooner we've left a port, given we've had the luxury of a proper supply."

Cook, a man larger than Turf, at least four and a half steps tall—well, Rose steps—came over to them and handed Violet a bowl and spoon. In a deep rumbling voice he said, "Here you are, Miss Violet."

"Thank you, Cook," said Violet in a pleasant voice Rose had not yet heard directed at her. Before walking away, Cook looked down and noticed Rose's bowl empty. He grunted, then took her bowl and spoon, and walked away.

Violet then joked, "I think he likes you."

"I'm sure," said Rose.

Violet then asked, "Are you washing your own dish right now?" then walked away to join the crew at a table. All of them moved out of her way, showing her highest respects.

A chime later after Gadriel and the "boyos" had second helpings of Cook's fine stew, and Gadriel paid Cook severe compliments for his work,for which the large man may have blushed. He, Shanks, and Rose made their way to Thinker's room. They knocked on his door politely, but there was no answer.

"I'm not touching the doorknob," Gadriel said out loud. Shanks motioned toward the doorknob then crossed his arms, as if expressing the need to wait inside.

"Oh really, Shanks, he probably *wants* us to go in? I'm going up top," said Gadriel, exasperated. Rose just followed, content with Gadriel's decision because she wasn't going anywhere in anywhere without explicit permission on this ship.

On the deck, Gadriel, Shanks, and Rose were temporarily blinded by a much more beautiful day than the one they left when they went below decks. The Midnight was at full sail and still moving with what felt like incredible speed, though Rose had no frame of reference. Many of Midnight's crew were on the deck, evidently enjoying the sunlight. Admittedly, Rose enjoyed its warmth too after being chilled by the open ocean; Lulin wasn't the warmest township either. Rose spotted the captain on the quarterdeck with Thinker. Shanks tapped Gadriel and pointed to the quarterdeck as well. Other than his very first visit, this was the most time afforded Gadriel on the deck of the Midnight, let alone one with any freedom.

"No, I don't really want to look over the edge . . . No, I don't want to look over the front, either, that doesn't make it any better," said Gadriel to no one. Fortunately, Rose was already somewhat accustomed to this and wasn't very bothered by Gadriel's behavior.

"Gadriel, I think we should go speak with the captain and Thinker," said Rose.

"I agree," said Gadriel, then sighed, "one moment," then quickly walked over to the rail of the ship, grabbed a rope tightly, and stuck his head over the edge, shouting, "There! Happy!?" Pushing himself back upright, he turned and walked back purposefully past Rose and on toward the quarterdeck, where several crewmembers were looking at him with peculiarity. Rose simply followed and smiled at the absurdity.

"Permission, uh, to, uh, come up there, Captain," said Gadriel with an unnecessary salute, flanked by Shanks and Rose.

Tiredly, Captain Tamara responded, "You're allowed up here as long as we're not in battle, not in rough seas, and don't think you'll fall off otherwise. And don't salute me, that was ridiculous."

"Yes Cap't," said Gadriel. The three ascended the short stairs of the quarterdeck.

Upon reaching Captain Tamara and Thinker, the captain said, "If no one has any questions, Thinker has need of Mr. Gadriel in his cabin to discuss the stone. And I have a ship to run."

"Actually I have one question, please Captain."

"Go on," said the Tamara.

"Where are we going and how long will it take us to get there?"

"I told you, or do you not remember? We're going to dock at Saints Rock, which is the better part of three weeks away—now the better part of two weeks and six days away," said Captain Tamara, again tiredly.

"No, I do recall that. Captain, but, forgive me. Saints Rock is south of Lulin."

The captain began to smile, then said brashly, "And what about it?"

"I'm no sailor, Captain, but we were headed into the sunrise and turned to port; that was north, not south. So, I'm simply curious. Where are we going, and how long will it take to get there?"

Both Thinker and Captain Tamara slow-clapped for Rose.

"Points for you, deary. There aren't a lot of people in my experience who catch that. 'Ow 'bout you, Think?" to which Thinker added, "Nope, you would actually be the first in my experience. At least the first who was not a sailor."

Captain Tamara tapped her own chin in thought. "The same is true for me—congratulations, Thorny, what a pain in my ass you are."

"Well?" asked Rose.

From the side of Rose, Thinker, and Captain Tamara, Gadriel said to none of them, "Well, if you also noticed, why didn't you say anything sooner? That doesn't even make sense, we were below deck . . . Ohhh because 'you' were above deck. Rrriiiight."

To which Thinker said to the group, "If you'll excuse us, I think I'll take Mr. Gadriel to my cabin so we can discuss the stone and his new . . . affliction . . . further."

Rose began to speak, but before she could continue, Thinker interrupted, "No, I will not hurt him."

"Mr. Gadriel, would you follow me, please?" Thinker announced. Gadriel smiled and followed him like a puppy. Shanks just shook his head and followed them both, leaving Captain Tamara and Rose alone on the quarterdeck with only Helmsman, who continued his duty in silence.

"We're headed to an island settlement called New Haven," stated Captain Tamara. "It is actually where Thinker hangs his hat, and we should be there in about the same estimated time," she added.

"Why not just tell us that?" asked Rose.

"Why would I tell you that when I could not?" asked the captain, adding, "unless we're advertising our speed, I don't make it a habit of telling dockmasters my next port of call, exporters where I'm taking my cargo, or captives where I'm taking them."

Rose nodded. The captain then said with a smirk, "We may make a sailor out of you yet, but you deary, are no scoundrel."

In Thinker's cabin, Gadriel sat at a large workbench across from Thinker at the far end of the room. Shanks sat in a corner as far out of the way as possible. On Thinker's workbench it was easy to see why he was often referred to as an engineer, and Gadriel thought this by just how much he did not understand what he was looking at.

"Gadriel if it's all right with you, I'd like to start off asking a few questions?" asked Thinker.

"Sounds acceptable to me; I am a captive on your ship, after all," Gadriel responded, to which Thinker couldn't help but smile, a rare show of emotion. Shanks from the corner of the room stifled a chuckle; even Rod from inside Gadriel's head reacted: "*Damn.*"

Thinker was a slight man but wired in muscle. His oak-brown hair was cut very short as to show ornate tattoos on the side of his head in addition to ones Gadriel could see on his forearms. The tattoos on Thinker's right forearm, however, were badly damaged from significant scarring that of which Gadriel had never seen, from Thinker's hand to passed his elbow. From what Gadriel had observed, Thinker had preferred to wear worn lighter leathers instead of warmer, thicker, wool fabrics, likely for the protection it afforded.

Thinker's dark brown eyes contained a radical and calculating intelligence capable of complex, if not terrible, things.

Thinker produced the stone from a strong box attached to his workbench. Being taller than Thinker, he naturally sat up higher than the older man on the same workbench and was able to see why he needed the strongbox. Within it appeared to be precious metals, other gems, even vials of liquids containing metal flakes among other strange solutions. Thinker placed the stone on the workbench at what was likely the exact equal distance between Gadriel and himself.

"Now that the stone is out of the lockbox, does it seem any different to you?" asked Thinker.

Gadriel said, "Yes, now Rod sounds like he's right next to me, in the room with us."

Thinker then asked, "And is Rod the name of the man within the stone?" to Gadriel's surprise.

"How would you—"

Thinker went on the explain, "I suppose knowing a little about what's happening and what I may know only helps the situation. Do you believe in magic, Mr. Gadriel?"

Gadriel said, surprised, "Uh, I suppose, maybe?" to which Thinker responded, "Well I don't. But I do believe in what is observable. And alchemy, on our plane of existence, has been observed. Souls and spirits have been observed."

Gadriel understood and nodded. Thinker continued, "Based on what I've been able to learn from my sect, and gather in my travels, Whisper Stones, as they have come to be known, combine alchemy and spiritual energy, when one thinks about it hard enough, in a truly horrific way."

"How is it horrific?" asked Gadriel, suddenly more nervous than he had been. Before Thinker responded, Gadriel heard, *Think about it, genius.*

"Well," started Thinker, "the most consistent information I've found suggests that the soul, or spirit, of a man is trapped, either voluntarily or involuntarily—"

"INVOLUNTARILY!" shouted Rod.

"—within the stone. As you've probably learned from your companion, Rose, these Whisper Stones typically only bond with one person at a time and, well, whisper to them incessantly, driving some men mad. I must say you're doing quite well."

"Well, thank you," said Gadriel. "From what I've been told, this isn't my first day being mad."

"Yes that's correct," said Thinker, then finished his lesson, "your madness may very well be how you're handling this so well. Now the day is young but we only have so many, if we may continue?"

On the deck of the Midnight, Rose stood at the portside railing where the sun was setting, likely in about a chime or so, Rose thought. She was joined by Violet not too long after finishing her conversations with the captain and being left to her own devices. Rose had spent time attempting to ask members of the crew who appeared the most welcoming what their jobs were—not many were. Rose figured if she were on this ship for "maybe three weeks," she might as well learn something.

Violet said out loud, "It'll be supper bell soon. I wager you'll soon be able to smell the galley ahead of time. I believe Cook is roasting chicken this evening."

"But not for you, right?" said Rose.

Violet showed her surprise for the barest of moments, then smiled, "Very good, Rose. How was this something you discovered so quickly, did a crew member mention it?"

"No, Ms. Valet, if that is proper deference. I noticed Cook give you a bowl of stew that appeared devoid of meat, and in a way that made your food look separately prepared; it wasn't a difficult assumption."

"I don't eat meat; most from my lands do not," said Violet.

"That I did not learn in my studies."

"Shall I accompany you to the galley?" offered Violet. "We will make it back with time enough to watch the sunset. In calmer waters with low risk, I rarely miss it if my lady does not have need of me."

Rose nodded appreciatively, and although she was sure this was only politeness and likely orders for Violet to keep tabs on her, if she didn't think about it too hard, Violet felt something like a friend.

"Is he in the room with us right now?" asked Thinker.

"NO, I'm saying he's in the stone, but he's in my head. In the room it's just you, me, and Shanks," Gadriel said, hooking a thumb over to the stool tied to the corner of the room. Shanks knocked his boots together with an attempt at humor; Gadriel was the funny one, however.

"Okay, so if I may, let us confirm what we've learned, and then we'll grab supper," Thinker prompted with incredible politeness from such a hard man. Going over his notes, Thinker summarized:

"This Whisper Stone contains the spirit of a man named Roderick who demands to be referred to as Rod. He cannot recall how long he's been in the stone, but it's been some time. He vaguely recalls his spirit being ripped from his body and forced into the stone; that much is true, just not details of the event. And he chose to bond with you because, and I quote, 'you're Mother damn hilarious.' Is that right?"

"Yep," said Gadriel. "Can't see him, but we can talk clear as day. He didn't like being ignored at all; I do have a request you don't lock the stone away like under a sack of flour—he didn't like that. May I keep it with me for now?" Thinker paused, clearly he didn't want to allow this.

"I cannot go anywhere, I cannot steal it, I cannot sell it, this is your ship," said Gadriel.

"This is Captain Tamara's ship," said Thinker, quickly, then he added, "But I see your point. Yes, all right. Please keep it in your pocket; do not reveal it to the crew. I will inform the captain of this decision. Can you see yourself to the galley?"

"Yes, sir."

"Thank you for your time, Gadriel," Thinker said as he excused him from his cabin.

Gadriel, Shanks, and Rose entered the galley at about the same time and entered the mess line.

"How'd it go?" asked Rose.

"Good, actually," said Gadriel. "Thinker was eerily polite to me. Which made what Rod was telling me even creepier."

"Why, what was he saying?" she asked.

"Basically that Thinker was a dangerous man capable of terrible things," shrugged Gadriel.

"Not capable, has DONE terrible things, don't misquote me, I can hear everything now."

"Right, sorry, has DONE terrible things."

Approaching Cook, chatter between the two died down, and they were each given a plate of delicious-smelling food. Each plate contained half a small roasted chicken, boiled and seasoned potatoes and carrots, as well as fresh bread—likely not baked on the ship, but again more fresh than Rose would have expected.

"Are you surprised about the—"

"Food? Yes and no," said Gadriel.

"The food is going to get worse as we get further out to sea; it'll be no fault of Cook."

Rose and Gadriel took a seat. Then Captain Tamara immediately sat down across from them.

"And a good crew runs on its stomach, I say," she said. All crew present that walked by their table, which was most, said a respectful "Cap't" as they walked by to find their seat. Tamara nodded every time.

"Hello captain!" said Gadriel cheerfully. "Yes, hello," added Rose.

"How are my two favorite passengers?" asked Captain Tamara.

"PRISONERS"

"We are good, thank you," said Gadriel.

Tamara added, "Our food is exceptionally good. When I can procure and afford it. Contrary to most captains, I love my men. Sailing ain't easy. I wouldn't want to do it if the food was shit."

"I can agree with you there," said Gadriel.

"Ah, have a lit'l experience, handsome?" asked Tamara.

"Something like that," Gadriel said while Shanks just nodded his head up and down.

A short moment later, Violet joined them with a slightly different plate. Her plate contained the same boiled potatoes, carrots, and bread, but it also contained cleaned and prepared fruits of apple and plum. Violet nodded her head in silent greeting to the table.

"Violet, in the morning when you happen to rise, I'd like for you to rouse Thorny here and meet me on the deck. We have some things to discuss."

"Should I come?" asked Gadriel.

"I said Rose, we, things, lady things, deary," said the captain, not harshly. She added, "Thinker will gather you in the morning for a whole fun day of research on the stone and Mr. Rod."

"Aw great," groaned Gadriel.

"What??" The captain, Rose, even Violet asked with concern.

"Now he's *Mr.* Rod."

That evening on the deck of the Midnight, Gadriel sat quietly on strapped cargo overlooking the ocean as the last bit of sun faded below the horizon. A crew member walked around to light too few lanterns for just enough light to see work, but not nearly enough to make spotting the Midnight easy. The Midnight did not have a crow's nest, but it did have a fighter's nest. Fighter's nests differed from crow's nests in that they were less for lookouts and more for battles, like their name suggests. Not usually located at the tops of masts, and more centrally located in the center of ships closer to the quarterdeck, they were wider and could at times sit more than one man. It didn't matter to Shanks what kind of nest it was, however; he found himself content to sit in either when unoccupied. Gadriel noticed that about the Midnight, Shanks preferred much more solitude than was normal, and he could understand why. He'd likely be the same way for obvious reasons.

After supper, Thinker collected the stone for research, assuring Gadriel and "Mr. Rod" that he would be giving the stone back to Gadriel in the morning. Passing by Thinker's cabin throughout the evening, a great many strange noises could be heard, like the buzzing of bees as an example. Not many understood Thinker or what he attempted to accomplish, and Thinker didn't mind it that way. Gadriel and Rose had no problems sleeping that evening. Rod was glad to have been able to interact with someone after what could have been a hundred years for all he could remember, and both were exhausted and well-fed. Shanks opted to stay awake and continue watch. And despite Gadriel's exhaustion, his nightmares persisted.

The next morning Gadriel and Rose were woken up by a knock on their cabin door. They opened it to find Violet with her arms filled with clothing.

"My lady wished you wear this change of clothes," she said. "Something about you didn't get a fair deal before we left. But she wanted me to make clear to you that 'you haven't earned your blacks.' After you change, if you could please join us on the main deck." Gadriel and Rose thanked her.

Having, in a way, done this before, each took turns changing clothes with their backs turned while Shanks slept facing the wall on the top bunk above Gadriel's. They decided not to wake Shanks as he was likely up throughout the night volunteering for watch duty. *Once a sailor, always a sailor*, thought

Gadriel, with a smile for his young friend. As the two climbed onto the top deck of the Midnight. Rose was again awed by what she saw.

About half a chime after sunrise, the Midnight had her men climbing on and checking her rigging and unfurling top sails. Rays of light skipped off of deep, emerald-blue waters, while the Midnight cut through it at a slight angle, her main boom pointing out the starboard bow. The Midnight glided on the water, as if this great infinite mass of ocean were nothing more than a frozen pond a gleeful child skated upon. Rose could feel this joy from the ship, feel this energy from her men as they sang their work, and if Rose were not careful, she would soon fall in love with this ship.

Gadriel and Rose were now dressed in garb not too dissimilar from one another. Violet was telling the truth when she said they had not "earned their blacks," as they stuck out from the crew quite starkly wearing white blouses and dark brown pants, leather belts, and leather boots—rugged materials to withstand life on a ship, to be sure, but it was clear they were visitors, or more accurately, captives.

Gadriel and Rose approached Captain Tamara and Thinker, who were atop the quarterdeck.

"Think, steady as she goes," said the captain clearly.

"HELMSMAN, STEADY AS SHE GOES!" shouted Thinker.

"AYE! STEADY AS SHE GOES!" returned Helmsman.

Tamara was the first to descend the short stairs and informed Rose that she would be working with her that day, then asked Gadriel if he would accompany Thinker, who wanted to do more testing. Gadriel nodded.

"Hey, ask him if he wants to hold hands."

"Shut up," Gadriel said aloud, as far as the others were concerned, to no one in particular. They knew, however, this wasn't the case.

Thinker and Gadriel left to descend the stairs below deck. Captain Tamara began walking over to a large lockbox that had not been on deck the day before. Opening the box and reaching inside, she quickly turned around, throwing what looked like a stick at Rose, then attacked her, swatting her in the thigh with a stick of her own.

"Ouch! What the Heavens, Tamara!"

"That's Captain, sweets, and watch y'mouth."

Rose looked down and she looked to be holding a wooden sword, a cutlass like the one that gave her the small scab she now had on the tip of her nose.

Captain Tamara had a similar wooden sword that she placed inside a belted sash, tossing a sash to Rose.

"'Ere, put this on. If they make holsters for wooden swords, I ain't buyin' 'em," said the captain.

Rose quickly tied the sash, copying Tamara as best she could.

"Al right deary, this is your first lesson. And it's painful, for both of us if you're good enough."

"I thought you were going to show me how to use that dagger?" asked Rose.

"We've got a few weeks, Thorny, pace yourself. Besides, you learn how to use a sword to survive a battle; that's a fight you don't get to avoid. You learn to use a dagger on how to win fights; half the time you get to avoid those. They'll use some of the same principles, but this 'ere is a cutlass, a true gentlemanly weapon, and the only one I'll use when the cards are down, if you understand." Rose nodded.

"Now, draw your sword and hit me with it."

However, Captain Tamara did not draw her sword. At this pronouncement, two young crew members ran quickly below decks, and a few men above them wedged their thighs, behinds, and biceps comfortably into rope of the rigging as to make seats to enjoy this entertainment. Slowly but surely, many crew members began filling the deck with as much nonchalance as possible, some carrying heavy items that didn't need moving, some bringing rope with them to tie that didn't need tying. Tamara couldn't help but smile.

"What are you waiting for, Thorny, hit me—this has got to be something you've thought about the last few days."

"You haven't drawn your sword?" asked a confused Rose.

"You don't worry about what I'm doing," stated Captain Tamara. "Now hit me."

With that, Rose began moving forward with an overhead, right-handed swing from right to left. Tamara took one step back with her left leg, shifted her hips and left shoulder, and leaned back slightly, causing Rose to miss entirely. Rose, embarrassed about missing her unarmed target with an audience, took another step forward with her left foot and attempted a left-to-right mid-swing. Throwing her arms up for balance and hopping back with both feet, Rose caught only a small amount of the fabric from the captain's black shirt—such a forceful miss off her less dominant foot did cause her to be off balance, which the captain was expecting, as she quickly palmed the back of her head and finished off Rose's momentum, pushing her to the ground. This swinging and missing continued for a quarter chime with Rose becoming more agitated, embarrassed, and tired.

"All right, all right, deary, that's enough; let us have a bow."

Captain Tamara spread her arms out wide and bowed deeply to Rose in a surprisingly respectful gesture. Rose mirrored her movement, and while her face was pointed toward the deck, she was shocked by a sharp painful sting on her behind. Rose yelped and jumped, and the men roared with laughter. Captain Tamara was now behind Rose with her wooden sword out of her sash getting spun around her wrist.

"What the Mother was that for?"

"Another lesson. We weren't done; I was still standing. You took your eyes off your opponent. You let your guard down. I let you try to hit me for half chime and you thought that was going to be the end of it? Naw, deary, you're too smart. The world isn't fair. Don't expect it to be or pretend that it is. Now ready yourself."

"What are we doing now?" asked a nervous Rose, holding her sword out as the captain just barely lowered herself to give her knees a slight, agile bend.

"Now, I hit you, but I'll let you try to stop me." Rose nodded. "Really? No protesting?" asked the captain.

"No, I'm here to learn." stated Rose.

"Okay, good. Then here we go."

And in that moment, the captain went from in front of her, to swinging her sword high in the air and her back to her left, then another stinging pain from her backside. The crowd cheered. Rose couldn't believe it. She was prepared and ready for her, yet the captain was able to go from standing in front of her, distract her high and to her right, then spin behind her and attack her from behind before she could properly react, or do much of anything about it.

"Don't feel bad, sweets. I've been doing this awhile. And you are a bit fatigued."

"I'm not just saying this; I shouldn't be this slow."

"Why do you say that, Thorny?" asked Tamara.

"I'm not completely ignorant; I've trained in bow staff," Rose said.

"Oh really," Tamara said. "Well," she continued, "with very few exceptions, is a light thin bow the same as a heavy cutlass? You'll just need to condition yourself. Now, get ready. 3, 2, 1 . . ." *Pop* . . . "Ow, damn it."

"Okay Gadriel and Mr. Rod. We're going to be doing some temperature tests today. If you could follow me please," said Thinker.

They then descended several decks to the personnel and facilities deck, where Gadriel presumed also contained a gun deck. They then passed the cargo hold, then they reached ballasts on the bottom of the ship, significantly cooler and more damp than the rest of the ship. In the deepest part of such a large ship, Thinker brought Gadriel over to a barrel, and when he looked inside he saw what looked like mostly ice floating in water.

"As you could've guessed, this is ice. I obtained it in Lulin before we left. I store it down here to slow it from melting, but this is a test we must do now before the ice is gone. I wanted to advise you . . . both . . . that I'll be placing the stone into this barrel, and I'd like it if you told me whether you or Mr. Rod, or both, feel any differences?"

Gadriel nodded. Thinker then held the stone under the iced water. Gadriel waited patiently and felt nothing in particular. Rod's voice was significantly muffled, however. After a full tock, Thinker removed his hand and the stone from the ice and asked if Gadriel observed any changes. Gadriel relayed only that Rod didn't like its effect. A short time later they tested the stone under heat to find no changes—only vulgar responses from Rod.

Over the weeks that followed, Thinker and Gadriel learned more about the stone, unfortunately only from an engineering perspective, not how to unbind him from the stone. Rose learned valuable swordplay from Captain Tamara, as well as more about Violet's culture and the lands of Rees. One late afternoon just before sundown, the two loud horn blasts sounded from the fighter's nest; Shanks had seen something. Gadriel perked up in the galley, which piqued the interest of Rose and Thinker, who had taken to spending much of his free time with Gadriel to observe the stone's long-term effects on a subject still alive.

Gadriel said, "Land, they've spotted land."

Shortly after, they heard a muffled shout from the deck, "LAND HO!"

Many crewmates took to the main deck. Thinker took a moment to write something in his notebook first.

Thinker and Captain ran up the quarterdeck and confirmed with a spyglass that it was New Haven island, which meant they did not have enough daylight to dock that day.

"Let's pull up and wait till morning; we'll just sheet out. We have too much time to stress the rigging if we're waiting till morning."

"Yes, Cap't," said Thinker, then shouted, "HELMSMAN, SHEET OUT ONE LEAGUE THEN COAST TO AN ANCHOR!"

"AYE! SHEET OUT ONE LEAGUE, COASTING TO AN ANCHOR FOR THE NIGHT SIR! AYE!" repeated the helmsman.

Rose asked Captain Tamara, "If we're here, why are we waiting till morning."

"Well, this place isn't just Haven by name alone, deary. Most of its shoreline surrounding the island is very shallow, making all but the smallest ships too dangerous to traverse unless they know the route in. Our Think knows the route in, but he must be able to see it from the bow and guide us in. So, we sit tight tonight." answered Captain Tamara.

"You, come with me," said the captain to Gadriel and Rose and began walking towards her quarters. Gadriel looked up to see Shanks in the fighter's nest give him a little salute, which Gadriel returned. He was glad Shanks was back in his element, but he would need to check in with the young man. This is the first either of them had been back on a real ship, and Shanks appeared to be taking it all too well.

Inside the captain's quarters, both were surprised by what they saw. Not that it was incredibly clean and squared away, but that it was also somewhat delicate. The captain's bunk, for example, was made with crisp linens and lines, but you could also see large, squishy pillows poking out from the top of the tightly tucked sheet and a not-quite-fluffy duvet neatly folded at the foot of the bunk. The head and torso of a mannequin sat in the corner of the room, which was used to hold her leather captain's jacket and cap. Her large desk, which served several purposes, was adorned with midnight-blue filigree around the edges, as well as her captain's chair, and the dark wood matched that of her ship. Gadriel and Rose separately thought this detail around the room was beautiful and fit the captain well. While it likely didn't surprise Rose, having spent time with the captain daily, it did well to serve as a reminder to Gadriel that while Captain Tamara was a captain first, she was still a person, if not a lady, despite her insistence to the contrary.

"Take a seat," ordered the captain.

Gadriel and Rose took a seat across from the captain, who also sat down with her back facing the bright, beautifully designed stern windows of her quarters; this left her face slightly darker and harder to read, and their own slightly brighter and easier, just the way the captain liked it. Before sitting down, the captain placed a bag on the edge of the desk but did not refer to it just yet.

"First, I wanted to thank you both for being excellent captives these last few weeks. Thank you, captives."

The good captain paused until Gadriel said, "Uh thank you?" then quickly, "Well, it was *obvious* she was waiting for it, pffft . . . sorry."

Captain Tamara smiled and said, "Don't mention it; I was." She continued, "How much do either of you know about New Haven? Other than it is where our dear Thinker comes from?"

Both Rose and Gadriel shook their heads, at a loss.

"Excellent," she said. "Please allow me to explain:

"New Haven is a settlement comprised of people like Thinker from under all of our stars that was formed several generations ago; Think was born there, ya' see. The settlement is well-established and well-known to ships like the Midnight for supply jobs and outfitting, and they pay well and complete very good work; we're delivering mainland cargo for them tomorrow, in fact, and we'll be paid handsomely enough that we'll eat just as well on our way to Saints Rock.

"It is called Haven because so many years ago, worshippers of Mother, and those of the Heavens Below, began to reject the learnings of newer sciences and technologies that engineers like Thinker pride and obsess themselves upon, to the point they'd run them out of towns and cities, and then escalated this to hunting them. They found it as some sort of sin, somehow insulting their faith to seek power already present on this plane—at least that's how I interpret it, if it could be understood logically.

"The island of New Haven was deliberately chosen due to its large size and many sources of fresh water, but mainly because of its wide, shallow shoreline. The only way we'd be able to unload cargo is painstakingly with skiffs and canal boats, which I've seen done for those who don't know the routes to their harbor, but it can be done, as the waves ain't nothin' in water so calm and shallow; canal boats do just fine.

"The original settlers of New Haven carved out the routes themselves, wide enough to allow larger ships to pass through, but the Midnight is just about the largest to fit; any larger and a captain would be a little insane and risking beaching their ship. Tomorrow we'll be heading into port with Thinker's guidance. Good luck anyone remembering the routes without having been raised on New Haven; I wouldn't risk my ship and her men. Anyone who beaches, or at least is far away from a safe route, is considered a threat and likely invader, which still happens by spiritual fanatics who find their settlement—they become beached a quarter league away from shore, much too far for any ship's guns to do anything about, but plenty close for the island's artillery to do plenty about. Then they complete a salvage mission, take prisoners, and then go about their lives."

"It sounds like a safe place. Is there no risk at all for them?" asked Gadriel, but also thought Rose, both always thinking and working angles.

"Y'know, Think and I had discussed that one night over too much whiskey. And I'm not going to tell you. But it would involve the Royal Navy."

Gadriel sheepishly apologized, and Rose turned just as red, though she hadn't even asked the question.

"SO. Why you're here." The captain re-railed the conversation. "First things first, this—" Tamara picked up the bag from the edge of her desk and dropped it into the middle of the desk. "These are your blacks. Now calm down. You're not part of my crew. But where we're going there is absolutely no need to advertise that you're anything different from my crew. So, pretties, stop primping, stop preening. Thorny, you're going to stuff those pretty doll hairs under a cap. Gad, I'm going to ask that you keep the self-talk to a minimum if ya' can. However, you've been given a high-collar coat—be sure to use it if you can't help it; I couldn't know what it's like to have what you have."

Captain Tamara scooted the bag over to the two.

"What about Shanks?" asked Gadriel.

"Uh, right, uhm. Well, Shanks will have to stay on the ship, I'm afraid. He does a great job in the nest, however," answered the captain.

"May I tell him?" asked Gadriel.

"Yes! I'd prefer it, he is clearly your man," stated the captain. "A few more things about New Haven," added Tamara. "Just because we're allowed there, doesn't mean we belong there, and it'll be made known that we don't, get me?" Both nodded. "It is why we're leaving the dock with only a small group."

"Why are we here, may I ask?" Rose questioned.

"Good question, Thorny," the captain continued. "Thinker needs to meet with his sect concerning the stone, and Mr. Mad Gad here. Not everyone on this island is the same, feels the same, believes the same. Thinker's sect is particularly interested and versed in technology surrounding the stone and can tell us, we hope, more about it."

"I thought you wanted to sell it," objected Rose. "I thought the last time we kind of worked together you were interested in duping the Governor out of the stone because you had a buyer."

Captain Tamara rolled her eyes. "I liiiiied to you, deary. The stone has great value, but if you couldn't tell, as far as money goes, I'm quite comfortable. Think is my first mate, and I share some of his engineering curiosities he shares of the world around us. I am personally interested in what this stone, of which, may be capable. And so far, I have not been disappointed. Speaking of—" Captain Tamara stuck her hand down in the bag, rooted around for a moment, then pulled out a thick, well-crafted boxed leather pouch.

"This is for you, sir," she said and handed it to Gadriel. "Think made it for you after deciding it is best for the stone to remain near you and not with us. He has heavily documented how it agitates the spirit and power within the stone and would rather not. This pouch, which he specifically made for you, will attach to a strap or belt and lock shut. There will be no losing it, or no accidentally dropping it from your pocket. It goes in the pouch, we lock it shut, you carry the pouch, got it? Can you eventually open it if you had long enough? Yes. Will you have long enough? No. Can you quickly show anyone the stone? No. Do we think you'll otherwise give the stone away? Also no. So we like this plan, ya see?"

Gadriel looked down at what looked like intricate, expert craftsmanship. The thick leather pouch with a boxed bottom was double-stitched so well that it didn't allow light to pass through its seams. Its lock sat nestled inside two thick pieces of leather to where Gadriel couldn't even see how it worked, and the stone nestled into the pouch and fit near-perfectly without rattling around. Captain Tamara watched Gadriel place the stone inside, then she reached over and locked the pouch herself. All three felt the ship slowing rapidly down and turning slightly to one side, causing them to, in a way, half lean forward toward the captain; the captain remained seated upright. Rose didn't know what "sheeting" meant, but this had to be the result.

"Get some rest tonight. We'll have a long day tomorrow. Remember, putting those on, you represent my crew. Do not insult my crew." Both nodded and turned to leave.

"And kids," added Captain Tamara, "try to stay calm after seeing the things you'll see on that island." Both nodded again . . . hesitantly.

8

New Haven

Gadriel, Rose, and Shanks woke up at the sound of the ship's bell, which was three lazy rings. Everyone needed to rise and needed to shine. Rose was quick to dress in her new clothes. She now had two daggers after training with Captain Tamara nearly every day. These were placed behind her back, hilts quickly accessible.

Without turning around, she said to Gadriel softly, "I'll head up top and give you two a minute." As Rose exited their cabin and took a sharp right up their corridor, she was tucking her hair under her cap as instructed.

Gadriel sighed and looked up at Shanks, who motioned with his hand up and down. "This wasn't my decision, dear Shanks. The captain has a limited number of people permitted on the island, and she asked me to tell you to please remain here on watch."

Gadriel was worried for his friend feeling left out, but to his surprise Shanks smiled and gave him the lightest of backhands to the face, which caused Gadriel to laugh, then Shanks laughed. *If that was the worst part of his day*, thought Gadriel, *then he'd have a pretty good day.*

Rose, again, was in awe at the site she found when reaching the top deck. This time it wasn't beautiful nature or wildlife like days before, and it wasn't a breathtaking sunrise. It was a marvel of an island she would never have thought possible. Upon reaching the top deck and looking up, she noticed a large, fabric bubble above their ship, which turned out to be a balloon, filled with hot air. There were two men in it looking down on them with spyglasses, and they were much too far away for the Midnight to do anything about it, Rose would imagine. Looking at the island, which Rose could just barely see a white glow leading up to its shores from the water indicating light reflecting off its shallow waters, Rose was taken aback.

There was much more in the air on the island than there was a single balloon above their ship. Many gliding pieces of fabric like large kites, some with unknown instruments on them, some being constantly pulled in then slacked out, all caught significant winds off the other edge of the island. She saw a much larger balloon, shaped more like a potato, taking off then landing. Plumes of smoke occasionally sprouted around the island as well; she didn't know if these were purposeful or failed experiments.

Gadriel joined her on the deck and looked up at the captain on the quarterdeck, who was giving orders to Helmsman, just more quietly than her first mate. Thinker, for his part, was leaning on the forward bow observing the water and directing the ship by degrees with his arms, which the captain, through years of practice, could easily interpret, much like Thinker did the other way around when they left Lulin at speed on their first day at sea.

Gadriel could slowly begin to hear sounds coming from the island, including what sounded like the large grinding metal of a moving artillery platform he felt was being repositioned and trained on their ship. With her spyglass, Rose watched a man on the windward side of the island running along the beach carrying a large kite-like piece of fabric pulled tight around a frame of sorts; she swore she saw him begin to fly like a bird. She also swore she heard him swear as he climbed higher and then dove face-first into the sand. Gadriel began laughing and said to no one, "Boy, that guy did eat shit, but you can't say he didn't fly."

Before long, the Midnight was met by the New Haven Harbormaster, named Webber, as they entered the harbor. He was met at Midnight's rail by Thinker, who introduced Midnight, Captain Tamara, and himself.

"Good Morrow, Think."

"May we interest you and your man in coming aboard? We may easily carry your skiff."

"No, thank you for your courtesy. In fact, please follow me precisely the last legs through the harbor, there are . . . dangerous areas. Also please respect harbor courtesy. Again, there are dangers."

Think nodded and saluted with a fist to his chest and a bow. The harbormaster did the same.

Rose quietly asked Captain Tamara, "What did he mean by 'there were dangers'?"

"My guess deary? That the harbor is filled with something like explosives underwater; at least that's how they're behaving," Tamara said.

"What? is that possible?" asked a concerned Rose.

"Hmm. Bump, kaboom, ahh oh no, the horror, New Haven? Yeah probably, too genius for their own good," said Tamara waving her hands for drama but smiling.

Rose swallowed hard and nodded. Helmsman overheard the captain, but deftly followed the skiff all the same, a drop of sweat now on his brow.

The skiff, which didn't seem powered by rowing, and no one understood how, pulled the Midnight the last several hundred steps and into its berth. The harbormaster was up, on the dock, and squared away before the Midnight threw down her mooring lines. With the harbormaster were a company of men that not only appeared armed, but armored. These men weren't there for labor; New Haven's equivalent job of longshoremen caught Midnight's moor lines and pulled them in the last few steps and tied off the boat. In such a convenient cargo berth, the Midnight was able to fully open her cargo hold, making loading and unloading faster and easier on all parties. Captain Tamara, Thinker, Rose, Gadriel, and four of her men, just as armed, just not quite as armored in their leathers, exited the ship while her crew behind them began unloading cargo onto the dock.

On level footing, Captain Tamara, leading the party, gave the harbormaster a slight bow.

"Captain Tamara of the Midnight at your service, sir." The rest of her company followed suit.

"Harbormaster Webber, Captain. Welcome to New Haven. I'm expecting a shipment, yes?" Captain Tamara thought to herself, straight to business, as always.

"Yes, sir. We have four flats of four of organic cargo from Lulin for your government here; I also have some live cargo, but we'll keep them in the hull until you have animalists available to take them? I believe the tariffs have been paid by the party initiating the import."

"Yes, Captain," said Webber. "Anything additional to declare?"

"Yes, actually," started Captain Tamara. "We have two flats of four, privately selling powder, happy to pay our fair tariffs on such an important import. We don't yet have a buyer, but I'm sure we'll find one."

"As long as it's dry, I'm sure you'll have no problem at all," said Webber.

"Of course, our hold is open to whatever your inspectors may need; please help yourselves," said Captain Tamara, to which Webber nodded.

"You're welcome to enter New Haven. I do believe you know the rules here. Please respect courtesy. You may keep your weapons, but should you use them, you best have a provable, justifiable reason. And of course, enjoy yourselves. Just not a lot," Webber said with a smile that may or may not have been genuine.

As Captain Tamara's party began walking down the dock, Rose could not help but look at the armed men, who weren't anything if they weren't soldiers, behind Harbormaster Webber. Their armor was strange, and not at all shiny like she had seen of royal soldiers who passed through Lulin or almost-shiny like Lulin's guardsmen. New Haven's soldiers carried a sword, but they also carried other things she couldn't identify; the two in front carried netted bags of what looked like small cannon ammunition. Some of the men carried long wooden sticks with metal pipes attached to them, others had short wooden handles with metal pipes attached opposite their swords on belts. Rose knew little of what these all meant, but she was confident she didn't want to find out; she was also confident she never wanted to have to invade New Haven.

The settlement of New Haven was built into the side of a hill with a small waterfall that turned into a mostly small but reasonably quick-moving stream flowing down the middle of it. The island contained a central mountain that could've been volcanic, but it was tall enough to hold snow during the right seasons and offered plenty of fresh water in addition to several fresh-water lagoons around the island, as it had been explained to the captain by Thinker over the years.

Despite looking like a warm oasis, New Haven was very cool, and it was likely very cold in the winter months. Gadriel's guess on what he heard was correct. As the group reached the dock's entrance, it was clear to see that large artillery platforms dotted the dock between berths.

"Wow, I wouldn't want to attack this place either," Gadriel said to no one.

Every single person in the group had a nervous smile on their face, as every single person—including the fearless captain—felt the exact same way, including the entity inside Gadriel's stone.

As they exited the dock, Thinker took the lead and first took them over a foot bridge crossing the stream, which took them to a building central to town. Rose and Gadriel guessed this was like a city hall; Captain Tamara thought of it as New Haven's only central government building. Thinker explained the night before that he would need to check in here upon his arrival and advise them he was back and how long he planned on staying, while also sharing any discoveries he had made. New Haven was built upon shared knowledge and comprised of sects, or like a family house in a place like Lulin, but it took a more community approach to everything: chores, raising children, teaching, learning, and so forth. Thinker belonged to the house, or sect, Atmos, studying the heavens, the stars, and observable power in the universe. He was raised with one brother and five cousins, but with how this society operated, they all were treated like other children would siblings. He hoped to see his family this trip, but understood this was business.

The plan was for Thinker to check in with the central building and offer his notebook for copying, not the one with all his real notes, just the one he was willing to share. This wasn't so much a pirate-smuggler-scoundrel thing as it was an Atmos thing, and it was an open secret. It had been eighteen months since he'd been home, and he needed to see Atmos's elder—whomever that was now, but he had hoped his oldest uncle—and discuss the stone in private with Gadriel to show him what he'd learned. As far as Thinker knew, this was the first documented case of a Whisper Stone not only bonding with a man, but that man not going mad immediately. Who knew what kind of secrets within the stone this could unlock, or what kind of power this could release or harness.

Upon arriving at the central building, Thinker asked them to wait outside while he entered. Rose and Gadriel didn't walk away, but they did mill about.

"Don't go far, dearies, listen to ya mother now," said the captain, adapting a matronly tone.

Both were fascinated by what they saw simply out in the open, fascinating inventions. One contraption smashed fruit in a rhythmic thumping while steam came out the top of what looked like a pot on a pipe; another was making what looked like lightning from a machine—how they did this without dying was anyone's guess as far as Rose and Gadriel, well and Rod, were concerned.

About a quarter chime later, Thinker exited the central government building and advised the captain that all was well. If she didn't need anything right away, he'd like to visit his sect if that was allowable. Captain Tamara gladly dismissed Thinker, then went about finding a buyer for two flats of black powder. The equivalent of a high street in New Haven was geared toward visitors, as their high-value wares were made for export and for visitors, not so much the island itself. Like Thinker explained, they more often shared resources and traded specialty items.

"Hey, hey, Captain there, you wouldn't happen to have that gorgeous ship down there, would'yea? How are its cannons? How's your ammunition? Moon sect, we bring the boom sect! Please at least see us before ya' leave, eh? Cap't??" said a barker shuffling alongside the group.

Before he retreated, Captain Tamara smiled and leaned over to one of her men, "Please remind me later, I want to talk to anyone that says they bring the boom?" The large man, Clancy if Rose's memory served, nodded.

As they walked down the street, which remained open on one side to show a beautiful view of the harbor and its giant terrifying guns, they reached a shop toward the end of the street that was apparently where they were headed. The wide shop had its outer wall completely open, having recessed into its roof.

"Banger!" shouted the captain. A man with one eye, one and a half ears, and seven fingers smiled and made his way out of his shop wrapping Captain Tamara in a great big bear hug.

"Tamara!" he said warm and happily. "Heaven's below girl, how 'ave you been?" he added with genuine interest.

"I've been good, Bangs! Here and there and business is good. How about you, young man?"

"Bah, young man. Old 'nuff to be ya' father, Silly," the man called Banger laughed.

"Their names around here sound literal, but I doubt they're ALL that way, don't be rude," Gadriel said to no one.

"Don't worry about him; he's pretty but he's mad," said Captain Tamara smoothly, to which Banger replied, "AH! Aren't we all a bit. Things are good here. Breechie's at home I hope relaxin' but probably cookin' up a feast. Can we tempt you for supper tonight?"

"With all these strapping lads? I wouldn't dare. But I do appreciate the offer, sweets; we'll be stayin' on the Midnight tonight. And I don't know how long we'll be here."

"Ah, I see," said Banger.

"Well," Banger said, knowing business had arrived, "business has been boomin' fer us, heh . . . "Y'know, there's a lad down the way from Moon sect that is ripping you off—says Moon brings the Boom or some such."

Tamara said, "Aw, yeah, it's the highest form of flattery it is."

"So what may I interest you in today," said Banger. "I have some very interesting things to show you, and two I made special for ya.'"

"I can't wait to see them," said Tamara. "But I'm here with something to interest you, actually. Two flats of four, black powder of the highest quality, well, highest you'll get that isn't refined here, that is."

"Oh *really?*" said poor-negotiator Banger.

"If you have your men wait out 'ere, I'd like to show you somethin' special inside."

"Of course, Bangs."

"You six, seven? Naw, six, whatevs, wait here."

A short while later, Captain Tamara exited Boomer's shop with two beautifully crafted contraptions lazily attached to her hips with clips to her belt, her cutlass and holster now resting on the right side of her behind. It was easy to see that Captain Tamara already loved these devices, whatever they were, but if the captain loved them, they were likely weapons.

"These, lady and gents, are called *pistols*," announced the captain. "They're tiny little cannons I can shoot from my hands, and their load will stay dry thanks to Bangs's genius here," she said patting his arm at the shoulder, to which Banger blushed.

"Clancy, you'll stay with me, Mad Gad, and Thorny here," said Tamara. "The rest of you, please return to the ship with instructions to deliver the two flats of four black powder to Banger's shop right here, please; do not pay their longshoremen, use their dock carts. When the cargo is delivered you'll be taking two crates back—Banger will give them to you; they're mine."

"Aye, Cap't," all said in unison.

"I feel like I'm getting a better end of this deal. May Breechie and I pay the import fee? It shouldn't be too bad this time of year, and it's considered research material," Banger said, concerned.

"Think nothin' on it, deary," Tamara then got on her tiptoes and kissed Banger on the cheek. "And yes, I shall inform your harbormaster that you may pay the fees," she said with a wink before departing. While still within earshot and waving to Banger, Tamara said, "Think and I will try to make it to see you and Mrs. Breecher before we must go!"

"Oh boy! Can't wait to tell her!" She then blew him one more kiss before turning around and becoming business-like Captain Tamara again. "Not a word, none of you. I'm a human as well; we've done a lot for each other over the years." All three of them, including Clancy, emphatically shook their heads.

Before leaving New Haven's merchant's area, Rose embarrassingly asked if she could get juice from the machine. "Well, I'd really like to see it work up close, and it seems like something nice Violet might enjoy."

"Ohh, really," said the captain. Then surprisingly, she said nothing else at all and placed a few coin in Rose's hand.

It was at that point Clancy leaned down and said, "The Moon Boom Man, Cap't".

"Ah, yes, thank you, dear Clancy. Please stay with our guests, and I'll return in a moment."

Rose, Gadriel, and Clancy approached the man and the machine, which looked to make juices.

Gadriel: "No"

Vendor: "Ello little lady, 'ello little lady. What'll it be, what'll it be? We specialize in juices, but I can also accommodate fruits wholesale."

Gadriel: "*Noo.*"

Rose: "Oh, uhm, just one, container? Please?"

Gadriel: "Absolutely not."

Vendor: "Of course, ma'am, just pick five fruits and I get to work; that's how we'll do it. Easy peasy."

Gadriel "SMASHER! I'm so sorry. If I don't ask if your name is Smasher I'll never sleep again."

Vendor: "Actually no, my name is Steamer."

Gadriel: "Whew," he breathed.

Steamer: "But my brother's name is Smasher—he'll be here tomorrow, is that all right?"

Gadriel: "MOTHER—" turning around and walking away, kicking the air.

Steamer: "Is he okay?"

Rose: "Yes. He does this."

Clancy, leaning down to be helpful: "He's just a lit'l mad."

After taking suggestions from Steamer, because she could not identify all of the fruits he had to offer, he made what Rose had hoped to be a delicious juice for Violet. Rose wanted to do something nice for Violet because although Violet had orders to help Rose, she had still been thoughtful and nice to her; she wasn't sure how much of that was orders, and she wasn't sure how much of that anyone would understand should she attempt to explain it.

A few tocks later, Captain Tamara rejoined them and stated, "Clancy, excellent work today. I've placed an order with Mr. Moon Boom; it is paid for, do not give him money unless you see something for yourself. Would you be so kind as to take delivery from him and transport it to the ship? Should the harbormaster ask you about export taxes, just say 'Moon' got it?"

"Aye, Cap't. Thank you, Cap't," said Clancy, his chest swelling with a little pride, taking off at a walk toward Moon sect's shop.

Captain Tamara added, "C'mon, let us go to the house of Atmos and find our engineer."

The house of Atmos, or the home of the Atmos sect, being scholars of the heavens, naturally had one of the physically highest houses in the settlement and also furthest away due to the nature of their experiments. This naturally led for them to be somewhat outcast or not as enfolded in New Haven society. But make no mistake, Atmos was very much a part of New Haven and greatly contributes to the community resources and nature of their society, just in ways that aren't always apparent to lower sects or those not in government.

The New Haven government was led by three elected officials called Justices, who carried supreme authority and made all significant decisions and decided trials jointly. The only time this was not the case was during wartime when the chief justice was given absolute authority, with the remaining two becoming second and third in command of New Haven's military forces, or what served as their military forces. To Captain Tamara's understanding, New Haven had not been attacked in over five years. And this had not slowed down their defense research in the least. As an example, Tamara and the Midnight had not been to New Haven in eighteen months. They had not added explosives to their own harbor, and their artillery platforms were simply heavy cannon. You could only describe Haven as fanatical, and you could only blame other worshipers for making them that way.

When Tamara, Gadriel, and Rose reached the house of Atmos, it was a wondrous site. Significantly colder than the rest of the island below, Atmos was more or less a glass tower half-built into the side of their main hill or mountain, depending on your frame of reference. As you approached the sect's house, you could see that near the top was an observation deck with what looked to be a large spyglass pointed at the sky. The roof appeared flat with what may have been twenty or more long spikes sticking straight up made out of some metal material. Rose later learned these were lightning rods, and Atmos would use them to capture lightning for their experiments.

Waiting for admittance as politely as possible, Captain Tamara leaned back to address Gadriel and said in a low, but strict voice, "I know we've had our laughs. But this is the time for you to shut. Your. Mouth. With all due respect, Sir Rod."

"Thank you Cap't, he appreciated the deference."

At that, grand doors clicked heavily and began to swing inward. As they slowly swung open to reveal polished, light gray floors, the three looked up to see Thinker standing there looking like a different man. Thinker was still Thinker, but instead of his leathers, he was wearing robes of gray and white, the sides of his head had been freshly shaven, and the tattoos on the sides of his head had been adorned with silver.

Despite the crooked smile on Thinker's face, you could tell he was uncomfortable, Captain Tamara knew it. And if it weren't for the larger man next to Think, she would have teased him relentlessly. Next to Thinker was a man half a step taller but just as thin, sharing many of Thinker's features. Oak brown hair, perhaps a few shades lighter, dark eyes, similar tattoos on the sides of his head, also adorned in silver.

"Hello good captain!" said the man, holding out his hands, which Tamara took and bowed in their way. "And you have friends—I am delighted;

I am Knowing. Who might you be?" Rose and Gadriel introduced themselves, copying Tamara flawlessly.

"I am the elder of this house, and as elder I am pleased at the prospect of new research! But as a father, I thank you captain for bringing my boy home for a spell!" he said laughing and wrapping an arm around Thinker warmly. "A genuine Whisper Stone! I'm sure however you came across it is quite a story. Do you have it with you, I hope?" Knowing prompted eagerly.

Captain Tamara played off her response casually while noticing a negative signal given to her by Thinker, a crossed pinky finger held down out of sight from his father, barely noticeable from under his robes.

"You better believe it, my lord. Quite a story indeed, quite a story. I'm 'fraid we don't 'ave the stone wif us. That be on the Midnight buttoned and safe, ya see," lied Captain Tamara, while also attempting to make herself sound unintelligent, thinking it better to be underestimated by a group of people who pride themselves on high intelligence.

"Well, there's always tomorrow! I've heard so much about it already from my boy here!" The proud father patted Thinker's back. "Please, stay for supper, and my wife and I insist you stay the evening with us," said Knowing cheerily. Thinker maintained their signal, which caused the captain to attempt to evade this invitation.

"Supper sounds lovely my lord. But it bein' gettin' late and it be best we get back to the Midnight for now. I have cargo to sort; I'm sure you understand."

The smile on Knowing's face began to falter when he said, "Please. I've insisted. You wouldn't want to insult my wife, would you? The cargo will still be there tomorrow. I'll send word to the harbormaster not to worry. I am Chief Justice of New Haven, after all."

If Captain Tamara were an amateur, her eyes would've widened, but she was not. "My lord, the last thing I be wantin' to do is insult your dear wife. It sounds, and smells, like my evening just freed itself up—smells delicious, sir!"

Knowing's smile returned. "Excellent! I will inform the house. If you don't mind, our house guards will collect your weapons. These will be returned to you before you leave, but I would prefer you not carry weapons where our children play; I'm sure you understand."

Captain Tamara bowed. "Of course, sir."

Thinker stated, "I'll take them to the guard captain father, this way."

While walking down the glass front wall to an enclosed room covered in one-way glass, Thinker leaned over to Tamara and advised, "I don't think this is good; I think we should leave as soon as we can without arousing suspicion. If he gets his hands on the Whisper Stone, there are good chances we never get it back. That was a risk we were willing to take. But the last time I was here, the Atmos elder wasn't my father, let alone the Chief Justice. Now? If he discovers Gadriel is who is bonded, as Chief Justice, none of us leave the island; it will be much easier to kill us on trumped charges."

Multiple guards exited the room, evidently a guard house of sorts, with a cart to meet the group still on the ground floor of the house of Atmos. Rose produced two daggers from behind her back and unhooked her cutlass from its holster, placing them on the cart. Rose took a calculated risk and did not remove her hideaway knife, which remained safely tucked behind her belt buckle. Captain Tamara walked up to the guards and first removed her cutlass, then her two new pistols.

"I've been informed the term is loaded, I wouldn't touch these."

She then continued. She produced two daggers from behind her back—one knife from her left boot, and one knife she once referred to as a "sticker" from her right, and one hideaway knife, again from behind her back, likely behind her beltline. She placed each neatly on the table.

"Uh, is that all?" said the guard captain from under the helmet.

Captain Tamara simply curtsied. Gadriel walked up to the cart and looked at the guards, then back to his people. Then placed his flute on the cart. Then backed away. The guard captain sighed and said, "Sir, you can keep this," and handed the flute back to Gadriel, which he gladly placed in his belt and said, "Okay, but I do damage."

"Master Thinker, do we need to shake these folks down?" asked the house guard.

"No. And please pay them proper courtesy; they are guests of the Chief Justice."

"Yes, sir," the house guard answered at once. "Thank you for your cooperation, my apologies, of course. If you should need any assistance, please see any member of the house guard, and I shall assist you myself." All of them bowed in thanks.

As they turned to walk away, Think quickly stopped Gadriel and walked back with him in the rear of the group.

"Gadriel. You'll all be given an opportunity to wash up before supper in a private room. I want you to remove the special holster and belt containing the stone and put it back on under your shirt, do you understand?"

"Actually, Think, I believe I do understand quite clearly. Also Rod is cooperating; he's quite frightened," said Gadriel. "As he should be."

Half a chime later they were sitting around a grand dining table with Knowing, his wife Andromeda, and Thinker's brother, Jupiter. Their extended family would not be joining them for this meal; they would be sharing a normal community meal in another area of the house.

"I hope everyone is hungry!" Knowing said, while everyone nodded politely. While servants brought out dishes of food, Knowing asked Gadriel directly, all traces of cheerfulness removed.

"Gadriel, correct?"

"Yes, Lord," answered Gadriel quickly.

"Why were you wearing a small leather box on your hip when you arrived and now you're not? You didn't turn it into the guard station. Is it a weapon?" Knowing said, staring Gadriel down without the hint of a smile.

Rose's eyes widened; being the most amateur member of the group this was not surprising.

Thinker attempted to interject. "Father, I—"

"I have asked our guest a question. I do believe he is capable of answering it himself, are you not, Gadriel?"

"Absolutely, sir. You see, I don't know how much Thinker has told you, but I suffer from a few afflictions. My name is Gadriel, but a lot of the boys in the crew call me Mad Gad because, well, I'm a little mad. But I earn my keep, yes I do," he said, taking out his flute and placing it on the table. "I work hard, I like playing music for the crew and telling jokes that—let me tell you, my lord, they are not appropriate for such pleasant company . . . Your son has been helping me manage my madness by studying herbs and medicines that help keep my afflictions at bay. These are what I keep in my little pouch. I didn't want to be rude and make anyone uncomfortable at dinner bringing it up or discussing it, so I thought I'd err on the side of caution and put it away under my shirt, and I apologize for any distress this may have caused. I do appreciate everything Thinker has done for me, however."

Chief Justice Knowing softened immediately and apologized to the table. "Thinker, son I didn't know you had an interest in the herbal arts. How kind of you!"

"It's nothing, Father; Gadriel I believe is a good man, and I just thought I could help. So, it isn't much. I have not noted anything about it officially."

"Oh, there's plenty we never note officially, right Andi?" Knowing said laughing for which his wife joined in, and so did Gadriel.

Rose and Tamara sat smiling. At about that time the servants finished dinner service, and Rose's stomach rumbled as she looked down at amazing, what looked to be expertly prepared food. Steamed lobster, which Rose had never had—only read about, roasted corn, a rice dish that smelled of rich herbs and cream . . . if she wasn't so terrified, she'd think she were in Heaven Below.

Over dinner, the group had the difficult task of discussing information the extent of which they did not know had been divulged to a powerful man that apparently had the ability to imprison them, and would, should he find out too much.

"So Think, Do you still like Think? You're pretty sure the stone is bonded, you said?" asked Knowing.

"Yes, Father," said Thinker. He continued, "It displays all the light-refractive properties of a Whisper Stone per the records, but has not communicated or physically affected any member of the crew with which I've tested it. My only logical assumption is that it is bonded and separated from its master, or victim, depending on what happened."

"I see," said Knowing. He then asked, "Captain Tamara, how did you come by the stone, again?"

"Like we said, quite the story, actually," said the captain. She continued, "In Lulin, just a few short weeks back, my men were attacked by a couple of local thugs. I don't know what their problem was, but they attacked them again in a bar fight, and this was lost by one of them in the scuffle. I say I'm not going to go on and give back precious treasures to ruffians that try and hurt my family. Thinker here recognized what it was straight off, and he knew its real value was priceless. My experience with that Governor 'ov Lulin ain't great. So what are my options? 'Oh, 'ello corrupt Governor, is this priceless stone *yours?*' Nah. We left and made a straight line for New Haven to help with research."

"Ah, so Thinker, do you believe it was one of the thugs that was or is bonded with it?"

"That is my assumption, yes," Thinker said. "This far away, however, with any luck it isn't driving the man mad."

"Interesting," said Knowing. "That's interesting," he repeated.

After an awkward silence, Thinker and the guests of Atmos looked up from their plates to find Knowing's eyes boring into Thinker.

"What is so interesting, Father?"

"It's just that, we've never had an opportunity to study a bonded subject, only the stones, yes? How would you know any measure of distance between a bonded stone and subject would have any effect?" Thinker did not answer.

"You've always been too smart for your own good, haven't you, son. Gadriel, you say you're a bit mad? Captain, I do believe there's something I'm not being told here. Has Gadriel here bonded with your stone, or are whomever they are simply on your ship with said stone?"

Captain Tamara thought about her words carefully and dropped all pretense of unintelligence. "First, my lord, please allow for me to apologize for being less than truthful with you in your own home. Subterfuge was not my intention coming here. It was to learn, a tenant of house Atmos."

Knowing nodded one time and continued his stare at the captain, unblinking, his dark eyes calculating.

"Second, if it is worth anything at all, your son was following orders, issued by me, to whom he has sworn duty, to myself and the Midnight until she no longer sails."

At this Knowing raised an eyebrow at Thinker, then turned back to Captain Tamara.

"Lastly, my lord, I ask you view this predicament from my perspective. Were I to admit that I had in my possession a lock and its key, would I ever see my ship again? Both are on my ship. And my crew have orders to destroy them should I fail to check in with them, either by word of code or with my person."

Chief Justice Knowing sat at the head of his table, stock still for a moment. He then dropped his supper knife for it loud enough to clang onto the table. A beat later the room was filled with house guards.

"Captain Oath, please take Ms. Rose and Mr. Gadriel into custody."

"What the Heavens is this?!" exclaimed Gadriel. "Aw, shit, tell me about it!" he exclaimed again.

"Tamara?!" a fearful Rose squeaked.

Captain Tamara said in a quiet voice, "Remember your lessons, girl. This will be temporary."

Tamara and Thinker remained seated while Gadriel and Rose were removed from the room. Before his removal was finished, Gadriel said to Knowing, "Lovely party, the food was terrific!"

"OUT!" Shouted the guard captain, lifting Gadriel by the rear of his pants.

"Was that necessary, Father?" asked Thinker, barely containing his rage.

"Well, I think so," said Chief Justice Knowing. "As we speak, Captain Oath will be forcing that container of Gadriel's open, where I may logically assume we'll find the stone?"

"Shit," Thinker said simply. "At least let me unlock it, I worked very hard on it."

Knowing held out his hand palm up, and Thinker placed the . . . less like a key, more like an unlocking bar, onto his hand. He leaned over to his wife, Andromeda, who was not Thinker's mother, and whispered into her ear, handing her the bar. She then excused herself from the table.

"Captain. I believe you were mostly truthful with me. Maybe. Whether your man Gadriel is mad because of the stone, or mad because he is mad, I'd rather not risk your men killing whomever may be on your ship that a Whisper Stone has established an honest-to-goodness bond. Thinker, this could be the Atmos discovery of a century, and this is how you behave—absurd."

Knowing continued, "Captain, you will be permitted to leave and return to your ship immediately. I will not release your cohorts, nor will I release my son. You will return here with either the person with whom the—"

Andromeda re-entered the room carrying a small lump covered in silver cloth. She placed it on the table in front of Chief Justice Knowing, which Knowing immediately opened and smiled.

"—this . . . with whom this stone has bonded. Or you will return with a patsy you want me to think with whom this stone has bonded. Either way.

What I want, Captain, is this stone, which I now have. And I want the human bond it has chosen, whom you claim to have. If you kill them, I will have your friends executed legally. Are there any questions you have for me, madam?"

"Yeah, have you always been an asshole? Or did it start after you somehow weaseled your way into the Chief Justice position?"

"GUARDS!" shouted Knowing, which arrived in moments. "See the captain out, please. She is dismissed. Notify me when she returns. She will."

Captain Tamara found herself alone, at night, reasonably far away from her ship, without her weapons. Let us be honest, though, she didn't give them all her weapons. Rose had the good sense to keep one; her Captain had the good sense to keep several. Though the settlement of New Haven was considerably more civilized than, say, some districts in a port town like Lulin, it wasn't without drunks, thugs, or thieves. There were always going to be idiots and opportunists, her mum used to say.

"MotherRestHer" she whispered to herself. Tamara set off on foot sticking to the main road, which was downhill from this point.

Crossing back and forth over the stream that ran down the middle of the settlement, the main road took her through much of the developed part of the island, which took her near all of its taverns. There weren't many, being a shared resource society and alcohol being generally frowned upon by most in Haven, but people are still going to get drunk.

Before reaching the merchant shops—which were likely closed by now, but they were a landmark for Tamara—the last switchback's bend contained a tavern, which hosted locals and visitors due to its close proximity to the docks. As she approached it, she almost absentmindedly didn't pay attention to the three men who paid her far too much notice from the porch of the tavern.

"Well look here boys, it's a little lady playin' cap't."

"Yeah, I heard one of the ships in the harbor had a little bitch at the helm; maybe it's this one."

"Nah, she doesn't look like a lit'l bitch to me. She looks like she could use some quality time, boys?" all three chuckled in a disgusting way.

As the three moved to intercept her, two were much more intoxicated than the charming gentleman in the lead. Captain Tamara had the advantage of starting the engagement from an uphill position, even if only from a minor incline. By the time the three men reached the center of the road, Captain Tamara was nearly on top of them and did not break stride as she used her momentum to hit the first man with much of her weight and both fists in the chest and shoulders. This caused him to scream out in unexpected pain and fall backwards, hitting the ground hard, where he groaned and began to rock left to right.

The two drunker men were confused by what had just happened, both by how their logic failed them and by the speed in which it occurred. Captain Tamara simply wasn't in the mood, snarling, "You bloody Mother damn cunts."

This caught their attention long enough for them to notice that her fists were dripping blood—well, not her fists, but each hideaway knife she was holding was dripping blood from the holes she placed in their friend. Tamara ruthlessly began punching holes in the men—a hole in the top of a thigh dropping one man to a knee, a hole in the side of a torso, a hole in a kneecap, a hole in the top of a shoulder. Tamara wasn't necessarily swinging wildly; she just didn't mind much where she found purchase—when she saw a good surface for the angle of her swing in progress, she focused there and let them have it.

By the time she was done, the three men laid on the ground, bloodied and writhing in pain, one of them crying. Tamara, breathing heavily but still in control, upset that the first man was only stabbed twice and while lying there leaving himself fairly unprotected on the ground, she wound up and kicked him right in his crotch as hard as she could with her little bitch cap't boots. Satisfied she felt something break that ought not to, she bent down, wiped her hands and her blades off on the cleanest parts of their clothing, put away her knives, and continued on her way—the entire exchange taking less than three tocks.

9

Shanks

Tamara reached the ship a quarter chime later. Chief Justice Knowing had indeed sent word to the harbormaster, but likely for ulterior reasons as harbor guards appeared on alert. Captain Tamara would give Knowing one thing: he didn't miss much. How could she use this to her advantage, she wondered. The captain's black blouse made blood less noticeable but did not hide it completely. She hoped that by walking with purpose, coupled with the dark of the night, this could go unnoticed, and thankfully it did so, or perhaps it didn't. The lead man, whom she very well may have killed, was a local. In the timing of events, who knows if the good Chief Justice really intended for her to make it back to her ship, or simply wanted to send her a message.

Clancy, in charge of ship security as third mate, was waiting and guarding the main cargo hold, which remained open and accessible to the dock barring additional orders from the captain or Thinker. Clancy had several fighting men with him; this was likely an unconscious (or thoughtful, Clancy could surprise you) response to the guard activity within the harbor. All men stood at attention, never mind the hour, at the sight of the captain as she rounded the prow of the ship and began marching down her length.

As Captain Tamara began marching up the side of the cargo hold, Clancy shouted "CAP'T ON DECK!"

"AYE!" the men returned, with a rattle of their equipment as they stood a little straighter.

"Clancy my dear, button up this hold, tell the men to wear their Sunday best, then quietly meet me in my quarters."

"Yes, Cap't."

Clancy could feel the change in mood despite how smooth the captain remained. This was all business for her now, which meant this was all business for Clancy. As the captain marched up the stairs, Clancy started with his men in the main cargo hold.

As the captain was rounding the second to last stairwell before reaching the top deck, she used her fist to knock on the bulkhead, which she knew could be heard and felt in Violet's cabin. As she reached the top deck she found two of her younger men playing cards on an overturned empty crate.

"You two." They sprung up, embarrassed for having not noticed their captain before she noticed them.

"Yes, Cap't."

Captain Tamara continued, "If you know where Helmsman is, send him to my cabin; if you do not, find someone who does. Now. I have a very important question, and I need you to tell me the answer; this concerns our family." One of the young men's eyes widened slightly.

"Do we have any men that snuck off the ship to go drinking or chase local strange?"

The inexperience of these two boys really showed when it was clear they didn't want to be the ones to rat out their mates, but it was clear to the captain that this was the case. Her men always did; she always had a suspicion that one way to guarantee they did was to tell them not to.

Captain Tamara used her thumbs to gently flick both of their noses to make them look up at her; she needed to see they were understanding her.

"Boys. I don't care. I know you all do it. I do it. If I didn't I'd go crazy. I don't care about that. What I need now is our family back on our ship. This is what I want you to do." Both men nodded quickly, both relieved and concerned over what was a drastic shift in energy and urgency for them.

The captain continued, "I want you to find another runner, send down one gang plank, and quietly enter New Haven. We haven't been banned from traveling, and you'll just look like three nice boys looking for some entertainment. Here is some coin." Tamara placed it into the hand of who she thought was the oldest of the men. "Use this to bribe your way out of trouble because I'm sending you on this errand unarmed. You cannot give guards any reason to arrest or hurt you, get me?"

"Aye, Cap't."

"Find our boys; you tell them I said to get their ugly, smelly, caught asses back to the ship quiet-like. You are in charge of finding everyone. Our guests and Think are not here. Get me?"

"Aye, Cap't," they said again somberly.

"Get along, get along," she said. And the men quickly scurried away. One began moving the gang plank, one ran below deck to find Helmsman.

Captain Tamara marched into her quarters, swinging the door open and hipping it closed behind her, placing her captain's jacket on her bunk, ripping off her shirt, then taking down her freshly pressed shirt from her mannequin, thoughtfully prepared by Violet. A moment later, Violet knocked softly twice and entered, closing the door behind her, the only person on the Midnight who did not wait to be admitted entry during non-emergencies.

"Captain you're bleeding!" Violet said, urgently rushing over with a basin of water and cloth.

"I'm not, deary, but thank you. It's not my blood, just three perverts."

Violet was immediately calm. "Oh, well thank Mother for that. I like it when it's perverts."

"Oh me too, deary, me too."

Violet helped the captain change her clothes and began re-outfitting her knives how she knew the captain preferred. Then she began fastidiously cleaning her hands and nails while the captain remained deep in thought, looking at herself in the mirror, but seeing something else play out in her mind entirely. When it came time to put on her jacket, Violet always took a small moment to herself because this was her favorite part of her duties as a valet, like finishing a painting because she felt the captain was certainly a work of art.

Violet was used to helping prepare the captain when she was leagues away in thought like this; she preferred it at times because she had more control over such a powerful and confident woman. Before reaching for her jacket, Violet pressed the palms of her hands firmly together and ran them down the captain's arms; this was both to pull down any wrinkles of her beautiful black blouse, which Violet prepared for her by hand with the finest silks they could acquire, and also massage the captain's arms before what could always be a significant battle.

After squeezing her shoulders and working the muscles of her upper back, Violet slowly and methodically rubbed out any wrinkles from the captain's shirt before taking her left arm and pulling it outward almost ninety degrees, which the captain held there for her. The captain still paid little attention to Violet's irreplaceable work; she was muttering to herself, working on the problem of a lifetime—that's what Violet told herself every time her lady needed her.

Violet picked up her black jacket from her bunk with reverence. The black leather was fashioned in a captain's style, but trimmed in midnight blue with polished black buttons that shined as well as any gold would have. Violet slid the jacket over the captain's outstretched right arm. She then took several side steps to the left, sliding in the captain's left. When she lowered her lady's arms, the jacket fit her like a worn glove, even making a soft thump as it fell into place.

Buttoning her jacket, Violet would try not to look in the mirror after this point, every time, instead focusing on what she called her battle braids of the captain's beautiful hair. When she was done pinning them up, she got chills as she completed her work of art, placing her captain's cap atop her lady's head, to make what she thought was the most beautiful, capable, cunning, and intimidating woman she had ever seen in her life. And Violet was confident that even if she did not feel she owed her a life debt, she would love regardless.

Absent her new pistols, Captain Tamara returned to daggers on her hips as well as a cutlass on her left and a hatchet on her right. Captain Tamara was angry, and she was ready for a fight; she didn't care how technologically advanced these people were—everyone bleeds. Tamara took a seat at her desk and set to writing quickly. A knock at the door brought in Clancy and the Helmsman, Midnight's second mate. Helmsman had a proper name, but everyone just called him Helmsman, and he didn't care—he loved driving Midnight and good food. Everyone including Violet took a seat, and Captain Tamara relayed what even she thought was an insane plan.

Two and a half chimes later, Captain Tamara, who was armed for battle, and Clancy, who was unarmed, began their walk through New Haven back up to the house of Atmos. Chief Justice Knowing didn't give her a time deadline, but seeing as how she wasn't going to rest, she thought it best to return at the most inconvenient time possible just before New Haven began to wake up. As they walked they were forced to check in with several guard patrols that all knew to expect her and one more. Tamara expected that if she had anyone else with her they would've been sent away. However, the moon was small enough and the strange lamps New Haven utilized provided so little light that she imagined she could've had a number of people with her that could've gone unnoticed by guards that had never been in combat before.

Upon reaching the last switchback that led up to the house, Captain Tamara turned to Clancy and said, "You're doing great, sir. Do you have any questions for us before we do this?"

Clancy was clearly pleased with the praise and said, "No, Cap't, I think I got it. Try not to say anything. And if I do, talk to the ground like we said."

"Yes, my mate, now let's get to it."

Captain Tamara and Clancy approached the door. To Tamara's surprise there were no guards out in front of the structure, but this was likely to show the Chief Justice's arrogance. In the most obnoxious way possible, Tamara "knocked" on the door by kicking it, hard, so hard she heard a small splash from the stream passing close to house Atmos. *I wonder if there are fresh water fish in that stream,* Tamara thought. The doors opened to smirking Guard Captain Oath and Thinker, whose hands were clearly restrained in front of him, but mostly hidden by his robes.

As the doors closed, locking in Captain Tamara and Clancy, Shanks popped his head out from the last stream bridge. It appeared as though Shanks had been trailing the captain and avoiding guards all through New Haven. Knowing Shanks, he had likely eavesdropped on the captain's quarters during planning. They had done this once on the Sapphire by dangerously clinging to the stern of the ship under his former captain's windows to win a bet—in Shanks's words, "Worth it." He might not have said that would he have fallen, however.

Shanks being Shanks set to climbing the outside of Atmos Tower to find a less protected entry to the structure—his money was the roof, but he hoped he'd find a window along the way; climbing was tiring, and he'd need some strength for what came next. Inside Atmos, Guard Captain Oath commanded Captain Tamara to disarm herself. She said simply "No."

Captain Oath wasn't expecting this, and said, "You . . . you have to."

To which Captain Tamara responded, "No I don't."

"Yes you do."

"No. I don't. The last time I came in 'ere, you took my stuff and didn't give it back. Like I'm just going to give you my stuff again. I have followed the good Chief Justice's instructions to the letter; none of those instructions outlined my disarming myself. I will wait here for you to wake him up and ask."

"... Come with us," said Captain Oath.

I can't believe that worked, thought Tamara.

I can't believe that worked, thought Thinker.

Don't say anything; look at the ground, thought Clancy.

Meanwhile, Shanks found it much easier to climb the glass-windowed sides of the structure compared to the rocky walls into which it was built. On one side of the tower, the ceiling of the ground floor was much of the height of the structure, about four stories; they didn't want to climb this as they would be incredibly visible. He did, however, take his chances climbing from room to room like he would from deck to deck on the other 'half' of the tower, and he was able to reach the observation deck without notice.

There were no guards on the observation deck. This did not stop Shanks from moving quietly and swiftly. He tried the double doors into the structure, which were locked. Shanks then decided he would finish the climb to the roof and check access there. He couldn't help himself, however, and first ran over and sat in the chair of the giant spyglass and looked at the night sky. What he saw was magnificent. And he couldn't know it, but what they were looking at was the Andromeda galaxy—neighbor to their own, and Knowing's wife's namesake. Afraid of being lost in some sort of magic trance, Shanks sprung up and ran over to the rocky sidewall and resumed his climb.

Inside, Atmos, Thinker, Tamara, and Clancy walked behind Captain Oath and four of his men; all carried clubs and pistols, with Captain Oath carrying something like a gladius on his back, which appeared very heavy. As immediately as the opportunity presented itself, Tamara passed Thinker a small, short dagger that was easy for him to conceal within his robes, regardless of his restraints, which Tamara felt for; unfortunately they were metal, fortunately they were in front of him.

"So, Captain," said Captain Tamara. "You seein' anybody?"

"What?" Captain Oath said, somewhat confused. "Just curious if you're seein' anybody. I think you look good, and maybe after you're done with these crimes against humani'y, we could go for a drink and talk about some bad things you could do to my humani'y personally."

Two of his men and Thinker couldn't help but snort. Captain Oath's neck turned red, and he did not turn around.

"Shut your mouth, you are one of the trashiest people I have ever met" said Captain Oath, to which Captain Tamara cleared her throat and said, "Hey. hey. I bet *Oathy* lives with his *mummy*," which caused one of his men to actually laugh out loud.

"Ope, sounds like I was spot on, Think—"

"SHUT UP YO—" started Captain Oath, which was cut short by a strong, deep command "Enough" as they walked into a chamber containing Chief Justice Knowing, his wife Andromeda, and Rose and Gadriel, who were sitting in chairs; Gadriel had clearly been beaten. Knowing clearly believed Gadriel to be bonded with the stone, and Gadriel was not revealing this to him.

"Well, they're alive, thank Mother for that," said Tamara out loud; she did not say plenty of her inside voice.

Knowing raised an eyebrow at Captain Oath and asked, "You didn't disarm her?"

Oath stammered slightly and said, "She did point out that you didn't say it was part of the deal."

Knowing let out a long sigh. "Please instruct the harbor guard to train two of our artillery platforms directly on the Midnight . . . make it four."

"Yes, Chief Justice."

"You are excused."

"Yes, Chief Justice."

Captain Oath and his men filed out of the room.

Thinker asked, "Is that really necessary, Father?"

"Yes, a moment ago I wasn't armed. Now I am. This woman will likely not harm me now," said Knowing.

"Yeah, he's got a point, Think," said Captain Tamara, then continued, "So how do you want to do this? I give you Clancy here then we all leave? I give you Clancy here and you murder us?"

"Well, I think the correct answer is, you tell me who is bonded to the stone, then if they're not in this room, you give them to me. Then you and the crew of the Midnight will be put on trial for crimes against the settlement. Should you be found not guilty, you may leave, and it will be requested you never return. Should you be found guilty, however, I will not be murdering you; the Settlement of New Haven will be executing you, then we will salvage your ship, try your accomplices . . . I mean crew . . . and use the proceeds to fund research." Andromeda beamed.

"So your plan is to murder them legally?" said Thinker.

"Oh you'll be tried as well," said Knowing, which caused Rose to gasp.

"You'd kill your own son??" accused the captain.

"No, *no*," said Knowing. "I cannot be accused of favoritism. It is well-known he is a member of your crew; you said it yourself he has sworn fealty to you. I am Chief Justice. Should he be found guilty, with the rest of you . . . people, then what happens is the rule of settlement law."

"So you're doing this to him because he has sworn duty to a different family, then," accused the captain again.

Knowing smiled, then said, "Is this the bonded man? Quite large."

Clancy looked at the ground. Gadriel looked up and saw Shanks's little face peeking in from outside a high window to the room and smiled; they continued their climb.

"What's your name, son?" asked Knowing.

"Uhm. Clancy, sir."

"Why don't you look up, my boy? We're all friends here."

Clancy, despite being four and a half steps tall, felt and looked like a large child without his axe, without his armor and buckler. He liked protecting his crew, and right now he felt like he couldn't protect anyone, but by Mother he was going to try.

Staring at the ground, Clancy said, "You don't feel like a friend, sir."

At this point Clancy wasn't really acting; he was just being Clancy. Chief Justice Knowing arose, walked slowly to Clancy, and produced the stone from his pocket, placing it in Clancy's large, weathered hand.

"Tell me what you—" Clancy began shouting, "No, no, no, NO, NO, *NO, NO!* ***NO! NO!!***" then dropped the stone and cowered away from everyone.

Heavens Below, thought Tamara, *We're going to start having theater nights, and Clancy gets a bonus.*

"Son, son, it's okay," cooed Knowing. "No need to be afraid of the stone. You're in the safest building, on the safest island, in a thousand leagues," he continued while Andromeda picked up the stone. "Andi and I think you'll love it here! We have the softest beds, feasts, ale, entertainment . . . We'll just study during the day, and the night time can be Clancy time, eh?"

"No, sir, no, sir, I wanna go home, sir, I wanna go home, sir," Clancy repeated.

"Clancy?" Knowing said, less softly. "Look at me." He reached up to use two fingers under Clancy's chin to move his head up slightly to look him in the face. "You *are* home."

"So what now, you take Clancy and you let us all await trial on our ship under your guns?" asked Captain Tamara.

"Oh, no. You know, for such a smart woman, and I know you are, you ask a lot of stupid questions," said Knowing with a slight wave of his hand. "No, you'll be searched and disarmed properly and await trial here. I'll be convening the justices in the morning, so, about three chimes from now."

"And my crew?" asked Tamara.

"Your crew will be relegated to your ship after settlement security finds them out and about. Then they'll be given instructions to stay aboard and guarded to ensure it stays that way."

Shanks reached the roof of Atmos tower, where he found several guards smoking various weeds and drinking. Apparently this had been where off-duty guards spent their time. In addition to off-duty guards, there were also several signal mortars positioned on the battlement; whether they meant different things or they were all a general alarm, Shanks couldn't know.

There was a door leading into a stairwell that Shanks was sure was left unlocked, at least now with five men lounging around on this battlement of sorts. Shanks climbed a little further until they were atop the housing of the stairwell door and waited patiently for someone to open it, preferably someone coming onto the roof. This took only five tocks; the roof was very popular.

As a guard opened the heavy wooden door, swinging it wide, this allowed Shanks to, for lack of a better descriptor, swing himself from the roof section, above the guard, and into the doorway as the door closed behind him. Light on his feet, Shanks didn't want to spend any more time than necessary in this enclosed stairwell with no exit. In a spiral pattern, every twelve steps or so were open doorframes of support stones and small windows, which likely used to be arrowslits every fourth quarter turn that faced outside as he went down. This let in enough moonlight to see by, but this was probably much more pleasantly lit during the daytime.

As Shanks moved down, deeper into the structure, at two points he needed to stop, climb up the sides of the spiral stairwell, hold himself in the air above the opposite side of a stone support doorway, and pray they weren't noticed by people moving up the stairs. Shanks's goal was to get to the ground floor without being noticed, as he knew that's the last place he saw the crew, and it was not looking like things were going their way.

And they weren't. Tamara knew that she could only think of one way out of this predicament, and every other logical scenario she could imagine ended up with the loss of her crew, the loss of her ship, and the loss of her life, in that descending order of importance. Captain Tamara and her first mate had been together for years. They didn't think exactly alike, and this was a good thing. When it came to strategy and what was best for the crew, however, they were almost always on the same page. The captain and her first mate regularly found themselves in positions to communicate wordlessly. And what she needed now was to communicate one of the most important, heaviest decisions she would ever have to silently communicate with another living soul. And she did so.

Tamara made flat, dead, eye contact with her first mate. There was no emotion. There was no smile, there was no inflection to her eyebrows, there were no classic wry winks, there was nothing joyous about this moment, not for her, and not for her man. Thinker matched this expression exactly. No wrinkling of his brow or pursing of lips or flaring of nostrils. They both understood what was being decided here. And they both understood why it needed to be that way.

Captain Tamara and First Mate Thinker were eager to reach New Haven on the hope that the Atmos elder was Thinker's oldest uncle, Patience, who was not interested in the politics of the settlement. Thinker and Patience had always had a special bond; Patience, like his name, was always able to tolerate Thinker's temper and explain things in ways Thinker could understand. Thinker was an incredibly intelligent boy that grew up into an incredibly intelligent man. But he thinks differently than was normal for those of the Atmos sect. Patience recognized this, something his father refused to do. And it was Patience that taught Thinker all the lore he knew about the Whisper Stones, even showed him the stone the Atmos sect already had in its possession—a large stone at least amethyst in color that seemed to entrance but never really whispered to anyone, nor would it bond. Thinker often wondered if it was actually bonded to his uncle; he just never let this on to anyone, knowing the implications. But this begged the question. Where was his uncle now? Seeing what his father was so quickly capable of, Thinker had a pretty good guess.

All of this flashed before Thinker's eyes, and he was filled with a strange sadness that may have been more regret than anything else—regret for what he believed was about to happen, regret for not spending more time with his house, regret for not being here to protect his uncle. But he did not at all regret serving Captain Tamara or the Midnight. They were his family, especially now. And with no reservations, Thinker's dead expression gave his captain the barest of affirmative nods, which set off a series of actions in extreme violence.

Captain Tamara was closest to Chief Justice Knowing; however, taking his life was not her place, so she kicked him hard in the middle, pushing him over a table and toward Thinker. Knowing was so incredibly surprised. Here was something he finally miscalculated, and he let out a startled shout of pain as his back slammed into furniture. Captain Tamara, originally contemplated sparing Andromeda if it came to this, began marching toward the tattooed woman who took far too much pleasure in the thought of killing her incredibly innocent crew. Andromeda screamed for just a moment until Captain Tamara plunged her dagger into her throat, riding her to the ground on her overturning chair.

Thinker, for his part, used his own restraints to wrap around his father's neck, silencing him as he pulled so quickly he began picking him up off the ground before Thinker wrapped his legs around his father's head to finish his hold. He pulled and his father kicked. He pulled and his muscles flexed. He pulled and his father dug his fingers into his hands. He pulled until he felt his father's neck sickeningly click and his body go limp. Who knows how long Thinker may have pulled until Captain Tamara placed a gentle hand on his shoulder.

"You've did it boyo, let's get a move on, eh?" Thinker opened his eyes, which were wet, and looked up at his captain. "I know, boyo. Trust me."

When Captain Tamara and Thinker sprang into motion, so did Clancy, first squatting down in front of Gadriel to work on his restraints. At the same time, who also joined the room was a fast and silent Shanks from a wide-open doorway in the rear of the house. Shanks had managed to sneak through

House Atmos unnoticed, and he couldn't wait to tell his best friend about it. But right now there was business. Shanks slid next to Clancy and Gadriel, tapping himself on the chest.

"Shanks!" Gadriel said in a loud whisper.

"*Oy! Hey there! It's the little guy!*" said Rod.

Clancy said, "I don't be knowin' what you mean, Mr. Gad. but I've almost got your ties off."

"No, my boy, don't worry about me. Shanks will sort me out—help Rose, help her!"

"Mr. Gad?" asked a confused and worried Clancy.

"Just keep working, Clancy, you're almost done, then you can help me, okay?" said Rose.

"Shanks! How in the Mother damn did you get in here, or out there, or up here?" asked Gadriel excitedly.

"Shhh!" hushed a nervous Clancy.

"Clancy . . ." Captain Tamara said quietly and plainly.

He looked up to see his captain handing him her hatchet, which was small in Clancy's hands, but he was used to the weapon type, which may or may not have been Tamara's plan. After a few quick motions, Gadriel and Rose were free.

"Thank you, good sir," said Gadriel. "Rod said 'thanks biggin,'" Gadriel added.

Before anyone could say anything else, Clancy's giant torso twisted quickly, with his large arm flying down in what took Rose a moment to realize was a throwing motion. A moment later they heard a wet, meaty crack and looked over to find a guard, pistol drawn, having had it raised at them, now with a hatchet buried in his face.

"Uh . . . Rod said 'Damn, really good job biggin,'" said Gadriel, shocked.

"*Xoxo* indeed, deary," added Captain Tamara.

Thinker was crouching down over Andromeda's body until he said, "I've got it; I found the stone."

"Is there a rear exit to this place?" asked Tamara.

"No, just the front, which is right next to the guard house." Shanks tapped Gadriel then pointed a finger up five times. "Shanks says there's an exit on the roof," Gadriel added.

The group stopped and looked at him. Then Gadriel stopped and said, "What, how do you think he got in, the front doors?"

Captain Tamara leaned over to Thinker and quietly asked, "Is that true?" to which Thinker nodded slowly.

"Well, seein' as I don't have fifty steps of rope, I think we still use the front door. There's what, five guards on duty in there—we approach dimwitted enough they'll send two to run for the harbor to relay the Chief Justice's orders."

"How is that good?" asked Rose.

"Oh, Thorny," the captain clucked her tongue. "They won't make it very far," she added with a grin.

There was nothing to do about Thinker's restraints at present, but he could swing his arms. Captain Tamara handed him her cutlass. She handed Rose one of her larger daggers and removed the other for herself. Clancy retrieved the hatchet and wiped it off on the guard, which was apparently a pirate scoundrel way of doing business.

Before they rounded the corner, Captain Tamara looked at Gadriel and said, "It's your time to shine, sweets." She grinned again. And they call *Gadriel* mad.

Gadriel rounded the corner with his flute, playing and singing his little bard heart out:

New Haven is like a commonwealth
New Haven is where I find myself

This place is like a cult with nicer rules
This place is a'lead by the wicked and cruel
Now I have no home and I have no direction
But I'd rather follow wind than these bad intentions.
Aw shit, I know you're all in there, are you serious?

A flabbergasted Gadriel put his fists on his hips, and tapped his foot, and started saying random offensive rhymes: "Captain Oath couldn't hunt, Captain Oath was a cunt" and "Captain Oath doddled his sister then Captain Oath couldn't fix her."

At that point, a red-faced Guard Captain Oath exited with nine more men. He held up his left hand with two fingers and waved it toward the front doors. Two men broke out of formation and ran for the door; as suspected by Captain Tamara and Thinker, these must be runners with Chief Justice Knowing's contingency orders. Captain Oath then held up one finger with his right and waved it to a stairwell behind them. Another man broke off and ran for the stairs.

There were now seven men including Captain Oath standing in front of Gadriel. Shanks was the first to run out and reach him; standing to Gadriel's right, they quietly leaned over to Gadriel, pointed upward, then made an arc, then explosive motion with his hands.

"Ah," said Gadriel and nodded. Captain Tamara, Thinker, Clancy and Rose then rounded the corner to stand with Gadriel. This engagement was about to be seven versus five, and the seven were more heavily armed, outfitted, and rested. Our not-quite heroes didn't care, however. They had faced worse odds, and this was business.

"Before we get started, uh, Captain. Shanks says there are mortars on the roof, likely signal flares," Gadriel said in a low whisper.

This appeared to concern the captain as well. She then said, "Well, we can't worry about that right now. When this goes down, just try not to get shot or stabbed. Maybe hit the deck, eh?"

"No *way*," said Gadriel.

"One chance, sow," said Captain Oath, adding, "You have one chance to surrender, right now. You'll receive a fair trial, even if you've murdered New Haven's chief justice. I can assume this is what happened, yes?" Silence settled on the scene.

That silence was broken by a charge from Clancy, hatchet starting in an across-the-body swing into the nearest enemy on the left. Thinker used Clancy's body as cover, moving forward towards his own house guards. Captain Tamara moved to the far right of the engagement to close the distance and separate the enemy's attention. Rose, for her part, at least initially, tried following the captain. Gadriel started scream-singing insults at Captain Oath, knowing nothing else to do being unarmed.

"CAPTAIN OATH MARRIED A WITCH! CAPTAIN OATH IS A WEE LITTLE BITCH! HE ACTS LIKE A CLOWN! HE PEES SITTING DOWN! AND HIS ARSE IS AS WIDE AS A DITCH!"

The enemy was quick to react; they didn't stand there doing nothing. Positioned in a column formation of Captain Oath at the head followed by two rows of three men, Clancy struck the first man on the left and nearly cleaved him in half, but the man behind him drew his pistol and was able to fire a shot cleanly enough to hit Clancy in his left arm well enough to lame it. It didn't blow it apart, so it likely was not a direct hit. Captain Oath drew his gladius and began a swing at Clancy, which was deftly blocked by Thinker wielding his captain's cutlass, a short heavy, deadly sword she kept incredibly sharp that was specially made for her size. This fit Thinker well, as he and Captain Tamara were not that far off in reach and stature, almost as if Captain Tamara thought of this as well.

The first position guard from Captain Oath's left fired his pistol at Captain Tamara but missed by a league. Tamara reached him quickly before he was able to draw his club and ran him through the stomach with her dagger and kept running, pushing back the man behind him to bowl them over as best she could. Rose observed the guard in the middle with his pistol, who could not have had a shot before, begin to train it on Captain Tamara as she moved into the fray. Rose panicked and screamed, running as fast as she could, tackling the man and punching him with the edges of her fists in a savage fashion. His pistol was discharged, but into the guard who was in formation behind him.

"OATH HAS A WEE WILLY! HIS MUMMY TELLS HIM IT'S SMELLY! HOW DOES SHE KNOW HIS WILLY IS SMELLY? BECAUSE CAPTAIN OATH IS A SICK BASTARD!"

Gadriel scream-sang once more then began blaring his flute as fast as he could play it. This was finally too much for Captain Oath who turned his attention away from Clancy and Thinker to draw his pistol and aim it carefully at what he thought was a crazy fool dancing around a battle with a flute.

He was smiling as he prepared to squeeze the trigger and end a man whom he hated the moment he met him. Rose was getting up from the man she had beat into a stupor on the floor. Thinker, Clancy, and Captain Tamara had the remainder of the guards occupied by flanking them from either side now that none of them had pistol shots left.

Rose screamed "NO!" as she jumped on Captain Oath's back. The imbalance was enough to jostle his shot so he only grazed Gadriel in the leg; although it was an imperfect hit, it did take the man down.

"Aw, you *BITCH!*" snarled Oath. He reached up, grabbed a handful of Rose's auburn hair, and yanked forward and down, hard. Rose squealed as she floated over the man. As she landed on her bottom, Oath forcefully let go of her hair. Rose was flat on the ground now and trying to draw her dagger. She did so, but Captain Oath kicked it out of her hand, hard enough that something in her hand moved in a way it shouldn't have. Rose wailed.

Oath was filled with rage—at his enemy, at what they had accomplished, and at Gadriel's taunts. He got down on his knees on top of Rose and said, "I'm just going to enjoy this one, just this one." Pulling a knife from a sheath on his wrist, he ritually prepared himself by steadying the knife over her throat with two hands, then lifting both up in the air, preparing to plunge the knife into her throat with both hands.

You put this in your hand and don't stop swingin' till yer free, y'hear?

In one moment, Rose was sure she was about to die. In another Lou's words echoed in her mind, then she remembered her hideaway knife. She didn't know if she had enough time, but she'd try. What happened in the following moments felt like heartbeats. Rose grabbed for the knife behind her buckle with her good hand. Oath's hands began to fall, and his lips began to curl in a sneer. Crow's feet under his gray eyebrows began to spread. Further his hands were falling. Then two, smaller, fingerless gloved hands appeared to wrap around his wrist from behind and hold them, just long enough for Rose's good hand to float up and jam the hideaway knife into Captain Oath's jugular. Rose stabbed again, and she kept swinging, and screaming, and swinging, and stabbing, and crying, and covering herself in blood, until Captain Tamara's completely gloved delicate hands grabbed ahold of Rose's good wrist and said, "Deary, deary, Rose! It's okay, Rose, we're with you. It's okay. Babe, it's okay."

Clancy with his good arm picked up Oath's leaking body and threw it, just like he would so much trash. Thinker was tending to Gadriel and allowed himself a moment to laugh, "Captain Oath pees sitting down, eh?" They both started laughing.

Shanks was next to Gadriel as well; Gadriel saw what he did and told him how proud he was of a job well-done. Shanks grabbed the sides of his shirt like he would suspenders, then swaggered away to check on Rose.

While Thinker tore pieces of his robes off to bandage and tie Gadriel's leg, Captain Tamara tore pieces of his robes off for the same to Clancy's left arm.

"Cap't, what about the runners?" asked Gadriel.

"Well, about that . . . About one chime ago, Clancy and I made our way up New Haven to House Atmos at a leisurely pace. Yes, it was to disrespect the Chief Justice, but it was also to give plenty of time for the squad of heavily armed fighting men covered in goose fat to finish the first mission I gave them, so they could then slowly climb their way up from where New Haven's freshwater stream meets the harbor to follow us along at such an hour when patrols and people would be low in number. They've been just outside this whole time. Settlement security hasn't known they've been up here, as the *former* Chief Justice opts for his own house guards, which we have made some short work of just now. The first runner earlier in the morning shortly after our arrival should've gone through, for better or worse; we still had hope we'd get out of here diplomatically. But those last two runners? Should be tied up like pretty lit'l gifts, just outside."

"That is genius," grinned Thinker.

"I know, but, what about the signal mortars Shanks reported on the roof?" asked Gadriel.

A concerned Tamara looked to Thinker, who said, "If they have them, that's new to me."

Captain Tamara then turned to Gadriel and said, gently, "Look, handsome. I think we need to talk. First I want you to know you're—" just then they group heard several unnerving whistles. They looked out the great glass-windowed walls and saw white flares of light glowing in the sky.

"How is that possib—" Captain Tamara stopped talking, then resumed. "Think, with me, let's get those restraints off, also let's get you into a guard uniform so you can run better than in the robes, unless you think your leathers are around here. Rose, find the weapons cart in the guard room; Clancy deary, help her. Gadriel, you and uh . . . Shanks, sit right here, all right? MOVE!"

Everyone sprang into action. In just a few minutes, Thinker was wearing his jacket and boots, but guard trousers, and the silver scratched off his head—from the red marks it looked to be forcefully. Looking at the pants, Tamara raised an eyebrow.

"I want to study the armor; I've never seen it before. It's lightweight, could be a game changer. Looks like I'll miss out on both my notebooks. Time we start a new one anyway."

Clancy and Rose exited the guard house with their weapons and Violet's jug of juice, which surprisingly had not been stolen. Captain Tamara said, "Okay, everyone outfit yourselves. Clancy, deary, Unless you've found a bigger axe in the guard house, I think the hatchet is the best you'll get, eh? Unless you want one of my other blades."

"Aye, Cap't, you know me, I like the snappy weight of the baby axe please." Rose held up her jug of juice for Violet with a questioning face for the captain.

"I'll tell you what, deary. You make it to the bottom of this hill and on our ship without breaking that jug; you deserve to give it her."

Rose smiled for the first time in a while.

10

An Alarming Letter

As the group exited house Atmos, Tamara and Clancy may not have been, but the rest were surprised to see Violet, dressed in black suit of a strange material, exposed skin glistening from grease, boots, and heavily armed for a valet. Violet was flanked by six men, all carrying new "blunderbusses," as Banger referred to them, on their backs. These, like her pistols, could keep the powder dry somehow, and for these, just like her pistols, Tamara didn't need to know how they worked. Off to the side of the road were two guards hogtied and gagged.

"Take their pistols and any coin from their pockets. Then put them in those bushes over there. Someone will find them eventually. Leave them otherwise tied up just the way they are. Give their noses a tickle with leaves or long grass right before you walk away.

"Violet, this is everyone as accounted for. We're going to have company. We don't know what those flares mean exactly, but it'll mean people coming up here. And a small amount of resistance coming from this house up from behind eventually."

"Yes, my lady, let us lead in shadow."

Captain Tamara nodded, and then everyone hustled as fast as their slowest member, and that was Gadriel due to his leg injury.

Captain Tamara and her people made it down two switchbacks before they knew they would not be able to bluff past patrols. Another series of flares was fired from House Atmos, this time bright red, and they could guess what this meant. Heading down a third switchback, they met one squad of settlement security, who apparently did not expect to meet anyone and were responding to House Atmos. The security men removed long pistols from their backs in a practiced manner, but thankfully the moon was weak and daybreak had not yet begun in earnest, because the six men in question were focused on Captain Tamara, Thinker, Gadriel, Rose, and Clancy, not Violet and her men in all black up ahead of them in shadow. Two of Violet's men and their blunderbusses incapacitated all six of the security soldiers.

Noticing a likely repeat of events, Shanks got Gadriel's attention then pointed at the stream, then made a quick swimming motion.

Gadriel gasped. "Cap't!"

"What's up, deary, we're a lit'l busy at the moment. Coast looks clear—Think, Violet, good to move forward," Tamara rasped.

"No, Cap't! Listen!" pleaded Gadriel. All stopped. "Shanks wanted to ask why weren't we just riding the stream down into the harbor and swimming back to the ship, thereby avoiding everyone? Apparently he used the stream to get up to House Atmos; it's also how he followed you. We could do it quiet-like."

"Violet?" asked Tamara simply.

"Actually, my lady, the stream is fairly smooth down the middle, and if we were to go one by one, we'd be fairly hidden."

"Okay," said Captain Tamara. "But Gad, when we get back to the ship and out to sea, we're having a talk."

Thinker and Rose said at the same time, "Can I be there?" Violet and Clancy sounded their desire to also be there having worked with Gadriel.

"Yes, yes, now can we save the lives of a bunch of people already? Heavens below," said an exhausted captain.

As was their way, they relieved the six men of their long pistols and any coin in their pockets. Then one by one, the group used the stream bridge to hop into the stream and float down into the harbor. It was decided Clancy would go last with Gadriel between his legs due to the nature of their injuries. Together, they'd be heavier and less likely to be slowed down by any vegetation in the water; additionally, should Gadriel's leg cause issue, Clancy had no issue picking the man up with his good arm.

For several tocks, all was going very well. Violet and her men went first and, given their camouflage, were too difficult to spot. However, Rose, still holding on to her jug, and Thinker apparently stuck out too much, because nearing the bottom of the settlement, a patrol shouted, "IN THE STREAM! THE MURDERERS ARE IN THE STREAM!"

From several steps behind the guards on the bridge, Gadriel could see that they were training their long pistols on his people riding the stream down in front of him, likely not realizing there were more in the stream underneath them due to the darkness of Captain Tamara's clothing. Again, not knowing what else to do to help, Gadriel did what he knew. Clancy was already holding on to him, so Gadriel blew his flute loudly as if preparing a base note, then shout-singed insults.

"IS THAT A FANNY? OH NO IT'S A CRANNY!"

It made one man jump and shout, "AH! WHAT THE!?" in an alarmed and startled tone that was normally more rugged and reserved.

One man fired, and Gadriel hoped he missed. Gadriel then played another little ditty and shouted, "THOSE WHO MISS CAN KISS MY WIT! HAHAHA!"

Clancy said, "Alright boyo! let's not make them too mad; they might jump in."

Before they knew it, all of Captain Tamara's crew were falling into the harbor, one by one, with Mad Gad screaming, "ROD SAYS 'OH SHIT'!"

After plunging into the water, the returning crew knew they were on the clock. Captain Tamara knew the men that spotted them were running down the main road and alerting guards along the way; there were already men running down from House Atmos alerting more that Chief Justice Knowing and his wife and his house guards were dead. Could they outrun how fast a man could scream? Not swimming unassisted in the water, that was for sure.

The returning crew swam as fast as they could for the edge of the dock. Per the plan, Clancy handed Gadriel to Violet, an accomplished swimmer, who began towing Gadriel to the dock about as fast as everyone else was swimming unencumbered. While everyone helped each other out of the water, they began to run together toward their berth. Clancy was half carrying Gadriel again with his good arm; Shanks was attempting to hold up his other side, but being so much shorter, it was tough.

Gadriel for his part was trying to shake the water out of his flute. When he finally did so, he blew one short but sharp note. As expected, it was enough for someone on the Midnight to look in that direction, which was a direction you'd never expect your party to come from, and the main cargo hold door dropped open for quick loading.

Everyone ran in, and the ship was buttoned back up. Violet's men, Gadriel, and Rose collapsed. However, Violet, Captain Tamara, and her first and third mates never slowed. They immediately moved up the stairs.

"Clancy, deary, remember that crate from Mr. Moon Boom?"

"Aye, Cap't."

"Find two strong boys and have them bring it up to the top deck, would you? Then join us on the quarterdeck."

"Aye, Cap't".

"Let's get a breeze rigging down; we're going to need tight and slow maneuvers if we're gettin' out of here, wouldn't ya' say?"

"Aye," Thinker said somberly.

"RUN OUT ONE HALF A MAST AND ONE FORE, NICE AND TIGHT! BE READY YESTERDAY!"

"AYE!" A wide man of middling height and a powerful mustache then pointed at four men on the deck then set to climbing and screaming orders.

"HELMSMAN, AWAIT STEERING ORDERS, RUNNING ROUND SHORT RIGGING!"

"AYE! SHORT RIGGING, AYE!"

Just then, Clancy came up the stairs with a full crate on a half cart. Captain Tamara and no one else knew what was in this crate, and she knew how heavy it was.

"Clancy! You sexy brute! I said find two boys. Set that down and get up 'ere."

"Aye, Cap't," he huffed and puffed.

Gadriel with Rose and Shanks's help limped up from below decks and joined the Midnight's leadership on the quarterdeck. Shanks climbed up to his favorite spot in the fighter's nest.

"Okay, here's what we've got. There are six gun platforms, some of which are pointed at us right now. But what we do know is that the order to fire upon us was never given by the Chief Justice. For that to happen, it'll take the other Justices, which they very well may do if they're roused fast enough and informed the Chief Justice has been killed." All nodded, and Captain Tamara continued.

"We've got a harbor we've been led to think is filled with stuff that goes boom. But I've gotta be honest with ye', I seriously doubt they've mined their own harbor. I mean, why would they do it, honestly? They already have the sandbar, and the artillery, and the balloons. But I'm not risking my ship. So Think, I'm going to steer the ship with Helmsman, and you're going to be at the front telling us where to go. We won't have time nor can we put the responsibility on you 'hoping' you can navigate some new explosive you've never seen. But—thanks to this crate here, we don't have to. These are high-explosive cannon munitions. We're going to have Clancy with you, you're going to fuse 'em, light 'em, and count 'em off, and then Clancy here is going to throw them and blow the ever-loving shit out of the water in front of the Midnight as we go—it won't matter about things that go kaboom if we blow them out of our way."

Captain Tamara's plan resulted in several sly grins, even on little Rose's face. Then Gadriel added, "Rod asked what about the giant guns pointed at us."

Captain Tamara's eyebrows raised. "Ah, well right now these platforms are pointed at us in a direct fire position. If you look at the platforms, you can see they're not really designed for that. As long as we get away from the harbor, we won't be in range again until the sandbar, is my estimate."

"Okay . . . and . . . what about them?"

"Yes, I can't help but also remain curious, Cap't," said Thinker.

"Well, about that . . . First, would you believe that Violet here, before she was trained as a valet, was trained in 'special assignments'? Which for our purposes mean special missions. Which is what she was sent on before she crawled up New Haven with some of our best to save us in case things went wrong. Second, before leaving Banger's place earlier in the day, I made a healthy trade with our dear friend for our excess black powder flats. He gave us one crate of wonderful shiny new 'hand cannons,'" said the captain.

Tapping the handles on her hips, she continued. "But another case is filled with a whole new instrument of death. They're a bunch of jars filled with a fuel that burns 'almost as hot as the sun,' and it's sticky! I was really thinkin' a' you, Think. I figured we can get black powder any ole' place. But this was big-ticket stuff; plus Bangs wouldn't rip us off.

"Lastly, I was so positive that the Chief Justice would double cross us and use these artillery platforms to do it, someone sent a gorgeous young violet-eyed valet, in a seal suit, to go off and sabotage the artillery platforms with this sticky sun jelly before harbor security was ever on high alert. Shouldn't smell like anything, shouldn't look like anything is a miss. They'll try to fire it and r-r-roasty toasty."

Violet was very pleased with herself. Captain Tamara was very pleased with Violet and herself. Everyone else stood there gawking at both of them, somehow even Shanks, halfway up to the fighters' nest.

"Uh . . . great plan, Cap't. Not ruthless at all. With your permission I'll get us underway. Then we'll get plan 'burn down the harbor and kill everyone' underway?"

"I never said kill everyo— oooh, it's made of wood. Well, you know what, to Heaven with 'em cowards. They'd be trying to murder us."

Thinker shrugged in a "well that's true, never mind" gesture. Even Shanks rocked his head back and forth in the same manner from the mast of the fighter's nest. And that was that.

Gadriel added, "Rod says he loves you people."

In no time they were at breeze pace headed out of New Haven's harbor, methodically throwing high explosives at high explosives in front of their ship. Approximately halfway out of the harbor, Gadriel heard it again, likely his musician's ear.

"They're aiming platforms."

"Helmsman, keep following first mate's instructions."

"Aye, Cap't."

Captain Tamara ran over to the stern railing and with her large spyglass watched four of the artillery platforms, the four that appeared in a position to actually hit them, moving from how they were pointed in a direct-fire position, to skyward to fire upon them more traditionally. Captain Tamara contemplated sounding general quarters, but the size of those guns? If their sabotage didn't work, there was no mitigation they could offer shipside. They were here or they weren't as far as the captain was concerned, and the crew already knew they were running through a minefield.

Captain Tamara walked down her quarterdeck, then over to Thinker and Clancy to tell them more privately, "They're preparing to fire on us. Think, is this something you want to see?"

After thinking about it for a moment, he shook his head no. She placed a warm hand on his neck and squeezed. Not in a rough, or toughen up way, but in a way that assured him he was not without someone who loved him, no matter how ruthless he may be. For Captain Tamara's part, she hoped Banger and Breecher were nowhere near those docks at the moment.

Hustling back over to the quarterdeck and taking the spyglass back from Gadriel, Captain Tamara watched as the first gun fired and the ammunition or round flew only half the distance in a flaming ball of fire. Looking back at the platform, there was a delay, but it was engulfed in flames. Men on fire jumped off the platform, and most made it into the water, but as Banger explained it, it would not help them. The jelly would stick and could not be washed off. As the fire began to spread to the base of the platform, several more explosions, likely its ammunition and propellant stores, began to go, blowing away that section of dock entirely while the platform just sank. For a moment Captain Tamara felt sick to her stomach at the thought of the men on fire, until they attempted to fire the second and third guns.

Fortunately, New Haven's harbor security did not attempt to fire the fourth artillery cannon they prepared to unleash upon the Midnight. However, now New Haven was missing over half of its dock, and its harbor was in shambles. Mother knows how many men and women were dead. And it was very likely Captain Tamara and Thinker of Atmos would never step foot on the Island of New Haven ever again. Captain Tamara would likely never see Banger ever again, who was likely the most like a father figure she had ever known. New Haven now had a generation of rebuilding to do, and they couldn't blame it on anyone but themselves.

So far the Midnight may have detonated one mine with their 'blow things up that blow up' plan, but their efforts appeared to be out of an abundance of caution. The failed artillery rounds didn't appear to detonate anything under the surface, either. As they reached the sandbar, they called off their water-bombing, and Thinker was content with staying at the bow, directing the ship out of New Haven waters.

When they reached open water, they began to open their rigging and rested the majority of their crew. Captain Tamara went below decks to thank the boys for a job well-done and was excited to announce that she purchased "a whole bloody cow for Cook, and it's steaks for everyone when shit calms down" and also "when we're done with that, we're going to use its gourmet guts and catch a whole Mother damn shark," which was met with a resounding growl of joy.

Clancy and Gadriel were in the infirmary with the Midnight's medical officer, Doctor Cutter. Clancy and Gadriel had bonded quite a bit over the last evening, and Clancy was becoming more used to Gadriel's afflictions.

Gadriel asked, "Hey Doctor? Please don't take offense to this, but Rod wants to know if you're from Haven because of your name. I'm sorry, he's on a kick now. I told him no because you do not have their traditional head tattoos."

"Actually son, I am from New Haven. I came aboard with Thinker a few years back. I don't have the head tattoos because it went against my oath as a healer. I don't do harm. I will only help. Tattoos are inherently harmful. My sect didn't like my oath. So I left. Easy peasy."

"That easy, eh' Doc?"

"Yes, Mate Clancy, now be still, you giant," he said with affection.

On the top deck Captain Tamara had excused herself to freshen up in her quarters and was closely followed by Violet, who was also trained in high-level medicine. Thinker, who had also been through an ordeal but had been given the luxury of sleep and food while staying at House Atmos, volunteered to take the ship.

Before Violet entered Captain Tamara's quarters, Rose intercepted her—bloodied, likely with a sprained hand, a fat lip, and a lump on her head—but still with an unbroken jug of juice.

"Violet. I . . . had this juice made for you as a token of my . . . appreciation for . . . Will you take this?"

"Y-yes. Thank you."

"I can't name all the fruits in it, but I asked the man before we were wanted criminals there, and he said it would taste good, and I wanted to thank you for helping me and goodbye now," Rose said too quickly.

"Again, thank you," said Violet, genuinely. "Let us try this together, later this evening? Right now I'm covered in goose fat . . . old goose fat."

Rose said, "Okay!" in a voice of a higher register, then walked toward Doctor Cutter's infirmary.

About two leagues outside New Haven, Shanks noticed a small vessel off their starboard side. It was waiting, and while it had not struck its colors, it was presenting a white flag, likely for parlay—they could be in trouble or interested in trading with someone leaving New Haven; they couldn't really know until they spoke with them. Shanks blew his spotting horn, but this spurred no reaction from Thinker. However, Thinker was soon to notice the ship and turned the Midnight to the south to intercept. There was very little risk; this vessel was in open water, anchored, and on the smaller end of the clipper class—small and very fast, used for messaging or transporting very small cargo or individual people, a common sight in their business and more civilized society alike.

In the captain's quarters, Violet was tending to Tamara's cuts and bruises gently while Tamara showed an ounce of vulnerability and was dozing off in her chair. Violet had a new shirt prepared for her—Tamara received a nasty gash on her side, likely from the stream-slide plan—and at present had it clean and her chest wrapped in white bandages. While Violet was wiping up dried blood that she was pretty sure was not all her lady's blood, she heard two thumps from Think's boots on the quarterdeck, the only man allowed to do that.

"Wake up, my love," Violet whispered in Captain Tamara's ear.

"I'm up you gorgeous devil, what the Mother is happening now, I was having a wicked dream. You were there, but you were covered in fat."

"Thinker needs you; it's important. He stomped."

"Ah shit." The captain threw her fresh black blouse on and began buttoning it while Violet tucked it into her trousers with care. Around the front of her belt, Violet took care not to cut herself on the instruments of death she knew her lady kept there, and pulled her hips into her own. She then kissed the captain on the forehead for good luck and placed her cap on her head in their way, cocked it a little to the side, then she moved out of her way, slapping her on the bottom as she did so.

"Clean yourself up, you filthy scoundrel," said the captain with a wink.

Captain Tamara exited her cabin, then rounded the short stairs to join Thinker on the quarterdeck. "What's going on? I was almost asleep, sir."

Thinker just nodded in the direction of the clipper that they were fast approaching. At this point they could see with their naked eye that they were presenting a white flag.

"Hmm, parlay, you think?"

"I think so," Thinker responded, then added, "as far out as I saw them, they had whites presented. Unknown if it's for us or for anyone. I say we talk with them. How many could they have aboard, eight? *If* it were cozy?"

"I agree. I'm going to finish cleaning up. Please invite them aboard and show all courtesy. This is a good opportunity for the boys to practice, fresh after a battle."

A quarter chime later, the Midnight was alongside the much smaller clipper by the name of the Peregrine. The Midnight, though it dwarfed the

Peregrine in size, soul, and cannon (the Peregrine had no cannon), maintained courtesy under the same white flag, which Captain Tamara and Thinker figured would be tough for the Peregrine to believe, as the Midnight had a reputation and there was little the Peregrine could do if the Midnight wanted to take her.

Captain Tamara stood at her starboard side railing, expecting to meet the Peregrine's captain, and she did. The other captain she would wager forgot more about sailing than she knew. He was a man of later years with gray, long hair fashioned into a tail and always seemed to have his right eyebrow arched. He gave Captain Tamara a crisp royal naval salute. Technically having been trained by the royal navy, this was not difficult to return just as well.

"I am Captain Tamara; this is my ship, the Midnight. May we be of assistance to you?"

"Pleased, Cap't. I'm Cap't Gint; this is my lit'l ship, the Peregrine. Knowing you're the Midnight, I can be of assistance to you, I'm afraid."

"Understood, Cap't, We'll lower our—"

"No need, Cap't Tamara. I have only this message to deliver and then I must be on my way back to Lulin."

"I see. And what is this message?" asked Captain Tamara.

"One moment," Cap't Gint said, grabbing a long pole and hooking the sealed letter onto it. "Just so's yer' aware, the Lulin Governor sent two ships, one north and one south, each in the direction of likely near ports. I almost passed by New Haven, knowin' how rare'a place it be. But then I saw it well, shootin' flares and on fire. I decided to wait 'ere in case that was you or anyone needed help I could provide. I wouldn't approach, not New Haven, no way."

"Thank you for the information, Captain," Tamara said, plucking the letter from the pole he had to attach three lengths to, or he would not have been able to reach the deck.

"Yeah, so's, I'm going to be headed back to Lulin, and I'll be goin' fast. I wouldn't want to race ya. You'll lose, I think," he said with a warm smile.

"Well regardless, how about we give you a head start, Captain?" said Tamara.

"Sounds good to me! Stay safe, youngins."

As quickly as the older captain could leave, he was gone. At full sail, Captain Gint and the Peregrine were headed south in the direction of Lulin. As they watched him go, Captain Tamara looked down at the envelope, in a heavy parchment. It was addressed to "Captain Tamara Midnight and the merchant ship Midnight." After giving a hand signal to gather up and leave, and congratulating the "boyos" on a professional job well done even though Captain Gint didn't come aboard, Tamara joined Think on the quarterdeck to read the letter.

Think said, "I didn't know your last name was Midnight."

"It isn't."

"What is it?" he asked.

"Well, not as intimidating as Midnight, that's for sure."

Captain Tamara Midnight,

It has come to my attention that you have left the port town of Lulin with either something that does not belong to you, or someone who has something that does not belong to you. If it is the former, please know that if you do not return it immediately I will be investing my personal resources into hunting you down and taking it from you, including appealing for assistance from His Majesty's Royal Navy.

If it is the latter, please know that Rose Baker is wanted in Lulin for questioning related to the theft of priceless property. Her father, Jerald Baker, is being held in the Governor's private jail, which was re-commissioned for this singular purpose of questioning related to the theft of priceless property. Soon her family assets will be seized, her brother, Julien Baker, will be arrested, and the life as she knows it here in Lulin will simply cease to exist.

I have sent two of the fastest ships available in Lulin to the two most likely ports of call for the Midnight. These letters will be left for you there, at the ports of Windmere and Saints Rock. Their captains will return and be sent further. If you're receiving them at either of these ports, good news for you; this is the soonest you could have received them. I look forward to discussing this matter with you in person.

Regards,

Governor Matteson

Lulin Township

"Aw, shit," said Captain Tamara.

"What??" asked Thinker.

Tamara handed her first mate the letter, which he read rather quickly. "Aw, shit" he repeated, then added, "Do we tell Ms. Rose now, or later?"

Gadriel and Rose, who were on the top deck for the exchange, saw their faces and became concerned. Gadriel and Rose walked up and asked, "What's going on?"

Captain Tamara said, "Nothing important."

Gadriel then said, "No, no, 'aw, shit' what?" to which Think said, "Damn it," then took the stone out of his pocket and handed it to Gadriel, which caused him to go "Hahhh."

Captain Tamara said to Thinker, "I know we went to New Haven to learn more about the stone and its potential applications, but I think it works great for spying on people."

"Yes," Think said flatly, clearly annoyed at not thinking of something clever.

"Look, Rose—"

The captain was cut off, at least for Gadriel, by a spotter horn blast by Shanks from the fighter's nest. Gadriel looked up sharply, then behind them. He sputtered for a moment, then his sailing days came back to him.

"Cap cu. Contact! Stern!"

Everyone turned around sharply. What was barely visible through the naked eye could be seen through spyglass, which Thinker and Captain Tamara had one with them. What they saw was a massive, tall, black ship moving toward them fast.

11

Ships of Legend

"May I?" asked Gadriel, Thinker absentmindedly reached over the captain and handed Gadriel his spyglass. The first mate began barking orders to the crew.

"RUN OUT ALL RIGGING, HELMSMAN FORTY DEGREES SOUTH BY SOUTH EAST, WE'RE GOING TO SQUEEZE ALL THE SPEED WE CAN!"

His orders were confirmed by a round of "AYES!" What Captain Tamara saw bothered her a great deal.

"Shit, they must have had another dock behind the island, apparently a dry dock where they could build a monster like that. Think, did you know about this?"

"OF COURSE I DIdn . . . I'm sorry, Captain. Of course I didn't know about this. I apologize for my outburst."

"Don't you think on it for one minute, deary. Doesn't it look like its gaining far too fast?" asked Captain Tamara.

"Absolutely. I know one of the sects had been working on a form of propulsion for years, but I didn't know it had been applied to ships, or even functioned on that scale," said Thinker.

Captain Tamara turned around to address her men.

"Well then, let's give these lazy BLOODY MOTHER CHEATS SOMETHIN' TO CHASE, BOYOS!"

The captain loved to rile up her men, although she thought of them as her boys most of the time. And one of her favorite parts was this: a resounding, chest-rattling, unified, loud and growled "YEAH!" as the Midnight picked up quick speed and expert men were trimming sails for more.

Although the situation itself was quite frightening when you imagined end results considering the enemy ship's size, Thinker and Captain Tamara were all business. Unfortunately for Gadriel, however, looking through the spyglass, his blood ran cold. He couldn't believe what he was seeing. His legs and back were rigid, and not from his injury. He began to feel a tickle in his chest that he didn't realize was there and could do nothing about. His heart rate began to climb and he started to hyperventilate. Gadriel dropped to a knee and everyone sounded far away.

"Gad? boyo? Get Doc up here! We've got time before general quarters!" he thinks Tamara was saying.

"No. No, there's . . . no time," Gadriel got out. Shanks was next to him now, helping him up. "Shanks!" he exclaimed. "Noo, no, no, no, Shanks! Shanks, you've got to get out of here, Shanks! Not again."

Gadriel was back in his nightmares. He was back on the Sapphire. He was back with young Shanks. From very far away he heard an echoed, *"NO TIME! SNAP OUT OF THIS GAD; I'LL NEVER LET YOU SLEEP AGAIN!"*

Suddenly, all he could see was white for a moment, which cleared up into a stinging then a hot pain in his face, and he was back to himself. Apparently Captain Tamara had slapped him in the left cheek, hard.

"Are you with us, bard?" asked the captain.

"Yes. yes I'm . . . I'm sorry," he said. "Captain, please let Shanks take a tender and go. He can go back to New Haven and say he was a prisoner of ours . . . He can't . . . Not again."

"He can't what again, Gadriel?" asked Captain Tamara. If they had been sitting down, Tamara, Thinker, Rose, and Clancy would be at the edge of their seats. Because they all had questions.

"There's just no time for this, Captain."

Tamara leaned to one side to look at the large ship, looked at the Midnight's trimming, then said, "If this wind keeps, it'll take them a chime to reach us at this speed. We've got time. Please continue."

"Shanks and I were crew on the Sapphire five years ago." Thinker and Clancy whistled; Captain Tamara said, "No, shit?"

"Yes. Long story short, we were run down by a large, tall, black ship with unexplainable speed—THAT ship right THERE!" Gadriel pointed in a frustrated and animated way. "There wasn't talking, negotiating, nothing. We were boarded and slaughtered. They wanted something of the captain's; all they left with besides general piracy looting was a small bag and my captain at the time. Not only did they slaughter almost everyone, but they set the ship ablaze."

"And you survived? You survived the Sapphire wreckage?"

"It wasn't a WRECKAGE! IT WAS A DESTRUCTION, AN EXECUTION!"

Gadriel began breathing too fast again. Captain Tamara put both hands on his shoulders, Clancy retrieved a barrel, and they sat him down on it.

"Here, there we are, you calm down now. Let's not give your right cheek to the same treatment, eh?" she said, hoping to make him laugh. "Please continue," she prompted.

"That's all there was to it. We had the fastest ship in the water, at least we prided ourselves on it. This monster ran us down, pulled up next to us, and all I remember seeing was a black wooden wall. Then it just rained violence. It was over so quickly; when they left I was trying to get our wounded out, but our powder magazine went and everything was on fire. I found Shanks and a piece of the hull in the water and tried to paddle us to Pope. We were almost there. I kept Shanks as warm as I could. We barely made it. Shanks and I woke up on the beach the next morning, the same piece of the hull beached near us. The biggest thing I remember that morning was how warm the sun felt. I lived and we didn't look back."

Rose asked, "Gadriel, may I ask a question? And I mean no offense, sir."

In his normal Gadriel charm, he accepted by saying, "Of course, madam, anything you wish."

"That morning you woke up on the beach, Shanks was . . . with you?"

"Yep. We got up, walked away, started a new life."

"And you never looked back, not for other survivors, not for bodies, and not at the hull?"

"Nope! New life, no more death. Just singing and playing and fun, nonviolent crime. Funny how *that* worked out" he began chuckling. "Yes I know, Rod" he said to no one.

Captain Tamara looked over at Clancy and said nothing, which Clancy understood. Clancy put out his giant hand to Gadriel and said, "May I? I'd like to see this awful ship."

"Of course, sir," he said and handed Clancy the spyglass.

Clancy placed this in his pocket and stood behind Gadriel, waiting. Tamara said to Gadriel, softly, "Love, it's important now that you listen to me, to us. I think at this point we've grown a bond, and you and Thorny I think of both as my crew now—you've earned your blacks, okay?"

"Wow really? That's great! I never thought I'd sail again, but Shanks and I will have to think about it, we've grown to rather like taverns and the road."

"Gadriel, that's what we need to talk to you about."

The captain continued, "Gadriel, listen carefully, okay? Shanks is gone."

". . . what do you mean?"

"Your best friend, Shanks, isn't 'ere, deary," the captain told him, sadly.

"But he's right here?" Gadriel said confused, pointing to where he believed Shanks was standing but, to the rest of his crew Shanks simply was not.

"No, Gad, we understand you see Shanks. That you speak with him, that you have conversations with him. That he's always there, yeah?" said the captain.

"Of course he's always there. What the Mother are you trying to say?" Gadriel began raising his voice.

"Gadriel, I need to you keep it together now," said Captain Tamara. "Shanks may be there for you, but he ain't for us, get me?"

Gadriel looked around the quarterdeck, and most everyone except Thinker was looking toward the ground. Gadriel turned to Shanks and said, "Are you in on this? C'mon be serious, you little scamp." Rose started to cry.

"Gadriel, you're going to need some time with this, all right? Don't you worry about this monster ship; we're going to take care of it. You concentrate on you," consoled the captain.

"Look I don't know what you're talking about, but I'm going to—"

"Gadriel!" interrupted Rose. "Stop this," she continued. "You're in denial, okay? Shanks doesn't eat. Shanks doesn't sleep. Shanks can be on watch for days on end. None of us can see Shanks. Shanks doesn't talk. Don't you understand? How convenient so much of this is? There's a little reason for everything. *He is not standing here.*"

Rose hadn't known Gadriel for many more days than anyone else on the quarterdeck, but this, for some reason, was breaking her heart. Eyes watering, she continued, "Shanks died. I know you kept him warm. I've laid awake at night listening to your nightmares for weeks, Gad. You did your best, but Shanks died and you never looked back."

Rose needed to stop a moment and sniffle, and in doing so revealed that big Clancy was also crying.

Captain Tamara looked up. "What?"

Clancy responded, embarrassed, "Well, I mean, it bein' his best friend and all, n' he just wants to save him all over again, and we've got to tell him so he don't hurt himself, but I was confused too and only just figured it out." He ugly-sniffled, then wiped his nose on his arm bandage.

"Gadriel," said Captain Tamara, "Clancy here can take you back to Doctor Cutter; there are some compounds he has that will help you calm dow—"

"No," interrupted Gadriel. "I don't believe any of you, but this is how you all feel, all of you, like you've talked about it?"

Violet offered, "Actually no, sir, none of us have discussed this; we've just all thought about it at length."

Gadriel, one last time, said, "Okay, so . . . for my peace of mind, ladies and gents. I'm going to call your name—you please tell me if you think Shanks isn't real."

"Then you'll go see Doctor Cutter?" asked Captain Tamara.

"Well, we'll see, won't we," said Gadriel, then called out the names of his maybe-crew.

"Rose?"

"Yes, I'm sorry, Gad."

"Violet?"

"Yes, sir."

"Cap't?"

"Aye."

"Clancy?"

"Yes, Mr. Gadriel."

"Think? . . ."

". . . Think??"

"Actually . . . no."

Captain Tamara, with wide eyes, slowly turned to her right to look at Thinker and said low, but loud enough for everyone, "What. in. the. *Think.*" Not so much a question, more of a strong statement.

"I'm sorry, Captain. I cannot in good conscience agree with your assessment when I have observed evidence to the contrary."

"Oh, boyo, I've got to hear this," said the captain, and the rest murmured an agreement, including Gadriel.

"Gadriel made observations at the house of Atmos that he noted were from Shanks that he could not have known otherwise. One example being, he said Shanks came from the roof and he observed mortar flares on it, as well as a rooftop entrance," said Thinker.

"That could have been a lucky guess by our bard; do we know if your father took him up there?"

"Or y'know, you could just ask me," said Gadriel, to which the captain blushed slightly.

"Okay, what about Gadriel's knowledge of the stream that he could not have? He said Shanks explained it to him because that's how he climbed up to Atmos," said Thinker again.

"That . . . that could've been common sense for . . . for nature things or some such," said the captain.

Thinker continued, "Oh, c'mon, Tamara. You have to admit there have too many small moments here and there, him seeing things off the deck with his naked eye? When if someone *were* in the nest they could see it? Just a moment ago, Gadriel was alerted to a ship in pursuit he likely couldn't have seen on his own. Just half a chime ago we were tricked into revealing an important letter because I had a stone with a spirit inside it, in my pocket, that told him about it."

"Perhaps . . ." said Captain Tamara.

Thinker finished with, "Let us not forget what we both saw on the floor of the Atmos last night."

"YOU . . . WE don't know what we saw," exclaimed the captain. Thinker put his hands up, in a "true true" gesture.

Gadriel asked the question everyone else had. "What, what did you guys see?"

Captain Tamara gave a quick non-answer. "No time for that now—that monster ship is catching up." She then belted orders: "Gadriel, I'm sorry nevertheless all of this went down for you today, and I'm sorry it had to be this ship. Go see Dr. Cutter regardless of what you're going through; you'll feel right as rain, promise. Think, I think I have an idea; call for general quarters in three tocks, then meet me on the gun deck. Clancy, you'll have the ship while Think and I are below."

Think and Clancy both said, "Aye!"

Gadriel had a different answer entirely: "This ship that's about to attack almost killed me once. I'm not going to hide from it again. Besides, I can tell you how it attacks. It'll open with its bow chase guns."

That caused Captain Tamara to pause. "That may change things. Thinker, three tocks!"

Then she headed down the stairs. Gadriel followed her. Rose looked at Violet, to which Violet said, "This is no place for us now, Ms. Rose. Let us go to our quarters—you may sit with me in mine; we'll try some juice."

Below deck Captain Tamara stood over Banger's surprise glass jars of sun jelly, thinking. She was joined by Gadriel, who was also using what he knew of this terrible ship to think about the problem. Tamara knew they needed Thinker for this problem. But if you call general quarters too soon, men will become fatigued, and every minute counts.

"You know, Cap't. I've been thinking about this ship—well, Shanks and I—for five long years."

"Okay, and what are your thoughts?" asked the captain.

"Well, for it to be that large and that fast, there has to be some form of propulsion, and if it's that large and that fast, it must be very heavy," to which the captain said, "Yes, I think we can all gather that right now."

"So if it's that heavy, that large, and that fast, then it couldn't possibly turn sharply, could it? Not without slowing significantly, not in a way a ship like Midnight could." Tamara looked up sharply.

"They destroyed the Sapphire by running us down, disabling us with chase guns, then pulling up alongside, and boarding with superior numbers; I don't know why they wouldn't do that again, just more efficiently now if it's a New Haven ship."

"You know what, I think you've just earned your keep today, handsome."

Captain Tamara and her first and second mates stood stoically on the quarter deck as they continued to run from this infamous ship, legendary for the worst reasons. The Sapphire was not the only ship reported destroyed this way, but Captain Tamara and Thinker could not think of a reason for Gadriel, and, they supposed, possibly Shanks, to know about that today. Standing center down the deck were several members of the crew holding onto rope that had been lashed in taut lines from port to starboard railings, near about dead center. Most men toward the bow held jars of Banger's sunny goo—Tamara couldn't think of what to call it, and neither could Bangs . . . Mother above, she hoped he was okay.

The pursuing ship was almost within range of them now; Shanks reported from the fighter's nest that they had run out their chase guns, two large cannons.

Gadriel used spyglass to observe then said, initially indignantly, "*Shanks pointed out*, that they've run out their chase guns. They have two; we only remember them using one years ago, however."

"Shit," said Captain Tamara in a volume only her quarterdeck could hear. She then raised her voice. "Looks like it's time we paid these New Haven FOOLS another SURPRISE, EH? GUN DECK AT THE READY!!" The crew, the ship over, screamed in delight, and also very real, denied fear.

Thinker then gave the order that would begin a ridiculous plan that would either end in steaks and whiskey and a legend of their own, or their complete destruction.

"HELMSMAN, BEGIN EVASIVE MANEUVERS!"

"AYE! EVASIVE MANEUVERS, AYE!"

"HELMSMAN, THIS IS WHAT YOU DREAM ABOUT!" shouted Thinker, to which Helmsman responded, "AYE! NOT BE HITTIN' US TODAY, SIR, AYE!"

The Midnight began gracefully, almost swinging back and forth, not following a specific pattern, but making themselves a more difficult target. It was not purely an advantage; however, this of course slowed them down and allowed their pursuers to gain on them faster. This was actually something the Midnight counted on now.

Port to Starboard to Port to Port to Starboard. The Midnight wasn't drastically losing speed as she was meant to be maneuvered in such a way, but it was their enemy who gained noticeable distance quicker.

"Oy Gad," said Captain Tamara.

"Yes Cap't," said Gad seriously, awaiting an order, his sailing days quickly returning.

"You know if this doesn't work you owe me a ship?" All smiled.

"Aye, Cap't," said Gadriel. Shanks took this time to exit the fighter's nest and join them on the quarterdeck.

The enemy fired a single chase gun that missed by less than a quarter league, so only a few hundred steps away from the stern of the Midnight. Clancy was at the head of the men in the ropes across the deck and looked over concerned. Captain Tamara gave him an "all's well" gesture, and he nodded.

Captain Tamara said, "Likely testing their distance; they'll soon fire upon us in earnest."

Thinker then added, "Concur. Helmsman, prepare—"

"NO! Helmsman, start now, I've seen this ship lame the Sapphire from just over this distance. I believe they're luring us into feeling safe, Cap't."

Tamara then ordered Helmsman without any hesitation, "Helmsman, begin your maneuvers," to which Thinker nodded his agreement, moving to stand shoulder to shoulder with Helmsman, just facing the opposite direction.

Helmsman said at a normal volume, "Aye' Cap't."

The Helmsman said to the captain, "By, Cap't," and Tamara began to shout, "RIG MASTER BOWSPRIT TO THE BY WIND, BEGIN YOUR TRIM, MEN READY HARD STARBOARD," to which all shouted, "AYE!" as the bowsprit, like a horizontal mast with a sail attached that could be quickly moved 180 degrees across the deck to catch specific winds, swung out over the men and out over the starboard bow. It wasn't as useful, but when Helmsman pulled the Midnight's rutter, forcing the Midnight into a hard right turn, it didn't take long for the bowsprit to catch slower but present "by-winds." They were also moving at a sharp angle away from their pursuer, who appeared to be slowing down considerably to make a turn sharp enough to follow effectively.

This gave Captain Tamara and her command a clearer view of their enemy, noticing what looked a lot like large pipes sticking out of the back of their ship, then angling and pointing toward the water. This was an angle that Gadriel had never seen, and something Thinker and Captain Tamara had never seen as sailors, either. This also gave Captain Tamara a view of the ship's forward bow, which with her spyglass was clear enough to read the name of this beast: NHS Retribution.

For two chimes the crew of the Midnight repeated this maneuver, while the Retribution closed more distance, little by little. There was no safety for them to reach; there was no help on the way. This is what Captain Tamara knew they could do, and they were doing it well. Her riggers were masters, trimming sails as needed, which was constantly. The Midnight's bowsprit swung back and forth to assist Helmsman, who could find currents in a closet. The Retribution had taken to firing upon them when closest, but due to Helmsman's skill, they never had a clear shot or favorable attack angle with their port, starboard, or forward chase guns. But they were now out of time. Soon their ability to turn sharp wouldn't matter, because the NHS Retribution could hammer them out of the water with a broadside if they decided to sit still.

"It's time, my old friend," said Captain Tamara.

"Are you speaking to me, or our ship, my captain?" said Thinker with a rare smile, to which the captain said, "I can care about two things, can't I?"

At the present, the Retribution was finishing its starboard turn to line up a chase shot on the Midnight's stern, meaning it was turning right to continue its chase of the Midnight and would fire upon them as soon as their guns slid into view of the ship and had a favorable attack angle with its front cannon. What happened next happened very quickly.

"THIRD MATE, READY YOUR MEN!"

"AYE, CAP'T!" said Clancy, who began running down his line of men, ducking under the taut ropes that had been lashed across the width of the ship.

When he reached about two-thirds of the way down his line, there were two men to a rope, and he began lighting torches of one man and the other held a bottle of rum with some of Doctor Cutter's bandage sticking out the top, soaked in the spirit. This is the only reason Captain Tamara had rum on her ship, throwing it away, sometimes on fire. She said real sailors drink whiskey, but she knew in reality, real sailors drank whatever they pleased—she just hated rum. But she often received crates as gifts and bonuses. Now they were going to gift it to the Retribution, in a manner of speaking.

"RIG MASTER BOWSPRIT TO PORT—WE'RE TAKING THE LARGE WIND. HELMSMAN, CREW, PREPARE FOR HAULING THE PORTSIDE ANCHOR, YOU LOVELY MANIACS!!"

Though the Helmsman didn't roar out of pure concentration, the rigging men did. In response the gun crews did. In response to that, Doctor Cutter and Cook and his junior did. The low-deck men did. Clancy did, his fighting men did, Gadriel did. Violet and Rose through her cabin door did. Thinker did. Even the captain herself did. But Shanks did, and let out the loudest roar of them all. A roar from a soul that had been waiting. The captain paused for a moment, looking back at Gadriel, who was grinning, because he knew she heard it. But no time for that now.

The NHS Retribution fired high, aiming for Midnight's quarterdeck—terribly contemptuous form against an opponent who never attacked you and has only run away, bad form indeed. Though the first shot did miss the quarterdeck entirely, flying wide and to the right, the second shot from the second bow chase gun was more on target, still to the right, but flying under the quarterdeck, slamming into Captain Tamara's quarters in an explosion that sent wood, metal, and cannon shrapnel through the wall facing the top deck and into several of the men holding lit torches and bottles of rum. These men hit the deck screaming in pain, lighting fires upon the deck immediately.

"NOW, HELMSMAN! HOLD YOUR LINES!" screamed Captain Tamara.

The fire made Gadriel freeze for a moment in pure terror. He quickly returned to his body with a stinging hot pain in the right side of his face, Shanks holding his shoulders, looking at his friend, shaking him.

"I'm here! I'm here!" Gadriel shouted. He saw the fire again, and Gadriel and Shanks began running toward the flames.

Per their orders, the fighting men held their line, moving out of the way and kicking at the flames. Though an alcohol fire on its own should burn off quickly, much too quickly for there to be fear of the weathered deck genuinely catching fire, the ropes protecting the men, which were dry braided fuel, were something different entirely. Gadriel limped toward the first fire and began stomping and smothering the fire with sail patch he took from rigging storage at the rail.

Gadriel fought the fire like a man who hated it. Because he did. He didn't want to be on the Sapphire again. He liked the Midnight. He liked loving the sea again. And he and Shanks thought it incredibly unfair they had to see this ugly awful ship twice. While he fought the fire though, his time for sure footing ran out.

When Captain Tamara ordered, "NOW, HELMSMAN," what had begun happening was the smooth start of a portside turn to begin the swing of the Midnight's bowsprit over to the portside bow. That had begun during the fire and destruction of the captain's quarters. While this was happening, expert riggers were trimming sail to take the large wind, the prevailing wind, as opposed to the by-wind, or short-wind, that they used to travel in the opposite direction, or opposite tack. Now that preparations were ready, Captain Tamara and First Mate Thinker were attempting a maneuver that could rip ships like the Midnight in half if not done correctly, or leave them sitting still to be fired upon if done poorly. They were going to drop their portside anchor in motion, called "club hauling," long enough to sharpen their left turn so dramatically, that if done correctly, it should force them directly into the large wind, and they should immediately pick up speed going in a different wind direction, or opposite tack. And in this insane case, they wanted to charge the NHS Retribution, and the angle could work if the Retribution were attempting to preemptively turn to catch them, which they were, again.

The captain, having taken up position at the front of the quarterdeck, ready to face her enemy, had tightened her cap and taken her stoic posture a captain takes before ship to ship combat.

From behind her, First Mate Thinker screamed, "NOW! PORTSIDE ANCHOR! HELMSMAN ALL THE WAY!"

A deafening screech of metal and rope moving far too fast than intended was heard as the spool spun out the anchor rope wildly. Clancy stood over it with the largest boarding axe Gadriel had ever seen. The ship yawed so severely to port that Gadriel lost his balance and began to float for a moment as the deck fell from under his feet. The sounds of stressed timber and cracking glass echoed in a moment of silence broken by two missed shots from the NHS Retribution that would have obliterated the Midnight would it had been where it was ten ticks ago.

Gadriel was still floating as he was still falling, but the deck was now moving rapidly away from him. He frantically reached for the nearest bracing rope to himself, which he was able to catch with his left hand, still clinging to his piece of sail with his right. He no longer needed it; he just didn't think to let go of it.

"CLANCY! NOW!" shouted Thinker.

Clancy, who had lashed himself to the portside railing, didn't hesitate. With all his might, injured arm be damned, his axe fell on the thick anchor rope like an explosion, a clap of thunder echoing over the deck. Despite the rope size and speed, Clancy cleaved it clean through, so hard that his axe was wedged into the deck. Gadriel for his part was still hanging on for his life, and much to his dismay, his arm was in searing pain. He looked down to see his rope had caught fire. Though the rope was thick and was not in immediate danger of breaking, this did little to help Gadriel who could not let go or risk going overboard.

The dropping of the anchor stopped the stress of the Midnight's drastic turn, and Helmsman and the Rig Master knew their craft. The Midnight seemingly bounced away from the sudden loss of drag, luckily did not roll or capsize, caught the prevailing wind with trimmed sails ready for the occasion, and began a steady lurch forward, continuing their turn to port. Only now, they were beginning to face the NHS Retribution, and they were within a range where its bow chase guns were no longer effective against the Midnight, and the Retribution could not turn or slow down fast enough.

Gadriel was able to let go of the burning rope and put out the remaining fires, though the spray and wind from the last maneuver helped a great deal; it is probably why Captain Tamara told everyone not to move. However, now Gadriel felt his job was to get the wounded below decks, which he set to doing with Shanks's help. In total six men were injured, two significantly—

one would likely lose his leg. Gadriel would feel guilty later for thinking about how it would make a great song. Gadriel returned to the top deck, took one of the extinguished torches recovered from the wounded, lit it, and waited with a man who had a rum bottle and no partner.

Despite their stark difference in size, what was occurring now was the Midnight was barreling down on the NHS Retribution, and each captain knew it. Thinker looked over at his captain and observed her hungry smirk, which gave him one of his own. Captain Tamara had one last gamble to make, and she made this decision after learning the name of the ship. If she were the captain of the Retribution, she wouldn't want the Midnight to be alongside her either if she weren't controlling the engagement. She also assumed that due to the size of the Retribution, the gundecks were too high to be of any use against the Midnight point blank, and judging by the height of her chase guns, this was true. However, would this captain be insane enough, hateful enough, to ram the Midnight rather than let her have an exposed broadside, despite the Midnight's cannon not being very useful against such a ship either?

Captain Tamara had to decide, because she couldn't have her decision both ways for her plan to work, and her plan needed to work. Captain Tamara decided that yes, at the helm of a ship like the Retribution, what she now knows of the Retribution, and of what the people of New Haven are capable, yes, this captain would rather ram the Midnight and risk sinking or significantly damaging their own ship instead of letting them have a close pass and *maybe* flooding a ballast or two. The Midnight was nearly out of time, heading straight toward the NHS Retribution, lining up just to the right of her.

"Helmsman, prepare to turn starboard on my signal!"

"Aye, Cap't!" confirmed Helmsman. Thinker was concerned but trusted his captain.

"Helmsman, on my mark, twenty degrees starboard, sir."

"Aye, twenty degrees, Aye," confirmed Helmsman.

Within one hundred steps of the ship's bows, Captain Tamara could see that the deck of the Retribution could no longer see the Midnight, and this is when they would have to turn into them to ram them if they so chose this course of action.

"Now, Helmsman," the captain said calmly, to which the Helmsman calmly said, "Aye," then calmly turned the Midnight. They smoothly shifted the Midnight to the right while the hulking behemoth of the Retribution roughly shifted to its left, right in the path of where the Midnight was. However, now the Midnight *was* alongside their bounty, right where they wanted to be.

Thinker screamed, "NOW! CLANCY! NOW!"

Clancy didn't hesitate. He threw the first jar as hard and as high as he could and started a chain of timed actions that were as beautiful as they were violent. As the Midnight coasted alongside the Retribution, as close as they were, and it felt like they scraped alongside them, but Captain Tamara knew this wasn't the case, the crew of the Midnight began throwing and coating the side of the NHS Retribution's hull with Banger's sticky flame jelly, almost down three-fourths of its length. Then began the flaming bottles from the Midnight—one man would light a bottle, the next would throw it at the jelly, as hard as he could. One by one like a choreographed dance, including Gadriel, blazing heat struck the Retribution, and it didn't matter that there was spray, or mist, or fog. There were one or two bottles that bounced off the hull, there were even a few that slipped from hands or were thrown poorly, missing entirely, but this is why they had a third of their men prepared to light the jelly ablaze.

By the time they finished their pass, in any other engagement they'd normally see a ship like the NHS Retribution making the sharpest turn possible to re-engage their enemy. But what they saw made it easy to see why this was not the case: The Retribution was on fire. Over half of its portside hull was ablaze, and there was no realistic way for them to fight the fire, not with it being on the outside of their ship in open waters, and because this chosen substance could not be removed until it ran its horrendous course.

Thinker and Captain Tamara watched its next movements in their spyglasses and a few moments later were glad to announce, "First mate, please announce to our crew that our enemy is running."

However, Thinker didn't need to. The deck was stock still and went wild at the captain's pronouncement. The Retribution miscalculated their opponent. And the sounds of utter destruction were fading as they sailed away from one another. The Midnight and her crew became the second legends on the water that day.

12

About Two Weeks

In the days following their victory over the NHS Retribution, the men did their best to repair the captain's quarters with the supplies on hand, but would need a proper port with better materials to make it as good as new. After the first day, when at least the outer holes of the cabin were patched and everyone was allowed to rest to some degree, Thinker and Captain Tamara sat down with Gadriel, Rose, and maybe Shanks in the captain's quarters and provided a briefing on the letter they had received from Captain Gint from Governor Matteson. Rose did not take the news well, opting to stay in her cabin for days, rarely coming out.

Violet attempted to tend to her as best she could, bringing her food and attempting to cheer her up. Gadriel, for what he knew how to do, tried singing to her, comforting her, even telling her filthy jokes, which did receive the occasional laugh. Shanks, who apparently didn't know no one could see him either and was running on the same level of denial as Gadriel, expressed ideas to Gadriel to help. Discussing the subject of Shanks with Captain Tamara and Thinker more, they remained undecided, though Thinker remained more convinced.

Gadriel continued to learn more about his affliction and his level of denial, or madness, depending on one's perspective, through discussions with Doctor Cutter and Thinker, who had a layman's understanding of mind medicine. Apparently when Shanks took it upon himself to eat, this was an affectation of Gadriel's madness. Shanks, of course, wasn't eating anything, not sausage rolls, not Lou's fish and chips, not drinking ale. However, this hadn't stopped Gadriel from ordering him helpings of food and drink for likely years. Growing up a hungry child, this made Gadriel feel sick, for which Rod was happy to lay on guilt for fun. "*Think of how many orphans could have made good use of that ale, you heartless brigand.*"

As days went on, the crew was able to have their cow and whiskey feast, though they were unable to catch a shark with its "gourmet guts." They did, however, catch beautiful tuna, of which Cook was pleased to prepare. Rose began venturing out of her cabin and stopped crying, and her guilt stopped getting the better of her every morning. Captain Tamara ordered her to train with the cutlass daily, not always with herself, sometimes with Thinker, sometimes training with a rapier with Violet, sometimes buckle training with Clancy. Gadriel and Shanks were there to cheer her on daily. In fact, many of the fighting crew took this as an opportunity to train and hone their skills in what became afternoon training chimes. After a week's time, Rose had come out of her shell.

With Captain Tamara's quarters so badly damaged, she was without a bunk. During this time, she initially bunked with the crew, who had no problem giving her the respect she deserved and a wide berth. This changed soon after it began, however, when Violet insisted the captain bunk with her in her officer's quarters, though it was not quite necessary. The Midnight had one captain's quarter, four officer's cabins, and two guest quarters. One of the guest quarters was unoccupied, as was an empty officer's quarter, as examples.

On about the seventh day of travel, Gadriel, Shanks, and Thinker made an important discovery that changed Thinker's spiritual understanding of the world as well as his opinion on Shanks and Gadriel's relationship. After Rose and Thinker completed their cutlass lesson of the day, Rose bowed to show gratitude, which Thinker returned out of respect to his student.

"You're getting better every day, my lady," said Thinker.

"Thank you, sir. I enjoy our lessons, especially ones that focus on movement of the body around a space, not specifically sword play only. I do love to dance," said Rose.

Think thought on it a moment, then said, "Now that you mention it, that is where you excel."

Rose beamed, which was quickly diminished when Thinker said with a smile, "Since you're so good at it, however, we should train in other areas instead," to which Rose replied, "Oh, of course."

Thinker said, "I'm only joking; we can go over evasive movements tomorrow." Rose smiled and bowed again, of which Thinker properly returned.

"Thinker, may I spar with you, if you have a moment?" said Gadriel. This caught the attention of several crew about the deck, which suddenly became the attention of several more, as a crew is wont to do.

"Of course, Mr. Gadriel. Care to use wooden practice blades?" asked Thinker.

Gadriel said, "Actually, if we promise not to kill each other dead, I'd like to use the dulled blades so I may be more used to the weight. I haven't fought with a blade in some time."

For a moment, Gadriel was back on the deck of the Sapphire, with the invading man run-through on his sword, Gadriel, inexperienced and screaming, trying to retrieve his sword from the man's abdomen . . . then he was back in the present moment.

At the announcement of using dulled, but real blades, two young crewmates acting as runners ran below decks. Before long, Thinker and Gadriel's training session was being treated like a duel more than it was practice. Thinker was an accomplished swordsman, trainer, and, importantly for the purposes of this practice session, dueler. Gadriel was the first to admit he was none of these things.

Each man took a dulled, practice cutlass. The short, heavy sword felt heavier than Gadriel remembered, but most people thought that after a significant absence, he thought. Stepping back from Thinker, he gave the cutlass a few practice swings. It wasn't until about this point did Gadriel notice the crowd that had been forming, with Rose and Clancy taking prime spots as the starboard rail.

"What do you say, Mr. Gadriel, no striking to injure, strike to touch. First to three touches wins, anything else goes?"

"Well, the way you say 'anything else goes' scares me, but that sounds agreeable to me," answered Gadriel.

"Please do not be concerned. I say that for your benefit, I am here to teach you and I want you to think and be creative," added Thinker with a warm, genuine smile, somehow able to completely block out the crowd that had formed. Thinker was already warmed up from previous training, but gave a few practice swings to insure his joints felt smooth and limber; Gadriel thought this was intimidating all the same.

"Attack when you're ready, sir," said Thinker.

Gadriel readied himself. Thought about the Sapphire. Thought of home. Then began moving toward thinking until a clear and commanding voice broke out over the group of onlookers.

"What in the bloody Mother is happening 'ere?" Captain Tamara came through a parting crowd.

"Nothing in particular, Cap't. Mr. Gadriel and I are simply sparring for training purposes," which prompted Captain Tamara to look over to Gadriel with side-eye, to which Gadriel nodded his head emphatically.

"Oh. Well in that case, carry on, boys," the captain said, continuing her walk through the rough circle that formed, onto the quarterdeck to where she definitely wasn't going to watch the sparring session.

Both men recentered themselves, and again Thinker welcomed Gadriel's first attack. Gadriel held his cutlass at a forty-five degree angle across his body from his dominant right hand. Thinker held his vertically, slightly in front of him on his dominant right side. Gadriel's first strike was not from left to right, which would follow the angle of his blade and match where Thinker was already positioned, but from right to left, quickly changing his stance before striking. Thinker was easily able to avoid this strike by moving to his right; he then slapped Gadriel on the backside with the side of his blade, hard enough to make a popping sound.

Thinker returned to the same stance, which Gadriel copied. Feet shoulder-width apart, slightly staggered, Gadriel's stance was excellent, if not unpracticed. Gadriel nodded to Thinker, welcoming him to attack, which welcomed a smile on Thinker's face and a smooth, graceful advancement. As Thinker got close, instead of striking at the man, Gadriel became overwhelmed and began to back up. Thinker used this opportunity exactly when Gadriel had become off balance to swing over and downward into a thigh slap, again hard enough to provide a crisp slapping pop; the only part of which Gadriel was thankful is that it was not his wounded leg.

Shanks then entered the dueling circle. Knowing now he couldn't be seen by anyone but Gadriel, he figured he'd at least try to use this to his advantage. Both men, copying stances from one another, began advancing on one another for what was likely the last touch-point by Thinker to end the sparring session. Shanks and Gadriel and Thinker knew this was the case. Figuring he could follow a "why not, what else am I going to do, apparently I'm dead" attitude, Shanks took a running start and kicked at Thinker's foot as hard as possible in an effort to trip the man. Though this didn't trip him outright, it did cause his foot to be gently slowed, almost unnoticeable to an observer, but not to Thinker—what he felt was similar to when someone is climbing stairs in the dark and believes they have one stair left and they step to find air because they've already reached the landing. This caused Thinker to lose his footing just enough for Gadriel and his cutlass to get inside Thinker's guard for a point.

Initially Thinker was left confused by what happened, enough that he looked down to see if something had caught his foot; of course there was nothing there. Shanks's eyes were wide; so were Gadriel's. The two men squared off in a similar fashion and approached each other the same way, with Thinker moving toward Gadriel in a business-like fashion. Shanks took a running start from across the circle and attempted to tackle Thinker. Though he could not and for the most part "bounced" off Thinker, Think certainly felt his body physically feel an effect, and although it did not affect his balance enough to distract him from the duel, Thinker struck Gadriel in his hamstrings to win the sparring match. He knew he had questions for Gadriel in private afterward.

Few hands exchanged coin amongst the crew, including Rose handing a coin to Clancy, and they broke up to return to their duties. After bowing and paying proper respects to one another, including Shanks, who bowed to Thinker though he knew he would not be seen, Gadriel was glad to help straighten up the training area.

As they finished up, Thinker said to Gadriel, "I do believe that you, Shanks, and I have some matters to discuss."

Gadriel thought it peculiar that Shanks was addressed directly by someone other than himself, but it made him very happy for his friend. "Please meet me at the quarterdeck in a quarter chime?" Gadriel nodded and left the area to get himself cleaned up. Thinker then approached the captain to share what he believed he knew.

Soon after, Captain Tamara, Gadriel, Rose, Shanks, Thinker, Clancy, Violet, and even Doctor Cutter were cozily huddled in Captain Tamara's cabin. Inside the captain's quarters, her bunk, most of her wardrobe, some of her weapons, and half of her personal effects had been destroyed by the chase shot from the NHS Retribution. What managed to survive, however, was her desk and many chairs, one full-pressed captain's uniform that had since been cleaned by Violet, one weapons trunk, and many smuggling spaces about the cabin, many of which were filled with expensive and/or priceless whiskeys.

Doctor Cutter was the first to chime in, "I don't mean to be rude kids, Cap't, but I have injured men in my infirmary I must attend. May we get this started?"

"Of course," said Thinker.

Thinker first explained what he felt during his duel with Gadriel, which caused Clancy to laugh and tease him good-naturedly.

"OH that's rich—you sassin' the boys every day and you trip one time and now a ghost did it. Hah hah hah."

"Listen here, biggin', if you keep listening, I can keep explaining," said Thinker testily, as being interrupted was one of life's tortures for him.

"It was not only the one time. Gadriel has shared with me that Shanks attempted to interfere with the sparring match twice, and I felt two significant times where I was physically affected by what I now believe are fractions of force applied by Shanks's will as a spirit or ghost or however we're classifying his existence with Mr. Gadriel." Thinker then added, "This is in addition to what we saw the night we escaped Atmos."

"Thinker, we don't know what we saw, and we agreed to drop it," said Captain Tamara, apparently tired of discussing it, but no one but her and Think could necessarily know how often they had ever discussed the subject, if at all.

Thinker explained that on that night, which had only been about eight days before when Rose was fighting Guard Captain Oath and he had her basically pinned to the floor, Rose did an amazing job taking him down with her hideaway knife.

"Thank you, sir," Rose added, mid-story.

"You're welcome, madam," said Think. He continued, "At about the time Rose was on the ground with Oath on top of her, Captain Tamara and I had finished dispatching or incapacitating the remaining house guards nearer the guard house within the main floor."

"Yes, what's your point?" said an impatient Clancy.

"His point is," said Captain Tamara, "When you've been on ships as long as we have, been out at sea or have made continental ocean trips like we have, there are too many phenomena the ocean has to offer for people on land to understand. So what a good sailor does is appreciate what they've seen, but doesn't dwell on it, because you aren't going to get good out of it, and typically you'll be laughed at by sane people. But this is our mark to bear."

"We saw Shanks," said Thinker.

Captain Tamara pinched the bridge of her nose and said, "You don't know that," to which Thinker said, "Cap't, with all due respect, he meets every descriptor Mr. Gadriel has given us. Gadriel, Rose, Clancy, Doc? Guard Captain Oath was preparing to execute Rose the other night when he lifted his gladius. Rose did the right thing and grabbed for her knife, but didn't get it out quick enough to stop that hammer from falling, so to speak. His blade was on its way down toward her neck. We watched his arms stop and jerk. We watched Captain Oath's rage start to die due to his confusion before he was rightfully put down like the dog he was. And more importantly, we saw *something* cause Guard Captain Oath's pause. And I believe it was a kind of spectral form of a young man, perhaps on both planes with Mother—"

"We had both just killed men; we could have just imagined seeing something," said Captain Tamara, both tired and annoyed.

Rose then interjected. "Excuse me. But. I saw something too, and it might help us put this confusion or debate to rest."

"Go on, deary," said Captain Tamara.

"Well," Rose continued, "seeing as how I haven't told anyone what I saw, assuming I imagined it too, if I tell Dr. Cutter what it was, who out of all of us wasn't there at all . . . then you all mention what you saw specifically . . . well, then, if there are matching details, wouldn't it prove that Shanks is here with us? Or at least was there with us that night?"

Thinker and Captain Tamara paused and looked at each other for a silent moment. Gadriel and Rose were beginning to dislike their ability to communicate so much information without saying a word, but Clancy was already accustomed to it. Noticing their annoyance, he cheerfully chimed in, "Oh don't worry, you get used to it, then it's like the wind blowin' or water bein' wet," he said.

"I can think of many dirty additions, Rod, knock it off," Gadriel said to no one.

After a tock or two, Captain Tamara announced to the group, "Okay, then, deary. Go ahead and tell Doc what you saw. Doc, we don't want any confusion 'ere, so we're going to 'ave you write it down, eh? Then we will describe what we saw in detail, and if there's a match, we'll be havin' a different conversation."

Doctor Cutter said, "That sounds like an agreeable solution. I'll go grab paper, one moment."

A short time later, back in the captain's quarters, Doctor Cutter finished folding a piece of parchment paper in half and set it on Captain Tamara's desk. Tamara and Thinker then went on to describe what appeared to be the spectral or faint form of a young man of about twenty or so years of age. He was wearing a white blouse, dark trousers, boots, had two daggers in his belt of a throwing caliber, and his fingerless gloved hands were wrapped around Captain Oath's, delaying the fall of his blade to finish Rose's execution before she could rightly defend herself. Doctor Cutter gave Rose, then the room, a most peculiar look.

Captain Tamara said, "Note please," to the room, to which Clancy reached across the large desk and slid the folded note over to her. Upon opening it she read aloud, "Half gloves . . . no finger gloves around guard's wrists . . . saved me." Captain Tamara then said. "Well . . . shit, I guess that's that, then."

Rose, Gadriel, and the men continued to train; the Midnight continued hard toward Lulin. With favorable winds, they made it to the Port Town of Lulin in about two weeks. However, they didn't think it was a great idea to just drive up and take a berth acting like nothing was amiss. Exactly when they arrived may have been nearly a week faster than how they traveled to New Haven, but Lulin didn't need to know that. No, the Midnight made it in about two weeks, and now it had dropped its remaining starboard anchor to formulate a plan that considered all of Governor Matteson's threats. And planning for threats, especially those that had already been made, was what Captain Tamara and her crew did best.

13

Julien

THE Midnight anchored off Lulin's coast several leagues to the south. In an effort to maintain a low profile, Captain Tamara assembled a team consisting of Thinker, Clancy and six of his men, Rose, Gadriel and Shanks, and Captain Tamara herself. The ship was left in the hands of Helmsman and Violet, with orders to take the Midnight into Port Lulin at speed should they not return in two days.

Captain Tamara used the Midnight's tender boats to transport this shore party to land in pieces. Once reassembled, they marched to the outskirts of Lulin's south-most district, mainly filled with work-houses, but what also was not far away was The Thirsty Goat. The Thirsty Goat and Lou's hospitality would be their first official stop in Lulin. While the others waited outside of the town limits on the opposite side of a canal, Gadriel and Shanks approached The Thirsty Goat like they had several times before, again using a rear entrance, though this time they wore dry clothes.

Using their newfound knowledge to their advantage, Shanks scouted ahead and entered the establishment first; though being able to talk and communicate was a challenge, they had been doing okay enough for the last five years. Shanks returned a short time later. Having been able to observe the main floor and shared hallways of the tavern, Gadriel asked if the coast was clear. Shanks shrugged and then shook his head after pantomiming several weapons. Gadriel understood his meaning to say it wasn't full of weapons inside, so no guards, and asked, "Did you see Lou anywhere in there?" to which Shanks nodded excitedly.

In the time leading up to their arrival to Lulin, Gadriel and Thinker didn't just train in swords, they also conducted research on Gadriel's relationship with Roderick and the stone, as well as how Shanks interacted with the world and the extent in which he could affect it and communicate with Gadriel. Though their research, one example they learned was that Shanks was some sort of spirit, but not unto himself. He could not float around like some wraith from storybooks or run through closed doors like an apparition from children's ghost stories. Shanks was very real to himself and to Gadriel, and "lived" that way. Thinker's theory was that this was contributing to how Shanks could continue to nominally affect the physical world; he was still, in a way, a part of it in his soul.

Gadriel and Shanks calmly entered The Thirsty Goat from the rear entrance. While attracting a minimal amount of attention to himself, as much as one could dressed like a pirate sailor ready for battle, Gadriel sought out his friend for hire, Lou. He soon found her as she exited the kitchen while he waited by the hearth to observe the room.

"Oh, lookie here. You just keep gettin' more handsome, my boy. Though you smell like you've been on a ship. Words been out you and your friend be wanted by the Governor."

"My lady, always a pleasure."

"My lady he says," Lou said with a musical chuckle, more to herself than to anyone else.

"Lou, the Governor is doing some pretty bad things to good people. I know it isn't your fight—"

"I can't get involved, handsome," Lou interrupted.

Gadriel pushed on. "My group and I just need a place to—"

Lou cut Gadriel off again. "I'm sorry, love. I can't be gettin' involved and riskin' everything I've worked my life for. Just last month I barely helped you, and it almost lost me everything. I'd do it again, handsome. But not if it be involving the Governor."

Gadriel knew he was asking too much, and he still appreciated Lou. He apologized for having asked or even coming there, sliding her some coin, then asked, "I understand completely, and I'm sorry, Lou. Can you suggest somewhere we can go?"

"Yes I can, love. You just better not be sayin' anything, to anyone, abouts' where you be hearing it from, y'hear?" Lou said nervously but directly and strongly while looking Gadriel in the eye. To which Gadriel returned her sincere gaze and said, "Of course, ma'am. Where do we go?"

About a chime later, Captain Tamara, Thinker, Rose, and Clancy and his men were filing into an abandoned workhouse in the fifth district of town, closer than The Thirsty Goat to The Wooden Leg, Bake Shop, and Town Center.

"Pretty boy 'ere must be a bloody terror of a negotiator because this place is perfect."

Gadriel responded with, "Thank you, Captain. But this was more groveling. Lou wanted little to do with us at The Thirsty Goat, nor would The Wooden Leg if the inn-keep recognized me and associated me with the non-fire-fire that Rose started."

Rose interjected, "Oh like they'd still be upset over a fire not happening at such a fine establishment."

The captain arched a brow. It was noticeable to most of their group now that Rose was back in Lulin, on her home turf, much of her confidence and light arrogance had returned. Gadriel and Shanks missed it and appreciated it; Gadriel had no idea what Thinker or the captain thought of it, but he imagined they liked it too, even if they couldn't express such things in front of their men.

Rose then asked the group, "So, what's next? We get my brother?"

The captain was quick to point out, "No, we should speak with your brother, but he should continue running the bake shop or tending to whatever he's been doing for these last weeks you've been gone. Anything else will alert the Governor that we're here, and Thorny, what is the biggest advantage to have in an engagement?"

Rose thought hard. "Ummm . . . initiative?"

"Very good, initiative annnd?"

"I don't remember."

The captain was defeated, then said ,"*Numbers,* Thorny—if you have the initiative and the numbers, you've usually won." Rose nodded in a way that chastised herself from missing answers on a test that were important to her.

The abandoned workhouse was used to manufacture some form of goods, but all the equipment had been removed. There was a hard foundation covered in garbage, filth, and oil stains surrounding where the equipment had been. There was also a second floor that contained an office overlooking the main floor as well as a scaffolded walkway so that someone in charge could observe what were likely children doing the work whenever they pleased.

"Mad Gad here and I will go speak to Julien. Rose, too hot for you right now, Think and Clancy stand out. My lovelies over there, well, you've all got one purpose, and it ain't walkin' about having pleasant chats with bake shops. Xoxo, dearies." All nodded. "Gad, are you ready, then?"

Gadriel confirmed, "Ready as I'll ever be, Cap't. Rose, anything special you'd like for us to relay?"

Rose became emotional, attempting to hold back much stronger floods, and said, "Please tell him I'm sorry." Before Gadriel had a chance to respond, the captain stepped in and looked Rose in the face.

"Listen here, Thorny—This is something you need to get over or lock up right now. I'm going to tell your brother that you're here to fix the mess the Governor has created because that's what happened. *You* didn't even take the stone. Gad did, and I did—doesn't matter what your designs were. You're a terrible thief, deary, and you didn't choose for any of this to happen, let alone have your dear old daddy drug into a conflict. The Governor is a bastard," said the captain.

Thinker said quickly, "Right proper bastard."

Clancy added, "Bit of a bellend."

Gadriel added, "I think he's a cock. Shanks held up the crux." Rose began to smile. "Wait!" said Gadriel, then finished, "Rod says '*Doddle that guy,*'" which was met with chuckles by most.

One chime later, about midday, the captain and Gadriel were on foot heading towards the Bake Shop. The Captain had surprised Gadriel by changing her appearance so drastically, not just by changing, but her ability to do so. The captain now wore her hair down, not in her usual braids, and not tight up in knots for difficult grabbing in combat. Her beautiful dark brown hair—*was it styled?* Gadriel thought. Instead of her black blouse and weapons belt, she wore a crisp pressed antique-white blouse that was in contrast with her deep olive, sun-kissed skin—no captain's cap, no captain's jacket, though she did wear silks of midnight blue. She walked with the same level of confidence, her air of command surrounded her, and her swagger still raised eyebrows as much as the corners of mouths, which is how Gadriel knew it didn't come from swords, or pistols, or fine caps, or captains' livery; it was pure Tamara.

"You look amazing!" Gadriel told the captain privately as a genuine compliment.

"Well, thank you, boyo. But try not to become attached. I look absurd. And I only look like this now because I don't want to end up in the Governor's private dungeon."

Gadriel, for his part, still looked much like plain old Gadriel, just somewhat like a smuggler of sorts. He wore his one white, laundered shirt, but dark brown britches with brown leather boots. He opted to leave weapons behind at the abandoned workhouse as well, but did carry his flute with him mostly concealed in his boot, and Rod's stone in his pocket. Gadriel's hair had grown quite a bit over the last month on the Midnight. Fortunately, Violet gave him a fresh cut before they arrived at Lulin, so chin-length chestnut hair it was again. In fact, Violet styled everyone on the shore party, including their fighting men, so that they may blend in with townspeople if the situation called for it. Captain Tamara wanted to take no chances on this trip.

Tamara and Gadriel opted to take a longer route avoiding the town center and noble district for now. Being home to the Governor's mansion, it would have the most guard patrols and also the most people who would be aware of what Gadriel looked like and why guards would want to speak with him; this was as opposed to lower districts, filled with people too preoccupied with surviving to know or care.

About a chime later, Tamara and Gadriel were across the street from the Bake Shop waiting while Shanks went inside to look. When Shanks came back and started speaking with Gadriel, Tamara waited impatiently, still having a hard time accepting the reality she knew to be true that her friend, or at least one of her crew, had a ghost in his head that could talk to him and walk around. Not to mention, he was also connected with his mind to a rock that had another spirit inside it, but somehow that was easier for Tamara to believe.

"Well?" asked Tamara. "Well, he said the sausage rolls looked heavenly—one moment."

"Oy. Shanks. Tighten up," Tamara said to where she thought he was, which turned out to be directly at his face. Gadriel then said, "Whoa, Shanks thinks you're spooky and said there were two guards waiting in the room directly behind the back counter; they'll be listening. At least I think? Yes, Shanks just confirmed this is the case."

"Okay then, I have an idea. Let us find the nearest butcher," said the captain.

A quarter chime later, right next to the town center and noble district, Gadriel and Tamara had located what appeared to be the nearest butcher in relation to the bake shop, Dresden's Butcher.

Inside, Tamara introduced herself. "Hello, I'm Tam-abitha."

"Nice to meet you, probably not actually Tamabitha. Name's Dresden. What can I do ya' for?"

This butcher appeared to be wise from a lifetime of experience. Tamara liked him. "Please just call me Tabitha for short. My friend and I were interested if you sold whole butchered sows and for how much, and if you prepared and made your own sausage?" asked Tamara.

"No problem, Tabitha, yes to all in fact. Let me get you a price list."

Tamara gave Dresden a large smile and said, "Excellent, thank you, sir. And may I have a small piece of paper from you, please?"

"Of course, ma'am." Gadriel stood there pleasantly, unaware of what was happening entirely.

Tamara and Gadriel were then on their way back to the Bake Shop, and Gadriel needed to know, "What was that all about?" and Tamara explained. "Shanks confirmed that there are watchers, guardsman inside the Bake Shop in a position to hear everything happening at the counter. We need to get Julien out of there to speak to him privately, yet he's the only one working the shop. We can't exactly wait for him to leave, nor can we follow him home without being observed. And I have no idea what supplies he has baking-wise. However, I know meat is perishable, and you will just not shut up about these sausage rolls. We can get him to the butcher shop to discuss an order he just purchased, where we'll wait for him."

Gadriel responded, "Ohhh, well what about the full pig?"

"Well, we live through this? I'd like to get a full pig for the boys. Dresden's shop looked clean."

"Why did I ever think it would be something different?"

"Beats me, boyo," Tamara said with a smile.

A few tocks later, Tamara and Gadriel entered the Bake Shop like any other customers. Julien recognized Gadriel and his eyes widened. Gadriel quickly made a "hush" motion with a finger over his lips, to which Julien nodded. Captain Tamara then handed Julien the note.

"We know about the watchers. Get to Dresden Butcher, say you have a sausage order because you do. We'll talk." Julien nodded again.

"Two sausage rolls, please!" Tamara said sweetly. Julien wrapped these up and handed them to Tamara and Gadriel over the counter and said with the most nonchalance he could muster, "Thanks for coming in, we hope to see you again soon."

Something about Julien's behavior seemed to spook one of the guards, as he opted to follow Tamara and Gadriel. Shanks and Rod spotted the tail immediately and informed Gadriel, who then shared this information with Tamara, who already knew. Now they could not go to Dresden's Butcher and would not be going back to the warehouse while being followed, either. Figuring this guard was not a soldier specializing in espionage, Tamara decided to lose the tail in a fun way: by turning around and letting him panic and burn himself. He either knew who they were or he didn't.

"You know what, love!" she said to Gadriel.

"What's that, darling?" he said without missing a beat.

"This sausage roll is so good, I just must have another."

"Aw, well, lovely wants, lovely gets."

Rod: "*barf.*"

Both then turned on a heel back toward the Bake Shop to find a single Governor's guard following too close, in uniform, with wider eyes and a guilty expression of a child caught stealing sweets. The guard simply fled the area. Tamara simply laughed.

Captain Tamara and Gadriel were able to then go to Dresden's Butcher after taking a slightly longer route and wait for Julien. Gadriel and Tamara did not have to wait too long. Inside Dresden's Butcher, when Julien arrived, he looked around the shop, where he'd been many times before, then made a straight line for Gadriel and wrapped him in a hug, saying, "Gadriel, I'm so glad you're okay. Where's Rose??"

Butcher Dresden, for his part, realizing he didn't want to observe such a conversation, quickly shuffled into the back of his shop.

"Rose is fine, deary," said Tamara. "Also hello, I don't believe we've met officially, I'm Captain Tamara of the merchant ship Midnight."

"Hello, Captain. Pleased to meet you. Rose has mentioned you before; I'm Julien, Rose's brother, and it appears she's in some serious trouble this time," Julien said, with added coolness that was not present for his greeting toward Gadriel.

"That she is, boyo," answered Tamara.

Gadriel then joined the conversation by adding, "Julien, we need to know what you know up to this point. We just got back to Lulin and may be behind on details."

Julien nodded, then added, "Sure, yes. By now, everyone in town is aware that the Governor had a priceless green gemstone in his office and someone took it. The Governor personally came to our home, spoke to me and my father, demanding we give him the stone. But Gad, I don't have—why? Where would I have it, how would I get it? I bake all morning then sell all day. This man wouldn't listen to anything."

"We get that, sir, please go on," said Tamara.

Julien, all but ignoring Tamara, continued, "Well, after it felt like the Governor was comfortable with the information I gave, that we didn't have the stone, after he had his men slap me around a bit, he demanded to know where Rose was. Well, that I didn't know either, and that just enraged him all over again. He then showed me this note Rose had apparently written that he told me he intercepted from a runner boy. Something about how she'd be home soon, she couldn't resolve the adventure that night? Aw, Heavens Below. It doesn't matter, he didn't believe me. He took our father and I haven't seen him since! That was almost three weeks ago. I've tried speaking and appealing to the Governor, and there's no helping it. I don't even know where he is."

Gadriel nodded, then said, "Well, let us share with you what we know."

After a few tocks, Gadriel was aware of the contents of the Governor's letter to Captain Tamara, but not about Rose's involvement in the stone theft, or New Haven.

"So he has him in-in-in a stocks dungeon?! In his house?!" exclaimed Julien.

Captain Tamara then said, "Now calm down, boyo, you're becoming awfully loud for such a nice little place; those guards aren't far."

"No I will NOT calm down!" he shouted. "Julien, I know this is hard, but we have t—"

"What would you know about how hard it is?? Breezing in and out of places. No, now I know where my father is, I'm putting an end to this right Mother damn now," said Julien.

"Now wait just a minute, deary," said Captain Tamara. Casually pressing her back to the butcher's block counter, she continued, "I hate to say it, but you're not doing anything of the sort as it puts a lot of people at risk—my people—we're in this together, and we must be smart about it."

"Oh, great, now I get to worry about a smuggler and her pirates," accused Julien. "You're probably the reason Rose is in this mess."

"Bad form, Julien," said Gadriel, pitifully.

"To below with both of you," said Julien before storming out of Dresden's Butcher, or he would have, if Captain Tamara had not clubbed him in the back of his head, as gently as possible, with the wide and flat edge of a butchers' hammer she retrieved from the counter moments before. Gadriel sensed this was coming, but it still came as a surprise to Shanks and Rod. For their part, Shanks ran over to the windows to act as lookout, and Rod simply exclaimed, *"Aw shit, that was great, do it again!!"* like a gleeful child.

Gadriel caught Julien before he landed on the ground. Captain Tamara returned the hammer to the counter and was quick to lift Julien's feet to expedite moving his unconscious form. As they moved Julien into the back of his shop, Dresden, the proprietor initially protested, this was until the captain gave him a significant amount of coin, upon which Dresden gave them access to his cellar storage area, which could be locked. Julien was restrained and gagged, placed in the cellar, and the cellar door locked. This was only temporary until they could calm him down or figure out how to get him onto the Midnight, or achieve their goals and get her men back onto the Midnight, Tamara assured Gadriel, who nodded.

Tamara and Gadriel left Dresden's Butcher, thanking him one last time, a little over a quarter chime after having entered. Tamara asked for five whole chickens on a stake before leaving, which caused Gadriel no small amount of confusion.

"What's more suspicious deary, a young vibrant couple such as ourselves entering a butcher shop for half a chime or so, then coming out with meat? Or spending half a chime or so in here then coming out with nothing?"

"I see your point."

"Besides, did you want to eat tonight?"

Rod: *"Pfft, 'vibrant and young,' right."*

Gadriel and Tamara soon found themselves back at the workhouse with the rest of the shore party. Clancy and his men had already begun building a small fire to roast the chickens after all excitedly thanking their captain for yet another tasty meal. "A good crew runs on its stomach," she always said.

A chime later, Captain Tamara was picking at a piece of chicken and a coal-fired potato expertly prepared by Clancy. Thinker and Clancy knew their captain didn't eat much before a fight, so she must have sensed one coming; they all did in fact. But they wanted to make sure she ate something.

"Cap't, is the food . . . wrong, Cap't?" asked Clancy, innocently.

"Oh, nooo deary, food is a delight. Just lost in thought," Captain Tamara responded absentmindedly, deep in thought, but resumed eating. Clancy turned with a big satisfied smile on his face. With his back turned to her, Tamara grinned as well.

Every day Gadriel spent with this goofy crew of misfits he realized they were more and more like a family that worked well together. They weren't even very dysfunctional like most families he'd read or heard about. Gadriel's family was like this growing up at the brothel. Gadriel loved his family of forgotten misfits sticking together to support one another in a world that didn't care about them. The crew of the Midnight were doing the same thing—knowing, supporting, and caring for one another deeply, just pretending they didn't.

After nightfall, Captain Tamara and Thinker thought it best to attempt to retrieve Julien from Dresden's Butcher. He had likely calmed and likely knew the Governor's mansion better than anyone in their crew, having just been inside it. Also, after tonight, they had one day left before the Midnight made a grand entrance into the harbor the morning that followed. They needed to get a move on and formulate a plan.

Gadriel and Rose stayed at the warehouse to watch their equipment while Clancy and his men, Thinker, and Captain Tamara, who had all changed their clothing into the blacks they wore on the Midnight, moved quietly through the shadows of Lulin, deftly avoiding guard patrols, even traversing two rooftops over a well-lit busy street crossing to save time. Tamara and Thinker were soon entering Dresden's Butcher where they met Dresden, who silently walked them to the cellar where Julien was still . . . anger was the likely emotion.

Dresden unlocked the cellar and Thinker and Captain Tamara descended the staircase. There was plenty of light from the back of Dresden's shop to illuminate their faces; Julien stopped fighting his restraints and gag at their sight. When Thinker removed his gag, he asked calmly, "Now you can't yell, we're helping you and your sister. If you endanger my men by being petulant, however, I will silence you."

Julien nodded and then said not in a whisper, "I don't want your help. My sister—we are in this mess because of you."

Thinker patiently waited for Julien to finish, then responded, "Now, that isn't true, and I believe you know that, being an educated man. Now we must leave this place; can you be trusted without restraints, sir? We're taking you someplace safe." Julien nodded indignantly.

Julien's hands were left tied in front of him with his apron laid over them should they be stopped. All other ties were removed, however. Captain Tamara thanked Dresden again for his courtesy, and out the backdoor and into an alley her crew moved, just as silently as they arrived, maintaining the same pace on their way back to the warehouse, despite having a "civilian," as the good captain would say, moving with them. As they quietly moved between the side of a building, likely a storage warehouse, and a small dune of seagrass being closer to the docks, they spotted a guard patrol of three men.

They had begun moving down this wall in darkness, but the moon had since come out behind the clouds, and they were temporarily exposed. The quick and likeminded decision was made to move into the seagrass and lay down to wait patiently for the patrol to round the corner of the building, pass them entirely, and for the crew to be on their way. The crew began to wait patiently and silently for the patrol to reach the corner of the building; however, Julien apparently had a different plan.

Julien began to shout, "Over here!" but made it as far as the "Ov—" before Thinker struck him in the throat, incredibly hard as to immediately silence him, and if breathing came difficult, that was a bonus. Unfortunately this attracted enough of the guards' attention that they began moving toward their direction instead of angling to round the corner of the building like it appeared they would have. So now it was time to improvise.

Three of Clancy's men moved deeper into the seagrass to wait. Clancy and his remaining three men began hustling in the same direction the guard patrol moved, just around the building and starting from the other side. The guards were halfway to the group from the bisecting side of the building now. Thinker and Tamara, for their part, hugged the corner of the building for a moment, waiting for the guards to get closer. As one of Clancy's men let out a soft sound, Captain Tamara stepped out from behind the corner of the building and said, "Here . . . Over here. I love men in uniform," then with a sultry sway walked back behind the cover of the building.

One guard said to the others, "Uh, you two wait here, I'll go take a look at this one," and they were misguided enough to do so.

The first guard tried to be cautious, but was too eager to follow the Captain around the corner. As he did, Thinker grabbed him, pulling him to the ground where he wrapped him in a hold around his neck and choked him until he no longer moved. The whole incident took less than forty ticks. After a few moments more, one of the guards sheepishly asked the night air "Sergeant? Sir?" which only prompted Tamara to walk from behind cover of the building once more to simply say, "He'll be right there, boys," then returned behind the corner with a nice sway with her hips as she walked.

"Oh I don't think so," said the second guard as he began to march forward.

Then he hit the ground, then the third guard hit the ground as Clancy's men clubbed them unconscious, running up on them quietly from behind. Clancy and company then dragged the two behind the building to join their crew. They now had three unconscious guards who could come-to at any moment, a gagging Julien, who would likely pass out and/or throw up from the physical condition he brought upon himself, and no realistic way to keep them all prisoner.

"I've got it," Captain Tamara said after a moment's pause. "Who here has any spirits on them?" No one answered.

"Oh c'mon, you're not in trouble, at least two of you beasts have flasks, give them up."

One of them produced a flask from their pack filled with a strong spirit likely distilled on the ship somewhere.

"Okay strip the guards," she said, which her men did, careful to collect all the clothing. Captain Tamara then opened the flask and upended it, pouring it all over the men and their faces. "Gag the young man, let's move."

They were soon at the warehouse, sitting around a fire, unhappily looking at Julien, who was also near the fire. He just could not move due to his restraints and could not talk due to his two uncomfortable gags. Gadriel and Rose had been briefed. Rose initially protested Julien's treatment until she was offered the same thing.

"Listen here, Thorny. There's only one thing dear Julien planned to do. He was going to turn us all into the guards in hopes that would be the end of this whole thing, and his inexperience shows." Rose stood there silently, knowing she was right.

"My men and I don't have to be here. We could have dropped you off and left. We're here because completely innocent people became involved, and that doesn't sit right on my conscience, helping Julien, now barely, and helping your father. So if you're going to speak with Julien, talk some sense into him, because I'll choose my crew over him every time." Rose nodded.

Back over at the fire, the Midnight's crew gave Rose and Julien some space. Gadriel also got up with a nod and walked over to Thinker and Captain Tamara to give them some privacy.

"Julien, I'm going to remove your gags, okay, but you can't yell or draw attention to this place." Julien nodded, and Rose did so.

"Julien, you don't deserve to be here or any part of this, but these people are only helping us when they don't have to."

"Sister, these people are all the Governor wants; they stole his stupid stone."

"So did I, Julien, we all did in our own way—it is why they're helping."

"Helping? If not to return the stone for father, how could they be helping? I'm going to turn them in, first chance, just not in a way that will get me killed. You should do the same."

Fifty steps away Gadriel, Thinker, and Captain Tamara stood there patiently, and speaking quietly. Gadriel then added, "Annnd, yeah, he's not going to come around. He just told her that he's going to turn us in as soon as he can and is urging her to also turn us in. So much for that angle."

"Oh Heavens Below," cursed the captain. She continued, "Well, better that we know now. All right, Think, you gag him, and we keep a man on him until we're headed toward home."

"Yes, Cap't," Thinker said.

Thinker and Gadriel politely waited until the end of Rose and Julien's conversation, which consisted mainly of an explanation of the night their father was taken, which did not differ greatly from the Governor's letter. As they arrived at the fire, Gadriel bent down and picked up his jacket, then removed the stone from its pocket, transferring it to his pants pocket. He did so in plain view of Rose so she could know they knew Julien's intentions. This way it didn't come as a shock when Thinker asked Julien if he was thirsty or hungry, to which Julien scornfully said no. Thinker then said, "Well okay, then," and reapplied both gags.

In a word: Ornery. That's how Julien the prisoner could be described. While Captain Tamara and her crew were awaiting midday, Julien fought them at every turn, attempted to escape when allowed to relieve himself, and even tried shouting once during a water break until the back of his neck was squeezed by Clancy. Thinker pointed out how much more peaceful and easier it would be for them if he were allowed to . . . dispatch Julien. They could then concentrate on saving Rose's father. Think was disappointed when Captain Tamara forbade this path, much to Rose's relief and Rod's dismay.

As the clock tower in the center of town struck twelve chimes, Captain Tamara, Thinker, and Clancy decided it was time to move forward with their plan.

"Danny, right?" asked the captain to one of Clancy's men.

"Yes, Cap't," said Danny, standing at a fine attention.

"Okay, Danny, you have an important job for your crew today," she said.

"Yes, Cap't," Danny said, showing high resolve in his tired face.

"Danny, we're all going to leave here shortly, but you need to stay behind with young angry Julien here."

"Yes, Cap't."

"Then after nightfall that can hide you, whether we're back or not, I need you to shoulder young ungrateful Julien back to the docks where Midnight is set to arrive at daybreak. Got it?"

"Yes Cap't. Wait for nightfall, take the runt back to the docks, stay hidden, board the Midnight."

"Excellent, deary!" the captain beamed. Not unlike Clancy, Danny's chest swelled with a little pride.

The captain selected Danny on purpose for being, in Clancy's words, the most gentle and patient out of his men. For what was to come, the captain thought, it was best she left all of her most gentle men behind and brought only her hardest forward. As far as Julien was concerned, the captain really, really hoped he didn't try anything too rash. Danny may have been the most gentle and patient, but he was the most gentle and patient out of Clancy's men. He was still someone Julien shouldn't test too hard.

14

The Governor

The Governor's Mansion was situated on the edge of the town center, nearly in the very middle of this edge. Once acting as a symbolic bridge between the noble houses and the merchant district, the mansion now felt more like the crest of an ominous wave ready to crash over people and historical merchant houses alike. The mansion sat two stories tall, with ornate white stone carvings marking its lines, along with large white stone pillars across its front. There was a large bay window in the top right of the building that always seemed lit, and it was common knowledge that this was the Governor's office.

The Governor's office window overlooked the town center, and from it one could see many noble houses as well as most of the first (high-end) merchant district. It was long chimes looking through this window did the Governor spend his time thinking through his problems, as well as many meetings spent looking through the window to intimidate his guests—much like he was right then.

The Governor was a powerfully built man. At least four and a half steps tall, he was as tall as Clancy, and rumor had it he was as sharp as Thinker. His prematurely white hair betrayed his young age, but his square, clean-shaven jaw did not. Though the Governor was apparently obsessed with what some may consider a stone ornament, he did not prefer affectations and overly fashionable or noble clothing, preferring high-end merchant clothes. He still wore working man's boots and working man's gloves, and he prided himself on a working man's handshake.

But it wasn't a working man's handshake. Like so many other small men in large bodies, the Governor's version of a strong handshake was to physically dominate another—to squeeze as almost to injure if the other did not submit to him and to laugh as if it were in jest when the pain was over, using his massive size he came by naturally, like many other things he came by naturally and did not gain through hard work.

The Governor wore a fine light-gray coat, white blouse, and brown trousers with black boots this day. He did indeed wear a working man's boots and a working man's gloves, but it was for practical reasons like the one sitting in his office flanked by two of his guard captains.

The inn-keep of The Wooden Leg sat there, shaking, not entirely sure why he had been collected and brought to this place so far from his home. He barely knew of the Governor and was content in his little corner of Lulin. He barely understood the Governor when he demanded answers.

"Tell me. Where is the man called Gadriel, Inn-keep?" asked the Governor, calmly, arms folded behind his back, back to the room, staring out his great window.

"I . . . I don't be knowin' a Gadriel m'lord."

If one listened carefully enough, like the guard captains, you could hear the Governor's leather gloves creak as they tightened in anger; this made them smile. The Governor slowly turned around and slowly walked over to the man in measured steps. This level of calm with the air of unease and frightening energy in the room terrified the poor inn-keep.

The Governor stood in front of the man, squatted down to eye level, somehow making the man appear even smaller, and said, "I know the man called Gadriel stayed at your establishment for days, he even played his instrument there for money. Where. Did. He. Go?" The Governor waited impatiently.

The innkeeper started to say "I . . . I . . . don't—"

At that the Governor stood up, smoothly picking up the inn-keep by his clothing like he were no heavier than a small child. Like you should not do to a child, or anyone, the Governor then slapped the man down onto the floor, where he bounced once and groaned.

"Captain Dushe," said the Governor, "Yes, sir," said Captain Dush, no longer laughing, standing next to another captain, stifling more laughter.

"Take this man to the cells. Let him think on remembering where this Gadriel man is for the night. Perhaps we'll talk more tomorrow."

"Yes, sir."

"That'll be all for now, Captain Dushe."

"Sir?"

"Yes, Captain."

"It's just Dush."

"Oh, I see. Thank you Dush."

After a quick elbow to the side, Captain Dush and his partner were carrying the inn-keep out of the office, and the Governor returned to his window to observe the midday town center.

While the Governor observed his subjects, he noticed a thinner but solid-looking man of middling height being escorted by three of the Lulin town guards moving across the city square toward the Governor's mansion. As the four men came closer, the Governor could see the man was in restraints and matched Gadriel's description the Governor obtained from his "interviews" over the last several weeks.

"Guards!" the Governor shouted. In moments, a sergeant of the Governor's house guard was in his office. "I want those men brought up here immediately; go out and meet them, extend all courtesy."

"Yes, sir," snapped the sergeant.

While the house guards were suddenly aflutter and preoccupied with the front of the mansion, Captain Tamara had just finished handing a healthy amount of coin to none other than Lara near the servants' entrance to the mansion. Lara, who obtained her position back due in part to no small amount of groveling, still had mouths to feed and a home to maintain. Rose and Captain Tamara were given servants' dresses and were both quickly changing in a supply closet behind the kitchen. From here, they planned on hopefully volunteering to serve prisoners their meals for fun and liberating reasons.

Gadriel approached the mansion at the front of their formation, house guards quickly approaching them. Clancy from behind him, wearing one of the re-appropriated Lulin town guard uniforms, said in a low voice, "Don't be worryin,' Mr. Gadriel. We're right behind you," to which Gadriel passed the barest of nods. It was at this point house guards reached the main wrought iron gate, spiked, with occasional baroque columns of intricate design. For a moment, Gadriel thought the gate was beautiful, till he thought about never crossing it again, never leaving again. He shook this off to concentrate on the task at hand.

"Good morrow, men. I am Sergeant Vow of the Governor's house guard. Who might you be, and who might this be?" he said politely and well within his prerogative.

"Nice to meet you, Sergeant. I am Sergeant Shamus, and I oversee these two lugs. We have here for the Governor a wanted man. A Gadriel the bard?" said Clancy.

"Excellent!" said Vow. "The Governor will be pleased! Please come with us," he added.

Captain Tamara and Rose began their work in the kitchen, volunteering for bread making, of which Rose was naturally in her element, and

Tamara was far from her own. Tamara kept trying to follow Rose's lead, which ended horribly. What happened most often is Rose worked twice as fast to fix Tamara's work to avoid suspicion coming from the both of them. Though Tamara was genuinely trying to bake and make breads, she was also paying close attention to the number of house guards, staff, and even servants she could count—taking notice of their equipment, how they carried themselves, all the while acknowledging the very real possibility that in a few short hours she may have to harm any of these people to save her people or herself. She looked at Rose and wondered if those thoughts crossed her mind, then shook her head slightly, imagining that they did not.

Gadriel was brought in past the front gate and through great, double, oak front doors. Rough men marched on deep, luxurious green carpet through a grand foyer that included two staircases curving elegantly up to the second floor. Gadriel had been here once before and remembered this route; what he hadn't been looking for was how to reach the cellar, and he did not see one now. Sergeant Vow escorted the group up the staircase on the right, then turned right down the hallway of the second floor.

The second floor of the mansion was also covered in lush, deep-green carpet and accented in oak adornments. Light creaking that added character to the house occasionally spoke to them as they shuffled down the hallway. Upon reaching the end of the hall, which contained a large plate window allowing light to flood the hall, Sergeant Vow lightly knocked on the office door.

"Come in!" said a muffled, deep, excited voice from inside.

The doors opened to reveal the Governor standing in front of his window, facing the door with a smile above his buttoned chin, his too-soon-white hair in perfect place, hands behind his back, his posture perfect.

"Hello again, bard," said the Governor. "Or should I call you, sign pisser? Gadriel? How about thief?"

Gadriel said casually, "Uh, well, I suppose Gadriel will do fine."

"Oh you do, do you?" the Governor said with an ugly chuckle. "Sit him down," he said to Clancy and his men, which they did roughly.

"To whom do I owe for this great act of service?" the Governor said, or more announced to the room.

Clancy replied, "Sergeant Shamus, my lord, just doin' me job."

"Ah, of course. Sergeant, your uniform is looking perhaps a little snug? Does the town not supply its guard with adequate replacements?"

"Aw, my lord, it's just the missus, ya' see. We just had our first and it's been feast, feast, feast at home. Lucky me, I've got a big appetite, eh?"

"Yes, feast after feast will do that to a man. You need more discipline, Shamus."

"Right-o I do, my Lord."

"For example, sir, may I see your club?" asked the Governor politely.

"Of course, my lord," said Clancy, unhooking his guard's club from his belt and then handing it over, which the Governor immediately used to break Clancy's knee with an outward strike.

Clancy hit the ground in wild pain but he did not scream, just clutched his knee. At this action, his two men were quick to act, but not quicker than the house guards who were expecting this, and they surrendered to save lives.

"Now in this example, 'Shamus,' you could have had more discipline by not giving your enemy your weapon. Or perhaps, not using the three ill-fitting guard uniforms you stole just last night." The Governor looked disgusted. "Like those men would not have reported it."

Gadriel, for his part, shied away from the violence, nearly cringing in his chair, muttering to himself, "No, it's not my fault, I didn't do it. It was their idea to put me in restraints. Yes, I know I went along with it. I know it was my decision."

"What the Heavens Below are you saying, boy?" asked the Governor.

Gadriel ignored him. "Of course he's going to know, hahahah everyone will know, idiot. No, you're the idiot, no you're the idiot. No you—"

"The Governor is speaking to you!" Sergeant Vow said forcefully. This snapped Gadriel out of his near-trance of conversation.

"Yes, sir?" asked Gadriel, sheepishly.

"What are you going on about?" asked the Governor, genuinely interested.

"Oh nothin'. I'm just crazy, don't worry about it," said Gadriel nonchalantly, then looked back to his left at nothing in particular and resumed his chat, presumably with Rod.

The Governor, a sharp man, thought for a moment, then his eyes widened.

"Do you have the stone?!" he shouted. "Guards! Search him with your gloves on! Find the stone!"

The guards immediately set to work, receiving lazy protests from Gadriel. "Hey, stop that, don't touch me."

"As for you three, what to do with you . . ." the Governor said, standing over a wincing Clancy and his two men on their knees. "It's been very popular today, but off to the cells with you."

"But sir," tried Clancy.

"But nothing, criminal. We're going to find out exactly who you are soon, and you can sit in our cells while we sort that out. Good day," said the Governor dismissively. Six guards then began moving Clancy and his men out of the room and down the hall to move them into the cellar where the definitely-not-a-dungeon jail was located.

Sergeant Vow and his partner continued to pat down and search Gadriel. "Hey, that tickles, buy me a drink first would ya," he said, giggling.

"Nothing of note, sir. Just his flute," said Vow.

"Oh is that what we're calling it now?" said Gadriel.

"Sit him down," said the Governor. And he was, forcefully.

"Ouch, watch it, I'm fragile," complained Gadriel.

Back in the kitchens, there were moments Rose was enjoying herself getting lost in the work; the prep, the mix, the proofing, the baking, the smells. She thought about how she wanted this to be over and how she wanted to go home. Then she reminded herself that it would likely never be that way again, at least not for her. Just then, Rose and Tamara heard a ruckus moving toward the kitchens. Rounding the corner were several house guards with her men in restraints. Clancy was being dragged on the floor, his knee bent precariously off centered; nothing about his dragging was gentle. He did not scream, nor cry, however. Most of the cursing came from the two, what appeared to be uninjured men, likely unhappy with the treatment of their third mate.

Captain Tamara almost jumped her counter to begin fighting with kitchen knives seeing the treatment of Clancy, but stopped herself. Clancy, for his part, managed a pained wink before getting dragged to the cellar doors of the courtyard behind the kitchens. Rose adjusted her hair again to keep her bun in place, while Tamara told her to keep calm. Seeing as how it was Tamara who needed the advice more, Rose went with it in hopes it would calm Tamara down, and it did.

Outside the kitchens, in the rear courtyard of the mansion, the men removed a large lock from two cellar doors, opened them, and entered, carrying all three men. The stairs did not make it easy to carry man or beast that went into the cellar, but it was still achieved. Walking down to the cells, Clancy saw an old man he believed to be Rose's father. An older woman, Clancy thought her name was "Loo-annie," the one from The Thirsty Goat. The little inn-keep from The Wooden Leg. And the last occupied cell before reaching empty cells of their own appeared to be the Dockmaster, without whom none of this would've been possible.

The three men were placed in a cell together, mostly because they didn't want to have to help Clancy do everything, but also because they were running out of individual cells; the Governor's private jail was large, but it wasn't a private prison.

Back in the Governor's office, Gadriel's "interview" began.

"So, Gadriel, what are you going to tell me first? How you stole my stone, or came by it? Where it is now? Or how you bonded with it? What was your little plan in coming here with your little miscreants, anyway?"

Gadriel looked over to his right and out the window; the sun was going down. Then he answered, "Well, to be honest, we were hoping to all get into the cellar to help free your prisoners, especially Rose's father, who is a good man that only wants to help people."

"Bah, no one only wants to help people, Gadriel," said the Governor. He continued, "You get to a point one must help oneself in everyone's life. It doesn't make you a bad person; it makes you in need of survival, just like everyone else. I am here because I'm very good at surviving."

Gadriel looked at the Governor inquisitively. "You're here, here and now, because you're 'good at surviving?' What about your father, the former Governor, growing up in this house? Attending school?"

"I'm not going to feel guilty about taking advantage of what life has given me. But I wasn't handed my Governorship. Nor am I handed victories over my enemies every day."

"Ask him about his dear old daddy and if he has a cough."

"How is your dear old daddy? Does he still have a cough?" asked Gadriel.

The Governor froze for just a moment, then resumed moving around to the front of his desk to stand directly in front of Gadriel. Gadriel cocked his head to one side, as if listening to a voice far away, then said, "Speaking of Daddy, when he was murdered—whoops, I mean died—how did you come by the Governorship so quickly anyway? It was almost like you knew he was going to die when he did." In response the Governor backhanded Gadriel across the face, whipping his head around and knocking him and his chair over.

It was at this time there was a knock at the office door. "Fire duty, my lord," a voice said from outside. Before speaking, the Governor pulled Gadriel and his chair upright, then said, "Yes, come in."

Tamara and a servant girl entered carrying wood and kindling to start the Governor's hearth; Rose opted to stay downstairs to avoid being recognized by the Governor. She was sure some of the staff had already vaguely recognized her. Though everything in here looked like a normal prisoner interview, they did notice Gadriel's face swelling and discoloration. He just smiled at them and winked with his good eye.

With the Governor's back to her while the servant girl tended to the fire building, Tamara made enough eye contact with Gadriel as if to ask if he needed out now. Gadriel conveyed that he was all right for their machinations to continue. Tamara nodded and turned around, just in time for the Governor, only growing in paranoia, to turn around only to find two servants lighting a large fire in the hearth behind his desk. When complete, the two bowed then left the room, closing the doors behind them.

The Governor quickly turned his attention to Gadriel. "I don't know where you heard your lies, but I don't want to hear them out of your filthy mouth ever again."

"We sure?" asked Gadriel, tilting his head again as if listening intently. "You sure you don't want to talk about Daddy's tea?" In response the Governor lashed out in rage and, Gadriel was sure, was very real fear. The Governor struck Gadriel, hard enough to knock him to the ground, then proceeded to kick him several times to the point Gadriel almost broke free of his fake restraints. At the sound of the commotion, Sergeant Vow re-entered the office from his post standing outside it.

"Sir, is everything okay?"

"Yes, sergeant. That will be all, thank you. Mr. Gadriel and I are having a nice chat."

Back in the courtyard behind the kitchens, the six house guards were climbing the stairs to leave the cellar. Once at street level, two of them closed the doors but found they were unable to secure the lock on the doors. It had appeared someone filled the lock with grit, fine rock, and carriage grease. Until these men talked to Sergeant Vow and had the lock taken apart and cleaned, or replaced entirely, they couldn't lock the doors.

Guard 1: "What do we do?"

Guard 2: "I dunno, what do you think we should do?"

Guard 3: "Well, it wonts lock, whats are wes supposed to do?"

Guard 4: "You idiots, we just gotta tell the sarge about it, eh?"

Guard 1: "So we just walk away?"

Guard 4: "Aw shit, yeah I see your meaning."

Guard 5: "What if we just stand here a bit while some of you go tell Sarg'?"

Guard 6: "That would mean not coming right back like he said, sounds risky."

Guard 2: "I think this is called . . . Crit . . . critty thinkin'."

Guard 4: "That's 'critical thinkin'," you dolt."

Guard 1: "Oh you're so clever, what do we do?"

Guard 4: "Let's just all go tell the sergeant, that way no one is disobeying orders."

Guard 5: "This feels like a worse option, but at least we'll all get in trouble the same way."

Guard 4: "Exactly, see? Perfec."

So out of fear of punishment, all six guards left the area to report the lock problem to their sergeant, leaving the cellar doors unguarded and unsecured. And as soon as they left the area, the perpetrators of lock sabotage, Thinker and the remaining three men came out from behind cover from within the courtyard to enter the cellar. Captain Tamara had cautioned against certain levels of force. Thinker was looking forward to ignoring this order, having seen what had happened to Clancy, and observed a worked-over old inn-keep, having been in position before the others.

As night began to fall, Thinker and his men opened one cellar door, which creaked, closing it behind them, then quietly descended the stairs of the cellar. On the stairs Think drew his short blades, disregarding blunt weapons; his men did the same with hatchets and short swords. They were surprised by and upon their first house guard quickly, who had apparently been attracted by the sound of the cellar door.

Thinker at the head of his group, the house guard on his own, both met as they each rounded the corner and nearly collided. The house guard shouted in fright then swung his club at Thinker, who was already headed low to the ground to attack the man's legs, and he did so, ferociously. The man began to scream out in pain, but one of the men grabbed his face and throat to stop the screams. In moments they were dragging his body back toward the stairs, which they placed underneath them for now. They then moved forward.

In the kitchens, Rose and Tamara were preparing supper with the rest of the kitchen staff, bread having been done for the day. Rose counted six guards returning from the six that left. This made at least fifteen inside the house, along with twelve staff members, not including themselves. They did not enjoy their mostly unarmed odds. Tamara didn't like not knowing what was happening with Clancy and Gadriel being too long with that sadist of a Governor.

She approached the chef and asked, "Mary and I can take supper downstairs if you like? Guards first of course."

The chef paused for a moment and looked at Tamara, who gave him a sultry smile. "Yes, yes. Start with the guards. Five plates, you will need sergeant to unlock the door and to also head count prisoners. I have better things to do than pay attention to their dealings."

Six guards, four of them proud of themselves, approached Sergeant Vow down the second-floor hallway, outside the Governor's office. The four guards who were proud of themselves became quickly not proud of themselves when Sergeant Vow began explaining to them how easy it would've been to guard the cellar doors to the very illegal jail cells they were supposed to protect and to get their asses back down stairs and check them "right Mother damn now." The six guards turned on a heel and hustled back.

In the cellars, Thinker continued to move forward toward another turn, not seeing cells yet but knowing they must be near, gauging on how long it took for Clancy and the others to be placed down here. Approaching a blind corner, Thinker's impatience got the better of him, and he rounded it with less caution than he should have used—right into the round from a long pistol fired from a guard who was waiting for him, striking him somewhere in the upper body, spinning him to the ground.

Gadriel was bloody, swollen, and still laughing. Shanks and Rod kept Gadriel company through his beatings, making inappropriate jokes and lewd thrusts around the Governor. Gadriel's lack of fear and occasional laughter only made him angrier. Soon Gadriel knew for his own life he'd need to stop taunting the man. But he also knew the longer he could keep the smartest man in this building occupied, the better chances for success his friends would have in extracting everyone in trouble, partly due to his actions.

Gadriel then did what Gadriel did best: annoyed others with a passion for music and the sweet sounds of his voice:

If I were the Governor
I too would be stiff
For in the night time
My wit would be limp
If I were Governor
I wouldn't be happy
For if I were Governor
I'd have killed my daddy.

"That's ENOUGH, you little SON OF A SOW!" shouted the Governor, picking up Gadriel, and his chair, and throwing him several steps across the room. Gadriel crumpled into a bookcase breaking the chair, and also breaking his restraints. It was now or never for him to defend himself against the Governor.

Gadriel got up with as much dignity as he could muster holding a chair leg and said, "Oh boy, you're in for it now" and smiled with far too much confidence, and likely concussed.

Thinker's men quickly dragged him back behind cover while two more rounds from long pistols were shot in their direction. His men assessed the damage and quickly identified a large wound in Thinker's right shoulder, which they began wrapping tightly as if it were a heavy stab or axe wound.

"Charge them now," Thinker hissed. "They're reloading." And his men didn't hesitate.

There were three guards at a guard station down a twenty-step hallway, all trying their hardest to reload long pistols, which despite their design were not very accurate at twenty steps; Thinker was incredibly unlucky. The guards were ill-equipped and ill-prepared to handle a threat like men from the Midnight charging them without the help of ranged weapons. Before they knew it, they were trying to drop their long pistols and retrieve swords, but it was too late. They were clubbed, repeatedly, likely too many times than was necessary.

The firing of their weapons would have alerted any additional guards in the cellars to their presence. Though Thinker and his men did not know this was only one, who was with the prisoners, they remained on high alert. Two of his men returned to Thinker to finish dressing his wound and moving him to a safer place.

Who also heard the shots, unfortunately, were the six guards standing outside the cellar doors on street level, who were inclined to investigate. Four of the men shuffled down the stairs, heading toward the sounds of Thinker and his men. Two remained outside the doors to guard them. But not for long, however.

15

Flashes of Light

Captain Tamara and Rose approached the two guards outside the cellar door with trays of food for the men downstairs. "Hello, boys," said Rose, "It's supper time."

"Sorry, ma'am," said one of the guards, "we're investigating something down there right now."

"Oh, well in that case," said Tamara, and she dropped her tray revealing a knife in each hand underneath it. And these weren't kitchen knives; these were knives made for one purpose. And she used them for that purpose on these two men, and she did so to save the lives of her family.

On the second floor, Governor Matteson laughed at the sight of Gadriel, swaying slightly, holding up his chair leg defiantly.

"You want to know more about the stone?" This gave the Governor pause.

"Yes, I do," the Governor said simply.

"Okay, then you have to sit down, with a thumb up your butt," he said, which caused the Governor to march over toward Gadriel with murderous intent. Gadriel swung his chair leg overhand as hard as he could, aiming for the Governor's head, which was easy for him to block with his forearm. Gadriel heard a crack, and he realized with a sickening feeling that it was the chair leg, not his opponent's arm.

The Governor didn't strike Gadriel in return, but he did press him up against the wall with all his weight, crushing him, slowly. Then he said to him softly, "Listen to me carefully, *trash*. You're going to start talking, or I'm simply going to crush the life out of you. You're bonded with the stone; this simply gives me a chance to bond with it after I kill you. Do you understand?" Gadriel didn't respond to his threat initially, for which he received a sharp jab to his kidneys, and he yelped "Yes! I understand!" already out of breath.

"You've bonded with the stone, correct?" asked the Governor. Gadriel nodded.

"Do you know where the stone is right now?"

Gadriel said, "Honestly, no I do not. I don't have it. It could be on the Midnight for all I know." The Governor pushed harder, with barely any breath, Gadriel wheezed, "My friends probably have it somewhere near; I can hear it."

The Governor allowed him to drop to the ground, gasping for air and clutching his chest.

"Vow!" shouted Governor Matteson. The New Haven-born man entered.

"Yes, sir?"

"Search the grounds for anyone that doesn't belong here; round up anyone who appears suspicious immediately."

"Yes, sir!" and Vow was off.

Thinker and his men quickly became trapped at the guard station between four house guard members coming from the entrance to investigate pistol shots, and at least one (but only one) guardsman was between Thinker and the jail cells. Though no one was armed with firearms, no one was excited to charge either enemy's position with unknown information behind so much cover.

"Come out of there, where are you going to go, you're surrounded?" said Guard Number 4.

"No, YOU'RE surrounded," said one of Thinker's men, to which Guard Number 4 asked his fellows, "We're not surrounded, are we?"

"Yes," said Captain Tamara and Rose as they ran upon the men. The first two men took vicious wounds and went down. However, the remaining two were able to return their aggression with club and fist. Rose took a nasty clubbing to her left shoulder, sending her to the ground. Captain Tamara, for all her maneuvering, missed the swing of her opponent's club but did not miss the follow-up fist to her face, which sent her to a knee.

Rose was jarred by her hit; Captain Tamara was not. Driven to a knee, Tamara focused through the stinging hot pain of her face and saw a booted foot. She savagely dove forward, raking the man's leg with her knives; he could not help but drop his club and scream in surprise and agony. This only drove Captain Tamara to faster movement and more violence. How dare these Mother damn bloody sons of sows harm her boys. How dare they throw them in a dungeon—no, they'll pay, she thought.

Rose tried to get up but putting weight on her left arm made her scream out in pain; she then took another strike across her back for her effort. What slowed her attacker, however, was turning to his left and seeing he was the last man standing, and Captain Tamara, covered in blood, was beginning to stand up. Holding her opponent's club, Tamara smiled at the man with an eager smirk; seeing Rose all but incapacitated on the floor, this smirk was wiped away to nothing but business.

Tamara approached the man at a steady pace, swinging the club back and forth once to test its weight, just like her cutlass; the club was actually a little lighter. It was clear to this man that this woman not only had more fighting experience, but her skill simply outclassed him. He was about to receive a proper beating, of which he immediately decided he was not interested. Dropping his club and putting his hands in the air, he got onto his knees in surrender.

A little disappointed, Tamara said calmly, "You move? You get a thumpin'." Tamara poked her head around the corner and not too loudly called out, "Boyos, one of you come up here; we've got someone to tie up and Rose to move."

Two of the men came over. "Cap't!" All were excited to see her. The house guard remaining of the four was efficiently restrained. Rose, who had difficulty moving, was carefully lifted and brought back to Thinker, who had stopped bleeding for the most part, but did not look his greatest.

"Think, how goes it, boyo?"

"I'll manage, Captain," to which Captain Tamara nodded, then asked, "What do we have?"

"At least one man that way; we believe the cells are around that corner. Several prisoners, from what we were able to observe, innocent people caught up in this."

Tamara nodded, then looked around them. "Well, look here, why don't we load these pretties and see how many men they do have back there, eh?"

Captain Tamara was met with devious chuckles.

Gadriel, being a little more cooperative now that he had been punched, slapped, kicked, thrown, and crushed, wasn't interested in more singing to antagonize this huge man that did not seem to tire. Gadriel was now sitting in a new chair, not even restrained, he was so damaged, across from Governor Matteson as if they were having an after-dinner meeting on any other evening.

The Governor was finishing, asking, "And the name of your spirit is?"

"Uh, Roderick, sir, but prefers to be called Rod." The Governor nodded.

"And how old is Roderick?" asked the Governor.

"I'm telling you the truth he does not remember. If anything, Rod sounds crazier than I do at times. He's chaotic, forgetting most things."

"Yes, yes, that can at times happen with Whisper Stones. He must be a powerful spirit to be that old."

"Well," said the Governor, producing a blue gemstone of similar size from his desk, "I have an empty vessel here. And I'd like Rod to enter it, please."

"I don't think it works like that, sir; he's within the green stone," a confused Gadriel responded.

"Oh, no, no," said the Governor, "he's half in the green stone, he's half within you, now, I want him out of you, and into here. You shall will it, or I shall kill you, and Rod will return to his vessel in full, which I will find anyway . . . Actually, killing you might be preferable." He produced a dagger from his desk as well, placing it on the table next to the blue stone.

Gadriel thought he might die soon anyway and decided to ask, "What do you mean, will it into the stone?"

"Ah, finally, a good question," said the Governor, like a teacher beginning a lesson and not like a man who just spent chimes beating on a man who could not defend himself. "Whisper Stones, or I should say, the spirits within Whisper Stones, are very deliberate about the living with whom they choose to bond, but as I'm sure you've gathered, it can very quickly make the weakest of us mad." Governor Matteson took his stance at his window, looking over the dark, dimly lit streets of central Lulin.

"A bond with a Whisper Stone is not permanent. Should a man, in this case you, not wish to keep the bond, it may take some training, but the spirit attached to him can be willed back into the stone completely." Gadriel nodded.

"The reason why a Whisper Stone bonds with only one person at a time is due to quantity; there is only so much spirit to be shared. Spread a spirit too thin, and it becomes something incorporeal in the extreme, even to its own existence."

"So I will Rod back into the stone, and you let my friends and I go, is that it?"

"Oh, Heavens Below, no, I have a reputation to uphold. But if my Whisper Stone is returned to me, whole, I'll stop hunting for it obviously. I'll have no need to continue the questioning, and the charges against Mr. Baker and his son Julien, as examples . . . it would be clear their involvement was nil. You, sign pisser, however, shall be tried for your crimes, and appropriately punished." Gadriel sat there quietly. "How many innocent people would you like to harm, is the question, Mr. Gadriel."

"Well may I have a moment to think about it?" asked Gadriel.

Underground, Captain Tamara and two of her men were armed with loaded long pistols, and she called out, "Hello down there. We're here for the prisoners; your boss is a terrible man. What do you say? You just give us the prisoners and you go home?"

A defiant voice came from the end of the cellars. "I am Captain Dush of the Matteson House Guard. I will remain at my post!"

Tamara leaned over to one of her men. "Did he say 'douche'?"

"I think it was more like 'Dushe', Cap't."

"Ah," Captain Tamara said at a normal volume, then shouted, "You are Captain Dush-oshe, and you'll be shot!"

"It's just Dush!"

Captain Tamara and her men with long pistols at the ready marched down the hallway and cleared the corner wide, where they found Captain Dush with buckler and pistol ready to fire upon them.

"Surrender now," said Captain Dush confidently.

"Listen Duosch," said Captain Tamara; this made Captain Dush squint his eyes closed in anger. And right then she shot him, in the upper chest, knocking him backward and off his feet.

"Welp, that's that boys," she said. Captain Tamara dropped her long pistol and removed a short sword she had appropriated from the guard station from her servant's belt, then walked over to Captain Dush, careful to step on his pistol hand first. There was no need, however, as he was dead and likely that way before he hit the ground with a wound like the one received from a long pistol at such a range.

Tamara removed the keys she found on Captain Dush's body and traded them with a loaded long pistol from one of her men.

"How about we free everyone, eh? I doubt there's anyone in 'ere who deserves it." The captain then jogged back to the guard station, where she helped cover Thinker and Rose from any additional resistance as they prepared to get out of there. Thinker looked the same, in pain but still functioning. Rose was not conscious, but breathing.

Without further incident, Captain Tamara and her team climbed the steps of the cellar and entered the rear courtyard of Governor Matteson's mansion.

"I don't know how many more guards are inside, but I do like the idea of a ridiculous distraction, Think."

Her men placed the injured Clancy and incapacitated Rose behind cover in the corner of the courtyard while they prepared to re-enter the mansion to recover Gadriel. Giving Clancy the two long pistols and a buckler, they told him they'd be back as soon as they could—they had to go save the crazy one. He smiled, having felt bad for getting caught so early.

Thinker, clearly finished with his thought, leaned over to the captain to share his idea. She cackled. It was time to get their madman back. Captain Tamara led Thinker and six fighting men into the servants' entrance to the mansion from the courtyard.

Upon reaching the kitchen, Tamara announced, not loudly, but loud enough to be heard by staff, "Go home, all of you. You don't want to be here." Absolutely none of the staff protested, all filing out calmly.

Moving deeper into the mansion, two of her men broke off to move to another area of the house to execute Thinker's scheme of distraction. The remaining six crewmates, including Thinker and the captain, moved forward toward the foyer, where they met their first resistance inside.

Four house guards, evidently brought down from the second floor to investigate why supper had not been delivered and the Governor's fire not refreshed, nearly fell upon the crew. Though they were not expecting to find the crew, they had the advantage of height from the stairs and were quick to use this to break through defenses and rely on their armor to protect them as they barreled into the crew. The tactic was successful, having wounded three of the four unarmored men, and gave Captain Tamara a gash for her trouble.

Being forced back down the stairs was difficult in this setting as it meant not harming their own men who could not move well while also defending themselves from attackers still on top of them. Thinker was the first to purposefully get low and attack less-armored extremities like legs, knees, and feet, which worked quickly. Tamara quickly followed Thinker's lead while the remaining crewmates stayed (mostly) upright and fought the guards. The guards slowly began to fall, but so did their crew. In total, three guards were incapacitated, but so were three of her crewmates, another seriously wounded. One guard was taken prisoner and simply lashed to the banister. Thinker was holding his side and breathing rather shallowly.

"Think, what's the problem, boyo?" asked the captain.

"If our other men succeed, we don't have much time; we've got to move," said Thinker.

Captain Tamara noticed blood seeping from a wound behind Thinker's hand. "Think, get back to Clancy."

"I'd rather not, ma'am," said Thinker, looking her in the face, giving her a slight nod, both smelling smoke now from Thinker's plan of grand destructive distraction. Captain Tamara grabbed Thinker's good shoulder, again, in a way that told him he was loved, and he smiled. They moved up the stairs and then down the hallway toward the Governor's office.

Immediately outside the Governor's office were Sergeant Vow and one more guard member, two having run to another end of the house to investigate a possible fire. Vow saw them coming from a distance; it would've been nearly impossible to have been surprised. Vow drew his pistol and raised it, waiting for them to come into range. Thinker smoothly moved in front of his captain, not breaking stride. Vow fired, missing both entirely. Captain Tamara moved out from behind her Thinker-cover.

As they reached Vow and the remaining guard, Vow looked at Thinker pitifully. "I know you, scion of a great house, pisses it away to play pirate. You look half-dead, Atmos."

"We just want our man," said Captain Tamara.

"And I just want my master's things back," said Vow.

"*Master,*" said a disgusted Thinker. Captain Tamara just sighed "All right, all right, let's just get this done, then."

At the very end of the hallway, Sergeant Vow drew his sword, completed two test swings, then posted himself in a powerfully intimidating fighting stance called the Schlüssel. Vow knew what he was doing, and he was not playing around, nor was he underestimating his opponents. His partner began moving to the left to separate their enemies. Without a strike attempted, without what was no doubt years of practice and expert skill applied to what would have been a glorious battle to Vow, Thinker simply dropped his sword, ran at Vow as fast as he could, and threw his body into a tackle around him, launching them both through the plate glass window at the end of the hall, at least thirty steps in the air.

Vow's partner was so shocked, as was Tamara; neither of them took advantage of the moment to attack the other. However, Tamara was quick to re-engage with the fight and was the first to swing on the man. The strike was a direct hit, but his house armor caused the blow to glance. The guard returned a strike that was missed as Tamara ducked out of the way, being much more nimble than the armor-clad man. Tamara struck again, this time hopefully through his guard to reach his armpit; the man turned quickly, losing her the short sword, and he smiled. He then mightily lifted his heavy sword for a cleaving downward strike, but by the time it reached Tamara, she wasn't there.

Having moved too quickly for such a slow and powerful strike, she was inside the man's guard, stabbing him repeatedly in his side where his armor tied but did not meet. She stabbed and stabbed until she heard the clink of the man's sword fall and he dropped to his knees.

Tamara was tired. She was bloody. She was injured. And was this even her fight? Yes, she thought, yes it was. Visible smoke was now reaching the second-floor hallway; she better move. Tamara walked over to the now open and broken window in hopes to see an alive and well Thinker; she did not. What she found was Thinker on top of Sergeant Vow, both run through by wrought iron spikes of the gate below. She felt incredibly too much too quickly for just a moment, then tried to not think about it at the present, there would be a time and place for that later. It helped Tamara to imagine that it was exactly what Think intended; she knew it was.

Captain Tamara then turned toward the doors to the Governor's office, took a step forward, and kicked the doors, which turned out to be locked, and heard them crack. She kicked again. She kicked again. She kicked a fourth time and they flung open, splinters flying, to reveal the Governor holding up Gadriel between himself and the door.

"Oh hi, how have you be—"

The Governor shook Gadriel like a ragdoll, cutting him off. "What did you animals do to my chef? I smell supper burning," said the Governor.

"You smell your mansion burning, big man," said Captain Tamara, she continued, "Give me the mad one and we'll let you live."

"Ha ha ha!" the Governor laughed, nearly hysterically. "She thinks she has some sort of upper hand. Oh, if Gadriel only knew the power he possessed," said the Governor to no one.

Captain Tamara lurched forward as if pushed from behind, stumbling as she was caught so unawares. The Governor dropped Gadriel like he would trash and methodically marched toward Tamara. Tamara's eyes were wide, confused.

"Oh it really is so much fun when they don't know what's happening to them."

Tamara raised her sword, wincing at the pain in her arm, and started to swing at the Governor, who again laughed and continued his forward movement. Something odd happened, a sensation stopped her, as if the blade were stuck, for just a moment. And all it took was that moment's delay for the Governor to reach her and back hand her several steps away where she dropped her sword, stumbled, and fell to the ground.

Gadriel was trying to rise to his feet on the opposite end of the room near the Governor's favorite window, steadying himself with a short bookcase. Once at his full height, Gadriel attempted to grab the Governor's attention with his classic prose, but Gadriel was simply too exhausted. At this point, so was Tamara. The Governor bent down and picked up Tamara and began squeezing her small frame together with his massive arms and shoulders.

"Give me the stone and I'll let *you* live," he said with a smile.

Captain Tamara did what she did best, fought tooth and nail, stubbornly, even petulantly, by saying in a slur, "Go doddle yourself and I'll let *you* live."

Before the Governor could begin trying to rip her in half, Rose was in the doorway to the Governor's office.

"WAIT!" she cried. The Governor paused. "Ah, Ms. Baker. Welcome. Just in time to watch your accomplice expire. One moment, please."

"You want the stone, Matteson?" Rose said, reaching up to her hair, beginning to undo her tight braided bun. Matteson, sensing what was about to happen, dropped Tamara and began moving toward Rose, who worked faster.

Soon Rose was holding the green stone, which glowed in the firelight, reflecting much more light than was in the room. She held the stone up, which caused the Governor to stop moving.

"Set it down, child," he said.

"Rose . . . no . . . run," Gadriel tried saying.

Tamara managed to sit up on the ground with her back to the desk. "He has a Shanks," she said, that was all.

"What the Mother damn does that mean?" Rose thought quickly—thought of everything she had learned on the ship with Shanks and Gadriel. Thought of all the testing done with Thinker and Gadriel. Thought of what it would mean for the Governor to "have a Shanks" and made a snap decision.

Rose turned and ran, but was immediately tripped by something that wasn't there. Rose hit the ground but sprung back up, expecting the interference. Anticipating it would be some moments before the Governor's spirit could affect her, again she turned around and shouted, "MATTESON! YOU WANT THE STONE!? TAKE IT!" and slammed the stone down onto the rich wood floor of the Governor's office.

"NO!" he screamed. Rose wasn't sure, but she may have felt his scream as well as heard it.

The stone struck the floor but didn't bounce as much as crack deeply enough as to split and begin to roll across the floor. Halfway between Rose and Governor Matteson, the stone exploded into brilliant light and deafening sound, with chips of the deep green stone floating across the room. What she saw she was unsure if she would believe if Tamara hadn't also seen it. The light coalesced into something smaller in a flash, then shot forward through Governor Matteson's chest, and into Gadriel's head. Gadriel laughed exactly one time, "Hah," and fell down. Governor Matteson, however, clutched at his chest, confused, frightened.

After several ticks, it appeared as though Governor Matteson could not breathe, or if he could, he was not getting any air. And he began to turn awful colors, as if his heart had just stopped, on an otherwise healthy, giant of a man. Governor Matteson eventually fell, face-first, onto the floor of his own burning legacy. After a few moments, a bright blue light emanated from the Governor's back, not dissimilar from what occurred with the green stone, flashed and coalesced into some form, then flew forward into the blue stone still resting on Governor Matteson's desk, which now glowed in a way similar to Gadriel's stone before it had exploded, of course.

"Oh, dear Mother," said Rose. Captain Tamara looked from Rose, to the Governor, and back to Rose.

"Thorny, how did you know that would happen?" Rose shook her head slightly and said "I didn't really. I thought it would just destroy the stone and the spirit, giving Gadriel back his normal life and stop the Governor from getting what he wanted."

Captain Tamara shook her head and said, "You know what, I want to leave. This is the kind of garbage that happens on land. Each time I've been on land over the last month, it's been shit like this. I want to go home now."

Captain Tamara and Rose got Gadriel sitting up, but this was as much as they could do considering everyone's injuries. Rose ran downstairs through the smoke to find healthier men waiting with Clancy and the other wounded in the rear courtyard. When Rose turned back around, she saw that the fire had taken to most of the home and informed the rescuers they had no time left. Before long, Gadriel was being carried from the home like a sack of potatoes, Rose was leaving under her own power, and Captain Tamara limped along assisted by one of her men. Before leaving the area, she instructed two men to retrieve Thinker's body as quickly as possible, and they did so. With sadness and relief, they were on the way home.

16

Goodbyes

When escaping the cellar and freeing the rest of the crew, true to the plan, the crew of the Midnight released all of Governor Matteson's prisoners. This included the inn-keep from The Wooden Leg as well as Jerald Baker, Julien and Rose's father. Rose hadn't been able to speak with her father then but would not miss the opportunity now.

The battered crew of the Midnight were on their way to the docks, much less clandestine than usual, mostly because they could not be. Their first stop was the abandoned workhouse to release Julien and retrieve their remaining man. Upon arrival, Rose, who had been patched up as best as field dressings could do, requested to be the one to ungag and untie Julien. And he was as scornful as he was angry. "C'mon, we're free to go, Father should be home."

"Thorny, be at the docks at first light; Violet and Helmsman arrive at daybreak, and we can't wait here any longer than we must for this town to put two and two together. Y'hear?" said Captain Tamara. Rose nodded, then began walking with Julien back to their home. Julien remained silent, a little to Rose's surprise considering his lack of concern for her injuries. But these were his feelings, of course.

Rose arrived at home and first retreated upstairs to clean herself and change into fresh clothes. When she came back down the stairs with a bag, Julien's mood darkened, if that were possible. Her father was happy to see her, seemingly unaware of the last several days, or even a week he spent in captivity. "Oh Rosey! You're home. I'll make tea!" he said excitedly.

"So that's it, then?" said Julien.

"Is what it?" asked Rose.

"You blaze in, literally burn down the town, then just leave again?" he accused.

Rose responded, "Look, I came back to help you and father. Tamara wasn't kidding when she said I didn't steal the stone. But I do admit I am associated with the people responsible. You and father are home safe now. Governor Matteson, probably one of the most evil people we've ever seen, is dead. That doesn't mean I can stay?"

"Why?" again Julien asked accusingly.

"I don't belong here, and I can't stay here for obvious reasons, brother," said Rose, not with any malice, just softly, and directly. "I don't believe I can go from seeing the things I've seen back to baking bread, even though there is nothing wrong with such a comfortable life." Julien stared at her for a long moment. In walked her father, holding a shaky tray of tea.

Jerald Baker sat down and poured the tea. Rose took his hands and said, "Father, I love you, dearly."

He replied, bright and cheerily, "Oh I love you too Rosey! Now drink your tea, young lady, before it gets cold, now." And she did.

Half a league away near the docks, Captain Tamara and her men, carrying Gadriel's unconscious form and Thinker's body, continued their march thankful for not running into patrols. And at that thought, they walked right into a two-man Lulin town guard patrol rounding the corner of an alley. Captain Tamara and all her men stopped, tired, but clearly willing to fight.

The two guardsman stopped. Exhausted, Tamara simply said, "Okay, how do you want to do this—do you want to have seen us or don't you?" Without communicating with one another, the two guardsmen simply turned around slowly and began walking the way they came, not saying a word.

"Finally," Tamara said.

Shortly before daybreak, Tamara and her men trudged toward the end of the dock, knowing that's where she'd tell Helmsman to aim her ship and knew that's where he'd aim it. Clancy, for his effort, kept trying to walk on his splinted leg, and kept getting chastised for it by nearly everyone. The captain knew it was because he wanted to carry Thinker. And she also knew that's why he'd been crying, not because of the pain of his leg.

Gadriel was rousing but still unconscious, so he was laid down on top of a crate. Clancy sat on the ground beside him. Captain Tamara waited patiently, glad to not have to lie, sneak, or fight. Glad to be near the water. Glad to know she was nearly home.

As the very first rays of daylight from the east struck the docks, Captain Tamara could see a beautiful sight at the edge of Lulin's waters. The Midnight was coming in at a disrespectful cruising speed, exactly as ordered; this pleased Tamara to no end.

"Alright boyos, up, up, up, this is no time to nap; we've still work to do. Up up. Let's go, ya' lazy lugs," the captain said, clapping her hands together to emphasize her orders.

As the Midnight continued its disruptive cruise through the harbor, the crew awaiting pickup watched as the Lulin Dockmaster and several guardsman were assembling at the dock gates, likely as a show of force to reprimand this ship upon its arrival. What they also noticed in that direction was Rose walking toward the end of the dock, carrying a bag over her good shoulder.

"I said before daybreak" said Captain Tamara, stoically.

"Well, I had shit to do, did'n I?" Both women laughed. Then Captain Tamara said, "That's the last time I'll get that sass, deary."

"Yes Cap't," agreed Rose.

The Midnight reached the exact berth Captain Tamara expected, cruising to a not-so-gentle stop with the help of her first moore lines tied down by Danny and another less injured fellow, broadside starboard toward the dock, bow pointed away from the Lulin, ready to leave. By the time the fresh crew of the Midnight lowered her starboard hold door, the Dockmaster, visibly angry by the Midnight's lack of courtesy, approached the group flanked by six men in what was supposed to be an overwhelming and intimidating show of force. It simply wasn't.

Captain Tamara looked over at the poor man, who, as he approached, realized he probably should not have attempted to intimidate. This man was stubborn for all he was full of poor judgment, however, and continued on his present course.

"Listen here, I don't know how you people do things where you're from, but here in Lulin we have courtesy and rules of our docks and harbor." Everyone simply ignored him.

As the men continued to load the wounded onto the ship, the Dockmaster continued. "You might have damaged our dock, or maybe our dry dock moving around like that, like you're the only boat in the water." The Dockmaster was of course correct, which was the greatest reason he wasn't thrown in the harbor already. That and Captain Tamara's plain exhaustion. They continued to ignore him, however.

Now everyone was loaded onto the ship except for Captain Tamara, who knew they would not be coming back to Lulin in quite some time for obvious reasons. She turned to the Dockmaster and waited, knowing he had more to say before he was finished.

"I ought to levy a fine against you for using this berth acting this way; our Governor would surely agree with me."

"You know, boyo, I don't think he would," said Captain Tamara. She continued, "You can plainly see how wounded my men were, would that not explain the speed in which our ship came to their aid?"

The Dockmaster paused for a moment, then said, "Well, there are infirm—"

The captain cut him off and continued. "How about yourself being a government official seeing private peoples with such damage? You didn't think to ask if we were okay or how it happened to us? Just wanted to attempt to show force over the speed of our boat in the water?"

The dockmaster paused again, then attempted to say, "I could hardly see that your men wer—"

Captain Tamara cut him off one last time. "Dockmaster. Are you familiar with grapeshot?"

"What?"

"Grapeshot, Dockmaster, are you familiar?"

The Dockmaster turned red then indignantly accused, "Are you threatening me, *girl?*" to which Captain Tamara responded, "Actually . . . yes." And at that, a cannon was rolled out from the shadow of the Midnight's hold to point in the general direction of the docks on which the Dockmaster and his port guards stood.

The Dockmaster, who was red with anger, turned a pale white, dropped his writing board, raised his hands, and took a step back. Captain Tamara smiled and said, "Hey, boyo, you started it; mine's just bigger." Then she turned on a heel and boarded her ship.

Gadriel was placed in his cabin and on his bunk to hopefully rest off the effects of whatever had happened to him inside Governor Matteson's office. Rose attempted to help Doctor Cutter in the infirmary as best she could, particularly worried about Clancy and his knee. However, Doctor Cutter advised the splint and set that occurred in the field appeared to be about the best that was going to happen for Clancy at present and the best he could do was stay off of it. According to Doctor Cutter, all other crew would live with time, clean wounds, and good nutrition.

"Aw, the pig," said Captain Tamara to herself in the infirmary. Violet, who could not stop herself from doting on Tamara as soon as she set foot back on board the Midnight, asked her, "What was that, my lady?"

"Aw, I bought a sow for the men but we had to leave too quickly. I didn't have a chance to pick it up or have it delivered."

"I'm sorry, my lady," Violet said sincerely, wiping Tamara's face of dirt and grime and attempting to clean her hands while Tamara attempted to shoo her out of Doctor Cutter's way.

"Aw, it's fine, if that's the worst thing that happens today, we'll be in good shape. I think," said Captain Tamara. She then stopped, suddenly less jovial. Doctor Cutter, while stitching her wound, expressed how sorry he was for Thinker, knowing how close they had been for years.

"You know, Doc, I don't think I'd be here, weren't it for Think. Crazy bastard took a man right out a window. And I honestly think he aimed for the gate, if such a thing were possible, calculated till the end."

"You know, with Thinker I'd believe it," Doctor Cutter said, thinking out loud with the captain having finished his work.

"Is there anything special I need to know about his burial?" asked the captain.

"No, I don't think so. Thinker was part of the Midnight. I believe honestly it would be preferable to him to be buried in Midnight's way, his family's way, not House Atmos." The captain nodded.

The next day, the crew all dressed in their finest clothes, with the exception of Gadriel who still lay in his bunk, were on the main deck of the Midnight. They surrounded their first mate, they surrounded Thinker. Captain Tamara had him dressed in his finest found in his cabin, but Captain Tamara also found fine Atmos robes hidden in a chest at the foot of his bunk. She shrouded Thinkers body in his robes over his clothing and jacket.

Clancy, with a much better and stronger splint, stepped forward and picked up Thinker's smaller, lifeless form like he was cradling a toddler. As he did so the entire crew stomped a booted foot and saluted as crisply and as sharply as they knew how. Despite the pain, Thinker's third mate carried him with reverence to the portside railing of the merchant ship Midnight.

I know not where we go when we're gone,
Be it Heaven Below or another beyond.
Please guide this soul to where he belongs,
Where his sails are full and the wind blows large.
For his time for hunger and pain have ended,
By the grace of the Spirit willing, please Mother, protect him.

The captain ended her prayer by walking over to Clancy and kissing the top of Thinker's head, then gave Clancy's arm a squeeze.

"Clancy at your ready," she said quietly, though everyone on deck could hear her clearly. Clancy sobbed as he laid the body of his friend to rest at sea, with his family, where they knew he would have preferred it no other way.

Captain Tamara watched her first mate sink with the weight of the cannonball lashed to his legs to afford him the dignity he deserved. After he was afforded the proper deference. The captain walked over to the ship's bell and gave it three sharp rings, dismissing the crew. She then shouted, voice cracking, "HELMSMAN! TO SAINTS ROCK!"

"AYE! SAINTS ROCK AYE!" confirmed Helmsman.

In Gadriel's cabin, he was finally waking up to the faint ringing of a bell. Laying there on his back, his head was pounding and he wasn't sure why. Oh! That's right, he was beaten within an inch of his life by the . . . Governor!

Oh. oh . . . He wasn't in a cell. He was looking at a bulkhead, he was on the Midnight, he was in his bunk! How did this happen? he wondered.

He tried to get up, but that made him feel nauseous so he laid back down to rest further. From the top bunk Shanks's head poked out with a smile and a wave, to which Gadriel responded, "Shanks! Dear Shanks, I'm glad to see you. I'm sorry you had to see all that at the mansion. Thank you for trying to help the Governor pull his punches. I do believe you did, really. NO I'm not just saying that."

A few moments later another head poked out from the top bunk with a smile, which at first, Gadriel was too confused to be terrified, then the very real fear set in and he screamed. "AHH! WHO THE BLOODY MOTHER ARE YOU!"

"Oh c'mon, it's me! Rod!"

"What . . . what do you mean?"

"It's Roderick, Rod, the fun one. This Shanks guy is funny, lemme tell ya."

"What?!"

"I'm saying Shanks is fun—you know what, never mind. So yeah, I'm in your head now."

". . . What?!"

"Oh don't act so surprised and dramatic. I know you're a dramatic man, but I'm also dramatic, and that's not going to be helpful at all if we're both dramatic all the time. Let's only do that to be funny, all right?"

". . . no, What?!"

"Okay, look," started Rod. "The Governor, for being all the giant bastard that he was, kind of already explained this to you, you fanny. Half of me was anchored to you, the other half of me was in my vessel, which was the stone."

"Uh-huh," said Gadriel, following, but still shocked coming to terms with what he was realizing was the case here.

"When cute little Rosey decided to SHATTER my vessel, I didn't feel like ceasing to exist, so I joined the other half of myself inside YOU! Tada!"

"Okay, so. . ." started Gadriel.

"So I think you get it, boyo," Rod said, with a large, genuine smile, then added, "We're going to have so much fun!"